ALCHEMIST

THE GUARDIANS OF TIME ● BOOK TWO

ALCHEMIST

THE GUARDIANS OF TIME • BOOK TWO

VIVIENNE LEE FRASER

www.viviennelfraser.com.au

Vivienne Lee Fraser
www.viviennelfraser.com.au

Cataloguing-in-Publication details are available
from the National Library of Australia
www.trove.nla.gov.au
ISBN: 978-0-6488860-1-3

Formatting and cover design by KILA Designs
www.kiladesigns.com.au

*For Jim, who is my rock,
and the rest of my Southampton family—
hope you enjoy the local flavour.*

PROLOGUE

Beta gazed out over the Ethereal City from his suite in the Council Tower, and marvelled at how the Time Guardians had built their home to replicate Earth's cities. Strange, really—how they were so reluctant to give up ties to their former lives. Their absence of a physical form meant they no longer actually needed buildings.

Sighing, he imagined himself standing and his ghostlike form complied. The Council meeting would start soon and he must prepare. No doubt someone would have questions about his protege Sigma's latest adventure.

'You're still set on sending Sigma to cover the New Forest situation?'

Beta hated it when Alpha spoke before he materialised. There was no time for greetings, and thus no time to prepare for the attack his fellow councillor would inevitably launch—not to mention that the very act of admitting himself without permission was intrusive.

'Must we go over this again?' Beta asked wearily. 'The Council believes his connection with the potential Time Guardians who will be in the area during the event make him the best suited for the job.'

'I hear he is planning to take Alain, the apprentice apothecary from the Middle Ages, along with him and Barwick. Is that a good idea? I mean, it's Barwick's final test before he rises to our ranks, so it is doubly important for him—I would hate to think his ascension was to be placed in jeopardy.'

Alpha's rehashing of old arguments was another trait that annoyed Beta, but he felt compelled to answer anyway. 'Again, Alpha, the Council believes because this group have teamed up successfully once before, that outweighs any of the other concerns.'

Beta paused for Alpha to respond. When he was met with silence, he continued his argument. 'Sigma could have left the boy behind but his incarnation at this time is living on a different continent and we were not able to speed up his return to England. In any case, a council majority agreed the benefits far outweighed the risks.'

'I know, but ...'

'Besides, his being taken along has some benefit for us. At the moment he is all set to abandon his training and leave for the New Forest to agitate in favour of returning crown lands to their original owners. Given his recent assistance to Henry, he might well be listened to.'

'Henry would not be so foolish as to handover land his father confiscated less than a generation ago. After all, King William conquered so much of Briton, it would set a dangerous precedent. Not to mention the ramifications in centuries to come.' Alpha sounded so sure of himself.

'My point exactly. Unfortunately, at the moment he believes the New Forest is cursed—two of King Henry's older brothers lost their lives in the area. You cannot blame him for thinking the royal forest best be handed back. There is a real possibility it will happen after the Time Wreckers' interference with the timeline. Now he is even more convinced the forest is jinxed.'

'Would returning the land be so bad?' Alpha mused.

Beta gritted his teeth. 'You know it would. The ripples through time would cause enormous disruption. It's only because the forest was a royal preserve that it was saved from overdevelopment, giving southern England one of its few national parks, and an area of great natural power.'

It was too much to hope that Alpha's silence indicated this conversation was over, but Beta found himself hoping anyway, only to be disappointed when Alpha said, 'And I guess we still need to deal with the problem of the boy learning to think before he leaps. A little time in the field may teach him to consider his actions first.'

'Yes, Alain does need to learn to consider consequences. He is young, yet...' Beta was suddenly reminded of Sigma, who was very similar at the same age, and his voice drifted off.

'Anyway, we have no time for pleasantries. I have called a special meeting of the Council,' Alpha interrupted. 'I proposed your team be pulled out and a more experienced one inserted in its place.'

'Oh, and what team would that be?' Beta asked the question, but was already sure he knew the answer.

'I thought as Theta was free at the moment ... ' Alpha

confirmed Beta's suspicions.

'Of course you did, and it would just be a coincidence that she was your trainee.'

'I am not sure what you are saying.' Alpha frowned as he stared directly at his host.

About to shoot off a stinging retort, Beta paused as something occurred to him, then asked, 'Alpha, is there something you are not telling me? Have you found some evidence this is more than a quick investigation to rule out foul play by the Time Wreckers?'

The air around Beta changed, indicating a rising tension in his companion. 'Not exactly'

Ha! Seemed like the Time Guardian couldn't bring himself to lie. 'Alpha?'

'Oh. All right. On her last mission, Theta picked up chatter about something going on in 2017 in England. I am concerned this might be part of it, and I am not sure Sigma has the experience to handle a full-on Time Wrecker attack and manage two untrained assistants.'

Beta sighed. 'You are right; that would be beyond his current capabilities. King Henry's coronation had some unexpected activity and Sigma handled it well. I am not sure though that he would be lucky enough to thwart a Time Wrecker incursion a second time. Perhaps we should go and find out what the rest of the Council think.'

CHAPTER ONE
JOURNEY'S END

The tinkle of the shop bell alerted the teenage girl to a new presence, and Jo raised her head from the book she was engrossed in. Jenna, dishevelled and looking every one of her fifty-plus years, bustled from the door towards the counter.

'Hi Jenna. Watch—'

The stand by the counter toppled as charms flew everywhere, eventually finding a place on the ground. Trying to step around them, the distraught woman knocked a pile of books arranged on the counter ledge to the floor.

'Oh ... sorry ... oh dear.' Jenna froze, then burst into tears.

No doubt drawn by the ruckus, Alice, the store owner and Jo's boss, popped her head out to see what was going on. Moving swiftly, Alice pulled out a chair by the counter and manoeuvred Jenna towards it, narrowly avoiding any further disasters as Jo went to clear up the mess.

Having picked up the stray charms from the floor, she placed them on the counter, re-stacked the books, then busied herself untangling the charms, leaving Alice to calm their visitor.

When the sobbing subsided, Alice said, 'This is so unlike you, Jenna. What has you in such a fluster?'

'It's Pepe. I have just dropped him at the vet. He came down with it this morning. You know, the same thing as all the other dogs ... the ones who walk the New Forest tracks. I have to prepare myself ...'

'Most of the dogs recover well if they are caught early,' Jo reassured the woman. Working at the local vet, she had seen a few cases of Alabama Rot come through. Unlike other places where outbreaks had occurred, all but a couple of their patients had recovered.

'I know ... but he is so ill ...' Jenna trailed off, clearly too upset to go on.

'Let me go and make us some tea,' Jo said, leaving Alice to comfort her friend.

'It must be difficult for you. Pepe is a great companion for you, especially with Bill travelling so much for work.' Jo overheard Alice say as she entered the back room.

'I'm not sure I could bear to be without him.'

'I am sure he will be fine.' Alice soothed Jenna. 'What did the vet say?'

'She said we caught it early. There's a good chance Pepe will be okay.'

'That's great, and as Jo said, not all the dogs who contracted Alabama Rot have died.'

'I know, but ...' Jenna hesitated, then blurted out, 'I was kind of hoping you might be able to do something.'

'Do something?' Alice's voice raised in query, and Jo turned the kettle off to better hear her boss's answer.

'You know ... do some of that stuff you do.'

Jo almost dropped the tea caddy. Alice was always complaining that in the ten years she had been running The Witch's Hat, her family and friends had studiously ignored the fact her store sold charms, trinkets, and all the items any modern witch would need to practice their art. If they mentioned the store at all, they described it as a tourist trap.

Was Alice's practical, non-believing friend now suggesting she use witchcraft to help with her dog?

Jo finished making the tea as quietly as possible, still listening to the conversation in the shop.

'Jenna, I am not sure what you think I will be able to do.'

Jenna sniffled before answering. 'I thought ... you know ... that you might be able to cast a spell or something to protect Pepe, or make him better.'

Jo almost snorted, unable to believe people really thought magic worked like that.

'Pepe is in the best place, Jenna. There are spells used in witchcraft that can certainly help channel healing energies, but they're no substitute for a good vet.'

'Are you saying you can't help me?' Jenna sounded defeated, almost as though she had written her dog off.

'Well, not exactly. There have been so many dogs coming down with this disease lately, more than in previous years. I've reached out to some, um ... friends ... who may be able to be of more help than me in dealing with the blight growing in our forest.'

Jo almost dropped the mugs in her hands. Who had Alice called to help them? And what would they be able to do that their own coven of witches could not?

'What will they be able to do that you can't?' Jenna asked, her voice sounding rather uncertain to Jo's ears.

'I'm not sure, to be honest,' Alice answered as Jo pushed her way through the curtain with three mugs of tea in hand. 'In this modern world we are so distanced from our ties to the land, the magic we can perform is limited compared to what it once was. I hope these people will have some ideas about how to, um ... help heal the land, I guess.'

Jenna sat forward in her seat. 'Who are they? Will they be here soon?'

For a person who was usually reluctant to acknowledge the existence of magic, Jenna was awfully eager to know more. Jo waited for Alice's response, but her boss was strangely silent.

Sometime later, once Jenna had finished her tea and left, Jo decided to ask her boss what was going on.

'I am sorry, Jo. I really don't want to talk about it. It was just something I tried on the spur of the moment—I am sure nothing will come of it. I only said it to boost Jenna's mood. If you wouldn't mind putting those charms back out for me, I still have some work to do in here.'

Sitting down at her desk, the shop owner turned her computer back on and straightened the pile of papers, ready to return to work. Having been dismissed Jo turned to leave, and knocked some files to the floor. She bent to pick them up and caught a glimpse of the spine of a book

ALCHEMIST

in amongst the paperwork—*Spells from Medieval England.*

As she replaced the files she slipped the book behind her back just as she was summoned by the shop bell.

Alain stood, wiping off his leggings, and slowly turned to survey his surroundings. Morning fog rolled across the grass and swirled eerily around them. The soupy substance was so thick the trees encircling them were merely ominous shapes.

'Are we there?' Alain asked through chattering teeth.

'Yes, I believe we are in the New Forest, although I have no way of knowing whether or not we are in the right year.' Master Barwick's answer was short and sharp as he rolled onto all fours in an attempt to get up. Alain reached down to help the rotund older man to his feet. As he did, a rumbling filled the pre-dawn air. Two glowing beams cut through the mist.

Whoosh!

Alain looked up in alarm. 'What ...?' His eyes grew round as the light swiftly drew closer, and there was another *whoosh* as a peculiar rectangular shape passed them by. The journey here must have scrambled his brain because he was sure he saw a face staring out of the contraption at him.

It was difficult to believe just seconds ago he had been standing on the wharf in front of Westminster Castle, his only concern whether to stay with Barabal or go home to Winchester. Now here he was, hundreds of years in the future, all because Lala had suggested this journey might be good for him to understand the importance of the New Forest remaining a royal preserve.

Now that very same Time Guardian was nowhere to be found.

Lala? Alain sent the thought out, hoping for some sort of a reply from the being who had brought them to this strange place.

'I can't see him,' Master Barwick grumbled as he turned in a circle. 'He must be here somewhere. He came with us through the portal in the Thames that brought us to this goddess-forsaken place.'

'Master Barwick, that is a little strong. We only just arrived, so we can hardly be judgmental.'

With his grey-white hair standing out in tufts from his head, and his robes damp and dishevelled, Master Barwick, apothecary to King Henry and part-time alchemist, glared balefully at the young boy.

'I may be having second thoughts about taking you on as an apprentice,' he said. 'Stop for a moment and really feel this place. Magic is weak here.'

Wrapping his arms around his shivering form, Alain calmed his nerves and allowed his senses to expand. He trembled a little, not from the cold—although it was certainly chilly—but from fear. Master Barwick was right. If he concentrated, he could just about feel a little tingle of magical energy. His whole life, magic had just been there; now, it was not. Its absence threw him off balance, reinforcing how far he was from home.

Master Barwick spoke into the silence.' The goddess holds no sway here. The people of this place no longer take care of the earth; the old ways have been forgotten.'

ALCHEMIST

Alain was prevented from adding to the discussion as more lights cut through the air, and a rumbling drew closer. Moving slightly nearer to his master, Alain asked, 'What is that and how do we fight it if we have no magic?'

'Um, I don't think we will be required to do battle with the machines. I am not one hundred percent sure, but they are similar to something I saw on my last trip with Sigma—I mean, Lala—although these ones are larger and move more quickly. I am sure they are manmade contraptions used to move people around.'

'You can have a laugh at my expense, Master Barwick, as this is the first journey I have taken out of my time, but eventually you are going to have to tell me what they actually are.'

Frowning, Master Barwick shook his head. 'I am not jesting. I seem to remember they are called horseless carriages. They are not dangerous ... well, not unless you stand on the tracks they run on, and one bowls you over.' Master Barwick chuckled. 'Come now. We need to find Lala. He has all the details of our mission, not to mention we cannot return home without him.'

Alain opened his mouth to voice his concerns about not being able to return to Westminster in time to say goodbye to Barabal, then he remembered how horrid travelling through the time portal had been and he shut it. When he had decided to slip away with the Time Guardian Lala, he had been so excited he had not thought about how they would be getting to their destination.

He had almost backed out when Lala had led himself and Master Barwick down to the water—the slimy, filthy water that ran through the city of London—and he realised how the Time Guardian was planning to transport them to the future.

Only an hour or so earlier he had watched Lala return John, a boy the Time Guardian had brought from Australia in the 1800s to help them save King Henry, home—through a swirling time portal in the same river he stood beside. Of course they would be travelling the same way.

Attempting to ignore the floating debris, Alain had taken a deep breath and followed Master Barwick and Lala into the icy-cold Thames. Concentrating on keeping his breakfast down, he'd been swept off his feet by a whirlpool of water as he fell into complete blackness, only to stop abruptly when his bottom hit the soggy ground of the field they now found themselves in. It was not a journey he wished to repeat anytime soon.

If the Time Guardian wearing a lamb's body was to be trusted, they'd left London in November 1101, and were now in the New Forest, Hampshire, in the fantastical year of 2017. Having transported them nine hundred years into the future, Lala had then abandoned them to go and do ... well ... Alain was not sure what, but it wasn't very helpful of him.

'You should know better than to bring a boy out to play your stupid medieval games in weather like this—and without his coat too.' The shrill voice broke through the morning air. Dressed in some sort of unusual cloak, and wearing trousers like a male serf, a middle-aged woman leading a dog emerged from the fog and confronted Master Barwick.

'It is bad enough you men must play at re-enacting the past, but to drag your poor children into it as well is too much. Look at him; he is soaked through. Take him home before I call the authorities and report you for child neglect.'

Child neglect?

All right, his vision was somewhat obscured by strands of black hair dripping with water, and he had forgotten his cloak—but other than that, he was fine. Was this woman actually comparing him to the poor souls who hung about the castle kitchens, begging for scraps? How dare she compare him to those starving mistreated children.

He opened his mouth to give her a piece of his mind, then closed it. No one cared about the maltreated children in his time; no one in authority would even consider answering a call to help them. It appeared 2017 might take a bit of getting used to.

Lala must be close by because I can understand this harridan, Master Barwick spoke directly into his mind.

Huh? It took Alain a moment to comprehend what his master was saying.

Have you lost all your wits, boy? We need Lala to translate for us. English in this time is quite different from ours. He ensures we hear what people say in our tongue, and our words sound like modern English to them. Master Barwick's tone was impatient.

Lost my wit? Perhaps this is an everyday trip for you, but I have never time travelled before. Alain was quick to defend himself.

'Were you listening to what I said, or are you deaf as well as stupid?' The woman asked, her shrill voice pierced Alain's eardrums and he had to stop himself from putting his hands over his ears.

'I am sorry, ma'am, did you perhaps leave your

manners at home this morning?' Master Barwick beamed, and his voice oozed with charm as he traded insult for insult. 'The boy asked to come with me today, and his clothing is made of the finest wool so he is warmer than he looks. Besides he will be heading home just as soon as we find the animal we lost.'

The woman's eyes widened, then she pulled her coat more closely around her as she huffed. 'Well, I did see a stray Cockapoo—just over there. Similar colouring to my own Cherry, it was. Perhaps it is yours.'

Without answering, Master Barwick took off in the direction she'd pointed.

'Ah, thank you,' Alain said as he left the woman standing in the drizzling rain.

Within a few paces, they found a fluffy dog with long ears and sorrowful eyes sitting under the shelter of a tree. As they approached, it shook droplets of rain from its coat then settled down again as if waiting for them to approach.

'Is that a Cockapoo? I guess it has wool similar to Lala, but ...' Alain laughed.

I prefer the term Spoodle, and I could not go about in this time as a lamb. They are not exactly allowed in homes here, the dog sent to his mind.

Alain was distracted by rustling from behind him as the woman joined them.

'We have found our friend Lala. Thank you,' Master Barwick said politely.

'Lala. An escape artist like that is more aptly named Trouble.' The woman tossed over her shoulder as she stalked off. 'And he should be on a lead in this part of the forest.'

'Trouble.' Master Barwick's laughter filled the morning, and soon it turned into a splutter he was unable to stop.

You would not ... Lala protested.

I would and I am, Master Barwick said.

Impressive, Alain thought as he watched Master Barwick's shoulder shake with laughter. *How is he able to mind-speak while laughing so much?*

Practice, my lad, Master Barwick said. *And you need to practice shielding your thoughts from others.*

Shivering again, Alain was about to send a cutting response when he decided against it. He was keen to go somewhere a little warmer, complete their mission as quickly as possible, and return home. Lala had assured him he would be back in time for dinner, but Alain did not know just how accurate this time travel thing was, and he had promised his friend Barabal he would be there to say goodbye when she left to escort the new Queen to her wedding.

'Master Barwick, can we get going?' Alain asked out loud to reinforce the urgency he felt.

Master Barwick took a deep breath while the dog stared mournfully at him. Catching sight of the dog again, he burst into fresh bouts of laughter as he choked out the word, "Trouble". The apothecary eventually managed to still his laughter to an occasional chuckle before saying, 'Righto, Trouble. What do we do now?'

If you don't want to call me Lala, use my Time Guardian name, Sigma.

'But you hate being called Sigma. And Trouble is a great name for a dog, and it is also an apt name for you, my friend.' Master Barwick smirked.

If I am having a name change, so must you. No one is called Master in this time, and Alain cannot call you Barwick as it would be disrespectful. You must be called by your Christian name—Barnaby, Trouble said.

'But I detest that name,' Master Barwick protested.

But you respond to it and that is what is important, Trouble's tone was matter of fact and Alain sighed with relief as their guide focussed on the task ahead.

'Humph.'

Trouble ignored Master Barwick's comment. *As you have already found, children are treated differently in this time. People cannot simply pick up a stray child and keep it.*

I am not a child. I am almost eighteen, Alain objected.

In this time in England, you are not legally an adult until you are eighteen. We could lie—simply tell people Master Barwick is your uncle, and he has taken care of you since your parents died. That way we explain why you have no family.

Sounds like a good cover story, Master Barwick agreed. *We also need to be from somewhere quite remote—somewhere no one has been—somewhere like the Scottish Highland.*

It was Trouble's turn to laugh, only it came out sort of like a barky snort. *I tell you things have changed a little since your time. People now actually live in the Scottish Highlands, and some even go there for holidays.*

Holidays? Master Barwick stroked his beard as he considered the word.

Yes, Barwick. That is when people take time off work to do the things they enjoy.

Master Barwick scratched his head. *Work is enjoyable.*

To not work? Now that sounds very stressful.

Come on, you two. I am freezing here. Alain attempted to bring his mentor's attention back to the task at hand.

Spoilsport. Right, let me see. Perhaps you could be from an island in the Scottish Hebrides.

'So, Uncle Barnaby, we have travelled with our dog Trouble from the Scottish Hebrides, but where are we going to?'

Trouble stood and shook water from his coat, spraying his human friends before walking over to a sign by the edge of the field.

That way. He pointed with his head.

As Alain passed, he read the sign—*Burley 3 miles.*

Trouble led the bedraggled group through the forest's back lanes until they reached the edge of a village. The fog was beginning to clear a little, and they were being passed by more of the horseless carriages, albeit going a little slower than they had been before. Still more of the four-wheeled vehicles were standing outside the enormous mansions they walked past.

'How do they work, Master Barwick? The horseless carriages, I mean. Is it by magic?'

The dog stopped and turned to face Alain, his head cocked to the side. *You need to get used to calling Master Barwick "Uncle Barnaby". And if you have questions about things in this time it is perhaps best you mind-speak them. You will appear quite odd to people if you voice these things out loud.*

'Sorry,' Alain mumbled. 'I will try to remember. You did not answer my question though, Uncle Barnaby.'

They have not been called horseless carriages for more than 100 years—they are called cars. They are mechanical contraptions, powered by petrol, one of the ingredients of your Greek Fire, Trouble answered before Master Barwick was able to.

Alain veered away from the "car" he was just passing. 'Don't they blow up?'

Trouble did that weird, yipping laugh again. *Good grief, no. There are so many of them; they're everywhere. This world would be very dangerous if they kept exploding all the time. They are perfectly safe to use—well, so long as they have a good driver behind the wheel. Come on, this way.*

The dog turned down a narrow alleyway, then stopped by a leafy green hedge. *We are here. You need to take the lead now, Barwick.*

'This is where we are going?' Alain whispered, his stomach clenching. He had managed to keep his fear of cars under control, but this was a step too far.

The two-storey house in front of them was painted white, and had more glass windows than he had seen in any dwelling other than Westminster Palace. Clearly the person living here was high-born and wealthy.

Looking around, he found the street to be full of similar buildings. It reminded him of the area in London where the barons and dukes had their city dwellings. Although he had spent time with King Henry, he was not used to actually staying with nobility, and he was not interested in changing that any time soon.

'It's very grand. Are you sure we will be welcome?' Alain said, a little louder.

'Don't worry. We will be fine.' Master Barwick placed a comforting hand on his shoulder. 'Things have changed much since our time. The general population of England has a much higher standard of living, and I think you will find the people who live here quite ordinary.'

Taking a deep breath, Alain followed Master Barwick to the veranda and waited while the older man knocked on the door. The master waited a moment, then knocked again.

'Hold your horses, I'm coming,' a voice yelled from within, followed by the sound of feet slapping on bare floorboards.

The door flung open and standing in front of them was a woman who barely reached Alain's shoulders, with short grey hair and intense brown eyes. She reminded him of someone, but he could not place his finger on it. She slowly looked them up and down, her eyebrows rising quizzically.

'Can I help you?' she asked in a voice that told them she clearly did not think she would be able to.

'I think, madam, you will find it is we who have come to help you,' Master Barwick said.

Frowning, the woman glared at Master Barwick, then shook her head. 'I am sorry, but I am not into medieval re-enactments, so I am not sure how you can ...'

'Medieval?' The word slipped from Alain's lips. *Oops, I really must stop letting my thoughts escape through my mouth,* he admonished himself.

It is what people now call the time you lived in—the

Middle Ages or the Dark Ages, Trouble told him.

Why the Dark Ages? Alain asked.

In later centuries, the so-called Middle Ages were seen as a time of artistic and intellectual decline, Trouble responded.

Alain snorted. *Dark Ages—well, that is downright insulting and ...*

... and not something you can do anything about, Trouble calmly informed him.

Still, I could name this period as dark given how much they have pillaged the land, Alain continued.

'Quiet. I am talking here,' Master Barwick admonished them.

'Well, I never —he only asked a simple question.' The woman placed her hands on her hips and glared at the man on her doorstep, then turned her focus to Alain. 'It is just you are dressed in costumes from the Middle Ages, young man, so I assumed ...' The woman stopped and stared at Master Barwick, who was blushing all the way to the tips of his wayward white hair.

Alain thought to himself, *How odd. She reminds me of Barabal—or maybe I just have Barabal on my mind.*

Wringing his hands, his Master started again. 'Please, this is not going so well. Perhaps we might start over. I am Barnaby Barwick, master apothecary and part-time alchemist. I have been led to believe someone at this address called for assistance from a group we believed long forgotten on this world.'

With her mouth hanging open, the woman swayed and clutched at the doorjamb before uttering, 'Oh my goodness. My spell actually worked? You are an actual guardian?'

'Well, no, not exactly. But I have been sent by them to help you out. Actually, we both have. This is Alain, my nephew and apprentice.'

'The guardians sent you?' the woman repeated. 'You're not having a joke at my expense?'

'Madam, I never joke.' Master Barwick pulled himself up to his full height and puffed out his chest. 'We call them the Time Guardians, and yes, they sent us. Do you still need our help? If so, perhaps we might come in out of the cold and talk about why you called for assistance. We have come a long way, and we didn't dress for this wet weather.'

There was a long pause as the woman stared blankly at Master Barwick, and Alain wondered if she might not be a little simple. Just as he was preparing to suggest they leave, the woman shook her head, and held the door open as she spoke. 'Yes, yes. Oh ... sorry ...please forgive me, it is just you took me a little by surprise. I didn't expect it to work ... oh, look at me ... where are my manners? Please come in.' She moved aside and ushered her guests past. 'Keep going down the hall. The kitchen is down the back and the Aga is on full, so you should warm up in no time.'

Alain warily followed Master Barwick in, but not before glancing behind to ensure Trouble was with them.

'The dog is with you? Is he okay inside?'

Looking down at the diminutive woman Alain frowned, not quite sure what she meant by okay. She had paused in the hallway, waiting for him to respond, so he said, 'Yes, he is with us and needs to come inside.'

'Good. I wasn't sure whether he was house-trained or not.'

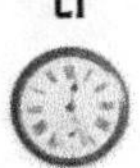

Trouble humphed his displeasure as their hostess shut the door, then escorted them down a narrow hallway. On the left was a room, and to the right were stairs to the second storey.

As he passed by a sitting room, Alain's eyes were drawn to a wall covered in books, showing how wealthy his hostess must be. Beside the books was a shiny rectangular black box on a table, and on the mantle next door was a gold pendulum clock. By the time he arrived at the doorway at the end of the hall, he was almost paralysed by the unfamiliar and expensive items on display.

The opening led into a kitchen which ran the width of the house. It was dominated by a wooden table that would easily seat ten people, and a huge stove to the left. The woman slipped by him and headed to the sink, which was under a window directly in front of them. She turned on a tap to fill a kettle before placing it on the stove. Alain's eyes widened—they had running water *in* the house.

To the right of the bench was another door with two rows of three glass panels at the top, framing a garden out the back. Nestled into the wall to the right was an odd white thing that gave off a faint hum. As he slowly moved inside the room, he bumped his hip against a floor-to-ceiling dresser with plates and serving dishes running along the wall.

Moving closer to Master Barwick, who had set himself by the stove, Alain enjoyed the delicious warmth encompassing him.

'You are both wet through, let me find you some towels to dry off. Where are your cases? Are they in your car? Perhaps you should get them and change into something dry.'

They must have looked confused, because she stopped and looked at them—really looked at them. Resting her chin in her hand, she circled them both, stopping when she came face to face with Master Barwick. 'Your clothes—they are not some sort of re-enactment garb, are they?' She reached out and rubbed the fabric at the bottom of the master's tunic between her fingers, then turned it inside out so she might better see how the garment was constructed. 'Your tunic is actually made of pure wool, and those seams are hand-sewn.'

When neither of them attempted an explanation, she said, 'When you speak, the right words come out of your mouth, but your lips are not making the shapes they should—it's like watching a badly dubbed movie. You have travelled from somewhere else entirely.'

How could he ever have thought this woman was addle-brained? Alain looked to his master, then at Trouble, wondering how they were going to handle this situation.

What do I tell her? Master Barwick asked Trouble.

Barwick, I see no other way than to tell her the truth. Lies are too difficult to sustain for long, and I think you and Alain will need someone to help you both adjust to the strangeness of this time.

'Umm ...' Master Barwick started, but was quickly interrupted by Trouble.

Best you don't say anything about me for the moment. Time travel will be hard enough to deal with without introducing the idea of talking dogs.

'Um ... yes, you could say we are from far away—another

time, in fact. Perhaps if you would not mind if we dried out, and maybe partake of a cup of tea once the kettle is boiled. When we are warm and dry we will tell you where we come from, and then you might tell us what is going on here and why we were summoned.'

The woman didn't move for a moment, then nodded once and swivelled on her heel. Over her shoulder, she said, 'I will get some towels. I think my husband's clothes should fit you, and I might find some of my son's things in the closets for Alain.'

She shut the door behind her. Alain soon heard footsteps on the stairs and the sounds of rummaging above. Wet and cold, they had little option but to wait for the woman who had called them to this time to return.

Sometime later, they were sitting at the table in the kitchen with Trouble curled up on a brightly crocheted blanket in front of the Aga. The clothes Alain wore felt strange. Alice, for that was the name of their hostess, had informed him the trousers were called jeans, and the warm top was a fleece. It was nothing like an animal fleece, but it was soft and warm, and cosy.

The clothes belonged to Alice's son, who was a soldier stationed in Afghanistan—wherever that was. His hostess was sure he would not mind Alain borrowing some of his clothes.

Master Barwick was dressed in something called corduroys, a shirt and a woollen sweater. They belonged to Alice's husband, who was on a business trip to another country called Hong Kong, and would not return for some weeks.

Warm, dry, and with their stomachs full, they were sitting with a cup of tea each. Alain rolled the tea around his mouth. It tasted different from the teas he was used to drinking. It was even more delicious when he followed Alice's advice and added a dash of milk from the jug.

'Right, now we are fed and watered, it is time to get down to business. Let's start with your names again, and where you are from.' Her brusque and authoritative manner really did remind him of his friend Barabal, so much so it brought a lump to his throat.

'I am Master Barwick, apothecary to King Henry when he is in London.'

'King Henry? Henry the Eighth?'

'The eighth? No.' Master Barwick shook his head. 'My king is the only King of England to have been called Henry.'

'Oh my goodness.' Alice's hand flew to her mouth. 'You are from around the time of ... oh let me think ...'

'We came from the year 1100AD,' Alain told her.

'Goodness, how strange all this must be for you.' Alice looked kindly at him, and he wanted to tell her how unsettling it actually was, and how much he wished he had not come. But she had been so welcoming, and she needed their help, so he mumbled it was not too bad, and carried on sipping his drink.

'How did you get here?' she asked.

'The Time Guardians can create time and space portals for travel,' Master Barwick informed her.

Alain waited for her look of confusion and some questions about how something like that might work.

Instead, he was treated to a nod as Alice commented, 'Of course they would be able to do that.'

As Alain pondered what sort of world this was where magic was all but gone but time and space portals were treated as an everyday thing, Master Barwick continued to explain their current situation.

'We arrived with only what you see. As you can imagine, anything from our time would make us stand out, and we don't want that. So I am afraid we will need a bit of support while we investigate your problem.'

A frown furrowed Alice's brow before she launched into organisation mode. 'I have my niece and nephew arriving today, so things might be a little cramped. Let me see. You can have my husband's office over the garage. You did say you are also an alchemist. Well, he is a scientist and you might find his equipment useful. He also has a pull-out couch you can sleep on.'

Alain and Master Barwick exchanged glances. *Pull-out couch?* Alain asked and his master shrugged his shoulders.

'Bebe can sleep in the guest room as planned. Alain can share with Lee in my son's room—I think we still have the old trundle bed we used to use when his friends came for sleepovers.'

Do not even ask. I have no idea about trundles and sleepovers, Master Barwick warned. *Trouble?*

The dog raised his eyebrows, but made no effort to enlighten them.

'Follow me. I will show you everything. Once you are settled in, we can talk about what drove me to ask you here. Will the dog be okay by the fire?'

ALCHEMIST

I will be perfect, Trouble told them as he rolled on to his back, legs splayed.

Alice led them out through the back door and up the wooden stairs to the room over the garage. It was full of bottles, and burners and jars of powders and other things Alain was unable to name—everything any alchemist might ever want and more. While he and Master Barwick gawped, Alice apologised for the poor selection. 'I can get you anything else you might need,' she added

'No ... really ... this will be fine,' Master Barwick told her. His fingers were twitching so much Alain just knew he could not wait to get his hands on the toys on offer.

If the chemistry equipment was not enough, there was also a sofa, which turned out to be a comfy chair for more than one person. To their amazement, it transformed into a full-sized bed.

Am I in heaven? Master Barwick asked, the grin on his face emphasising his delight.

They re-entered the house through the front door, and their hostess led them up to a room which was obviously intended for sleeping, but contained some other strange items of furniture.

Retrieving something metal from under the bed, Alice asked him to help her pull out the legs. Once extended, it formed a kind of cot. So this was a trundle. Alice then led him to a cupboard in the hallway and asked him to pull a roll from the top shelf.

He unfurled the mattress out over the metal frame.

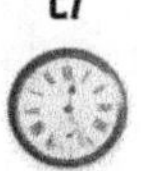

Alice then passed him another mattress, called a topper pad, and some bedding. When he had finished making up the trundle, Alice came back with two pillows and a thick blanket she called a duvet.

'I am sorry. It is not the most comfortable of beds,' Alice said as he sunk down to test it out.

Expecting it must be as hard as a board, he found himself enveloped in the comfiest bed he had ever lain on.

'I would let you have the other one, but Lee is quite a bit larger than you, and I suspect this thing would not hold his extra bulk.'

'This is perfect,' Alain assured her as his eyes began to close and his mind drifted off, revisiting all the strange things he had seen so far that day. Alice's voice pulled him back to the room.

'Here take this.' She handed him some sort of fabric bag. 'Open it for me and I will put some of my Tom's clothes in here. That way, my niece and nephew will not suspect where you came from.'

Turning the bag over in his hands, Alain found the mechanism keeping it closed, but he had no idea how to open it. Peering over the pile of clothes she had taken from the drawers, Alice laughed.

'Sorry, I should have thought. This is called a zip,' she explained as she pulled at a metal tag, which moved smoothly down to reveal the inside of the bag.

Placing each pile of clothing inside, she named them for him. 'Jeans, T-shirts, sweatshirts, underpants, shirts and underclothes. Hold on a moment; I have an extra toothbrush here and some toothpaste.'

Alain's head swam. It was obvious what the toothbrush

was used for. People here must use them instead of wooden sticks for cleaning teeth; but what on earth was toothpaste? His confusion must have been written on his face as Alice demonstrated how the paste was put on the brush and used with water to clean teeth.

It was all too much for Alain to take in. His head was spinning, and he was sure it would explode if he had to learn about one more thing.

'That's you sorted. Now it is your turn, Barnaby.' Alice handed Alain an oblong black box and said, 'Here, perhaps you could watch some telly while I sort him out.'

No doubt realising her mistake, she quickly grabbed the item back. 'This is difficult. This is a remote, it works the telly, or television, which provides entertainment.' Alice's hand swept towards the rectangular thing sitting on top of a dresser. It was a smaller version of the black box he had seen in the sitting room earlier.

Alain stared at his reflection in the shiny surface. How was this meant to entertain him?

Alice continued, 'It shows plays, and news, and, well, some other truly dreadful stuff you should avoid if at all possible.'

Alain looked blankly at her. She sighed and ran a hand through her hair. 'Let me see. Do you know anyone who can scry using water?'

Alain nodded. It was an advanced skill some druids still practiced. He had only seen it once, but he was fascinated by the images they conjured.

'Good. Well this is like entertainment in a scrying bowl.'

Nodding, Alain watched as Alice pressed the remote. A buzz caused him to turn just in time to see the thin black oblong thing light up, and people appear. Alain's jaw dropped. this was more amazing than the transforming sofa in the room above the garage.

'Re-runs of *Emmerdale*. Perhaps not so good for your first day in our time; it might give you the wrong impression.' Like a blinking eye, the picture changed and some of the strange horseless carriages appeared in place of the people.

'You cannot go too wrong with *Thomas the Tank Engine*,' Alice said as she pressed another button and the sound of voices filled the room.

Alain jumped back. 'I can hear them speak.'

'Ah, yes. Think of this as superpowered scrying.'

Master Barwick and Alice left him alone, and Alain sunk on the bed, entranced by the modern scrying device. Once he stopped wondering how machines had evolved enough to speak, he lost himself in the story of *The School of Ducks*.

He marvelled at how the engines worked to help the children get home after their school building was destroyed. He learnt some useful concepts about this world. The first was, all children seemed to go to school, and they had a special name for making use of things rather than throwing them away—recycling.

Alain chuckled as the engines looked through the debris people had discarded—there was even a table with a broken leg. Back home, if a table leg broke a new one was made. Even the broken wood would be carved into a spoon. No one would consider throwing out anything as valuable as a piece of furniture—they could not afford to.

He was disappointed when Alice reappeared and turned off the telly and urged him to come downstairs as they still had things to discuss.

Alain reluctantly followed her back to the kitchen. 'Alice, I have a few questions I would like to ask Thomas and his friends. Is it possible to visit and ask them myself, or should I write them in a letter?'

Alice tripped on the stair and he prevented her from falling and helped right her before she answered, 'Oh Alain, that was a story. Engines don't talk; it is just a make-believe show for children to watch, sort of like a play.'

'But I thought you said it was a scrying machine, and you can only scry actual people and actual places.' This television thing was really confusing. Surely if Thomas was like a play then there really were talking engines.

'Oh dear. I see I am going to have to be very careful how I explain things to you. Perhaps we should steer clear of the television for a while.'

'So the engines aren't real?' Alain plonked down in the chair beside Master Barwick, shaking his head. 'Perhaps it was a mistake coming here. I don't understand anything at all and the machines ...' he whispered to Master Barwick.

The older man squeezed his arm in understanding, then nodded towards Alice, who stood by the fire, ready to explain why she had called them.

'Before I start, I must address something. Perhaps your guardians were a little optimistic sending people from so far back in time to look into our problem. Since you arrived, I have found so many things that are new to you or that you don't understand. Modern technology and furniture aside, society has advanced so much you both stick out like sore thumbs.'

'We were led to believe there might be some sort of magical interference, and it has been a while since true magical practitioners walked the land in England, so what were the guardians to do?' Master Barwick countered on their behalf.

'I appreciate that, but your investigation might be hindered by your limitations in the modern world.'

I believe your skills far outweigh the disadvantages. Trouble raised his head and looked at them. *You just need to find a way to work around being in a different time.*

'Are you listening to me?' Alice asked, and Alain and Master Barwick turned to look at her.

'Sorry. We were thinking,' Alain explained on their behalf.

'I said, perhaps we tell the others Barnaby has come from somewhere quite remote to use Donald's equipment to run some tests on the problems we've been facing. I am sure you could play the eccentric scientist.'

Master Barwick nodded. 'We already thought of saying I live in the Outer Hebrides, and that Alain, my nephew, came to live with me as a small boy.'

'Good.' Alice nodded thoughtfully. 'If we explain how you homeschooled him because your island is so remote, and you never introduced him to technology because you don't believe in it—that will explain your lack of skills. But why would you bring him here now?'

Alice drummed her fingers against her lips. 'I know. We have a good school nearby, the Ballard School. It is small and select, and is the perfect place to send someone to finish their A levels before heading to university— especially someone who needs to get to grips with the modern world.'

'That is a great story,' Master Barwick acknowledged. 'Can we tie any of this in with what is happening in the New Forest, so it sounds less like a story and more like what might have happened?'

'Of course.' Alice appeared shocked that he would question her ability to produce a believable cover for them. The more she spoke, the more Alice reminded him of Barabal—his friend had the knack of turning every situation to her advantage as well. He had never met Barabal's mother. She had passed away when his friend was not much more than a baby, but he imagined she would have been a lot like Alice.

It is not so strange that she reminds you of Barabal. Alice is a distant relation of your friend —a many times great-grandchild, Trouble informed him.

Hold on a moment. I might have plans for Barabal and myself. Does that mean she is a relation of mine as well?

I am unable to say, Trouble responded.

I won't be upset either way, Alain reassured the dog. *Well, not much ...*

No, I obviously have not made myself clear. If I say she is or is not, that tells you something about your own future, and therefore might change it.

'Alain. ALAIN!'

'Sorry, Barnaby. My thoughts wandered off on me,' Alain was still looking from Trouble to Alice, unable to get his head around the idea that this woman who was old enough to be his mother might actually be his many-times-removed granddaughter—or not.

'Please pay attention, Alain. This is important. Alice

is ready to tell us why we have been called here.'

'I will start again so we are all on the same page,' Alice said, then waited as though she wanted to make sure she had their attention before continuing.

'For some time now, dogs in the local area have been getting ill. Many of them recover, but one or two have not pulled through. Local vets have not been able to identify the problem, but they have managed to narrow down the victims to dogs who are walked near here—in the New Forest.'

'Well that is a start,' Master Barwick commented.

'Yes, I guess it is,' Alice agreed.

'So, what are the symptoms?' He encouraged Alice to continue.

'The first signs are ulcers around the legs and chest, followed by lethargy and fever. This is as far as it goes for most dogs, but there are a few who advance on to renal failure—sorry, liver failure—and, in most of those cases, death.'

'Would you call it a mass outbreak, or an epidemic?' Master Barwick sat forward in his chair as he asked the question.

'No, not an epidemic. Well, not until recently. The number of incidents in our area have been growing exponentially compared to other places where the problem has been found. Still, I would not call it a full-blown epidemic, but I didn't want to wait until it reached that level before I called in help.'

Alain had been following along, and one question stood out, so he held up his hand to speak.

'You don't need to raise your hand; just ask what you

want to,' Master Barwick told him.

'Alice, you said you called us here because more dogs are getting sick. Have there been any cases in humans?'

'Goodness no. Whatever this is only affects dogs.'

Master Barwick ran his hand through his hair, causing it to stand up even more. 'All right, now we have cleared that up, Alice you said local vets have been looking into the cases you have had?'

'Mm, yes.'

'Right. First off, what is a vet?'

Alice laughed. 'Of course in your time you probably treated both people and their valuable animals. Now, doctors who look after animals are called vets.'

'Ah, so the animal doctors are looking into this. If that is the case, why have you called for a more, shall we say, mystical form of help?'

Alice coloured a little, and seemed to be searching for the right words to explain herself. 'This might sound odd, and maybe like I am a little crazy, but I have walked the forest where many of the dogs walk, and it ... well, it feels a little off?'

'A little off?' Master Barwick asked.

'This is difficult for me. I am the wife of a scientist, and my family laugh at me for it, but I have always been able to sense the energies of a place. I can tell when something is in balance, and when it is not. In my own small way I work to bring the balance back.'

'You are a witch?' Alain asked in surprise.

'Well, yes. Perhaps not in the way you mean, but I am certainly a modern-day witch. So when I say there are places in the New Forest that are "off", I mean they are out of balance with nature.'

'And you have not been able to fix it?' Master Barwick probed.

Alice frowned. 'No. I don't even know where to begin.'

I believe this suggests some sort of outside interference, just as the Council thought, Trouble said as he rose and moved to sit beside Alain.

Running his fingers through the hair on the dog's head, Alain attempted to sort through the information in front of him. 'Do any of your ... um ... vets know whether it is an illness passed from dog to dog? Or is it something from the earth or in the air?'

'They are not sure. Scientists are researching a number of theories on what causes the illness, but have not come to any conclusion. And, although they have found some animals respond well to blood transfusions, they have not been able to develop a cure.'

Before Alain could ask what a transfusion of blood was, Trouble provided the answer. *Modern man has found a way to replace a body's blood with blood from another like being.*

Oh, how exciting. I wonder if I could see them do that? Alain's curiosity was piqued.

With your penchant for blowing things up and pulling them apart, I do not think that is such a good idea. Trouble nudged Alain's hand with a cold, wet nose.

Yuck, what are you doing? Alain pulled his hand away.

A little scratch under my ears would be nice.

Alain obliged and returned his attention back to the main conversation. Master Barwick had already moved on.

'Right, I propose a three-pronged attack to investigate

this problem. Firstly, we need to walk around the part of the New Forest you say feels wrong. Secondly, we need to take some water and soil samples from the area to analyse. Finally, do you have access to a diseased animal? Studying one would be useful.'

'By studying, do you mean cutting one open to see how the disease has affected them internally?' Alice's tone was matter-of-fact.

'Heavens no. What a barbaric thought.' Master Barwick blanched. 'I want to study the animal's behaviour, perhaps take a little blood or saliva, and maybe a scraping or two from one of the sores.'

Alice expelled a breath and smiled. 'Oh, that is easily arranged. My friend has a dog that's taken ill; it's at the local vets. I'm sure she wouldn't mind you having a quick visit with Pepe. I'll give her a call now and arrange it.'

Alice hurried from the room.

'Give her a call?' Alain asked. 'Does she live close?'

People in this time have a way of communicating that is similar to mind-speak over great distances, Trouble explained as they heard Alice talking in the next room. *Maybe not so much mind-speak; it's more like being able to project their voices.*

Moments later, Alice returned. 'Jenna said she will talk to the vet and see what she can arrange for tomorrow. Before we go, we can head into the forest and I will show you around.'

'Perhaps we should go now?' Alain said. The sooner they solved this problem, the sooner he would be home.

'I would love to. How long would we be?' she asked, checking the clock on the wall.

'That depends on what we find,' Master Barwick said. 'I would like to walk the entire area and collect samples to test. If the area is large we might be two or three hours.'

'We will need to wait until tomorrow then; I need to be back here in an hour or so. My niece and nephew are due to arrive from Australia, and I want to be here to greet them. In the meantime, perhaps you can make yourselves comfortable while I start on a meal for this evening—I think I can make what I have stretch to feed us all.'

Alain laid his head on his arm as Trouble wandered back over to his place by the Aga. Closing his eyes, he blocked out the room he was in and imagined himself back in the servant's hall in Westminster Castle and the tension immediately left his body. Why did I ever think it was a good idea to come here?

CHAPTER TWO
THE GANG IS HERE

Tracking the path of a raindrop down the car window, Bebe sighed. It reached the door and slid from view. Leaning back on the seat she thought of her friends, who would no doubt be down at the beach. Hold on—they would be tucked up in bed having spent the day sunning on the sand, while she was speeding along a motorway in dreary old England.

Half-turning in her seat, she glared at her brother, who was perfectly calm and relaxed beside her. Lee sat there, his shirt un-rumpled, his hair perfect, looking no different to when they had boarded the plane in Sydney thirty-six hours ago.

On the other hand, she was clothed in a wrinkled jacket and had dribbled coffee on the collar of her shirt at some stage during their journey. Nothing she could do about that. After touching her greasy hair, she pulled a hairband from her wrist and twisted it into a messy bun. Taking a discreet sniff, she cringed at her own smell before reaching into her backpack. She found her emergency deodorant and made use of it. There—that was the best she could do in the circumstances.

Rainwater swished up as the taxi changed lanes, and Bebe braced herself against the door. Why had her father agreed to take a new posting in Brussels now? Why had her mother decided to go with him to set up house? Why had they both thought it a good idea she and Lee go and spend the time after exams with their aunt in some tiny town in the middle of nowhere, England? She sighed again.

'Honestly, Bebe, it is not the end of the world. Burley is near Southampton, and there are trains up to London. It is not like we are going to outer Mongolia.'

'You sound just like Mum and Dad,' she snapped.

'Perhaps, but they were right. This could be a fun break for us.'

'Trust you to support them. We are not all followers like you. Some of us have minds of our own.'

The hurt in her brother's eyes tugged at her heart and she bit her lip, unable to take the words back. Their parents' last-minute decision to send them across the other side of the world wasn't his fault.

'Sorry,' she mumbled, slouching down in the seat. She couldn't do anything right.

'It's all right,' he said, placing his hand over hers. 'It's just I want to make the most of this holiday. These are my last few months of freedom.'

'You chose to join the army and go to the academy.

ALCHEMIST

You can't blame me if you're worried about giving up your freedom,' she said. 'Sorry, that was mean. I'm just feeling blah. School is over, and I don't have a plan like you. I should be spending this time looking at options for next year, not having a break.'

Instead of the sympathetic noises of support she expected from her brother, he burst out laughing. 'Come on, Bebe. We both know over summer you'd work in the ice-cream parlour or laze on the beach with your friends. Only when everyone started up at uni in the new year would you start seriously looking for something to do with your time. At least this way we can tour around England, and I can help you get motivated. Maybe together we can come up with some options for you.'

Although she hated to admit Lee was right, he probably was. Most of her friends had provisional acceptances into courses for further study next year; the rest had jobs. On the other hand, she had no idea what she wanted to do beyond not making ice-creams for the rest of her life.

To make things worse, her father had been offered the posting of his dreams just as they were about to finish their final school exams. He had spent most of his military career in Australia, taking local postings because it was better for his family. With both his children finishing school, he'd decided to put himself first and had accepted a post as liaison officer to NATO in Brussels.

Lee had congratulated their father. With his future sorted and his accommodation provided at the military college, he was hardly affected by the change at all. Already in limbo, Bebe found it harder to be pleased for him. At first, she'd thought she would remain in their four-bedroom house by the water while she sorted out her life. When she'd said as much, her mother had looked genuinely shocked.

'Bebe, honey, we are renting out the house and taking an apartment in Brussels.'

'But I don't want to live in Brussels,' she'd protested.

'Actually, darling, while you will be welcome to visit any time you like, we were not expecting you to come live with us.'

'What?'

'You don't speak another language, so working or studying in Brussel's is out,' her father interjected.

'But what am I to do?'

'We thought you might go and spend some time with your Aunt Alice in England. Her husband is away lecturing at a foreign university while he works on some sort of advanced research project. And her son is stationed away with the British army. Given the circumstances, she might enjoy some company. Lee can go with you if he wants to,' her father had said.

'Dad and I would join you at Alice's for Christmas before sending Lee off home to begin his studies and moving to Brussels,' her mother had added.

'And what would I do after Christmas?' Bebe had still been rather shocked at her parents abandoning her without a second thought.

'Well, darling, we rather thought you might like to stay on in England. There are way more opportunities for you to consider in the United Kingdom than here, and I am sure Alice would love for you to stay a while longer,' her mother had offered.

Bebe blushed with shame as she remembered the argument that followed; she was still embarrassed by her own behaviour. Worse still, in the two weeks that had followed, she still had not looked into a single option for her future.

On the night before she and Lee had departed, her parents had held a party to celebrate their eighteenth birthday. With exams done and summer break on the horizon, her friends had bubbled with excitement. They'd wanted to enjoy their time together before they headed off in different directions. She, on the other hand, had been unable to enjoy herself as she was not yet ready to leave her life behind.

She leaned her forehead against the window. Beside her reflection, the scenery passed by—grey houses and grey roads appeared even more dismal in the drizzling rain. Smiling wryly, she considered how the day reflected her mood—dreary. How was she to find something to excite and engage her in a strange country in the middle of a winter?

Sickened by her own depressing thoughts, she asked, 'Do you remember Aunt Alice?'

'Not really. We were only about five or six when she came out to Australia for Grandad's funeral. I think I remember her face.'

'I don't even remember that. All I remember is Dad teasing her about selling magical things in her shop, but that may be from later conversations.'

'Yeah, that's strange. Here, look at this.' He passed his phone to her. He had googled their aunt's shop—The Witch's Hat.

Bebe took it and scrolled through the website. 'Oh my goodness. I thought it was like a touristy sort of thing, and some of it is. But see? It says the shop stocks everything the modern witch or wizard might need to practice their craft. Sounds like she must be pretty kooky—not like Dad at all.'

'I don't remember her being particularly odd; just sad.' Lee took his phone back as he spoke.

Staring out the window of the car as they left the motorway and headed into the New Forest, Bebe held back yet another sigh as the sun attempted to break through the clouds. The fields they drove through were green compared to her beloved Australia.

'Did you see that?' she exclaimed, pointing towards the forest. 'There are horses over by the trees, and they are not in a paddock—there are no fences to keep them in.'

'New Forest Ponies—they're a protected species.' Lee had an answer for everything. He would have thoroughly researched this place before they'd even set foot on the plane to get here. He leaned around her as if attempting to catch a glimpse of the native horses, and she sunk back into the seat so he could see better.

Only moments later, the taxi slowed down before pulling to a standstill outside a large, two-storey house. The door opened and a woman about Bebe's height rushed out to greet them, a large grin on her face.

'Welcome, welcome to Burley,' she said, pulling them into a big hug.

Bebe disentangled herself as soon as she could, observing the stranger who they would be living with for the next month or so. She glanced around the country lane that was so far from Sydney in summer. *Nice though all this is, at the moment I would rather be anywhere else than here.*

Lazing in a comfortable armchair in front of a blazing fire, with Trouble curled up on a blanket beside him, Alain had spent a pleasant afternoon reading a book, much to his surprise. After lunch, Alice had encouraged him to search the shelves and find something to while away the winter afternoon. Shocked at such a waste of time, he had first offered to help Master Barwick go through the alchemical equipment in the office.

'I'm not sure what Alice's husband keeps in the garage, so I think I would rather look by myself and see if there is anything we can use,' his master said before heading out the back door.

He means without your constant questions, Trouble clarified, with a snorting chuckle.

Turning to Alice he had asked, 'Is there anything you would like me to do?'

She considered his question then shook her head. 'It is too miserable outside to do gardening. I cleaned the house within an inch of its life yesterday for my visitors— so not really. I am going to do some accounts. I guess you could help me with them if you have any experience in that area?' She raised an eyebrow in enquiry, and he grinned sheepishly in response.

'Accounts? Numbers aren't my strong suit,' he admitted.

'Well, I guess an afternoon with a good book in front

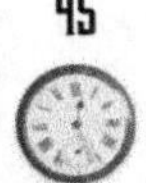

of the fire it is then.'

After searching the bookshelves, he found a book on the modern history of England. The first few chapters had his head spinning—there was so much to take in. When he complained to Trouble, the dog told him no good ever came of learning about your own future and suggested he try a work of fiction.

Being compared to wealthy noblewomen, who were the only people he knew who had time to read story books, was plain insulting—as if he would be interested in romances anyway.

Perhaps Trouble was reading Alain's thoughts as he told him, *Don't be so quick to judge; some of those romances are great reads. However, times have changed. Books are now mass produced and affordable. Many people from all walks of life read for pleasure, and there are a wide range of options to choose from.*

Encouraged by his Guardian dog, he returned to the shelves and started reading the titles. Finally, he found one he thought he might enjoy—*The Lord of the Rings*. It was not the tale of noble doings he had anticipated; in fact, it was a fantasy book about elves and hobbits set in a fantastical world. Although the story was not what he'd expected, he was too comfortable to move, so he persevered.

Alice came in to place more coal on the fire, and he never stirred. Nor did he stop to drink the tea she placed on the table beside him, or raise an eye when she came to in draw the curtains in preparation of the coming evening drop in temperature.

'Oh, they are here!'

Alice's exclamation pulled him from the world of Middle Earth—that and Trouble stretching beside him. Master Barwick wandered in from the kitchen as Alice flung open the door and ran outside. Moments later she returned, leading a boy and girl into the hallway. Alain's jaw dropped. Standing in front of him were the two people he had left that morning: Stanislaus and Barabal.

Shut your jaw. You look like a half-wit, Trouble told him.

But ...

... I know. It is not by chance I asked you to come here. We thought getting the old team together might give us a chance to resolve this problem a bit faster.

They cannot be ... Alain stumbled

They are not, Trouble said, transmitting his impatience along with his words.

They are reincarnations?

Finally you get it.

'This is my friend Barnaby Barwick,' Alice said, and Master Barwick nodded hello. 'And this young lad is his nephew, Alain. They both arrived today as well. Alain, meet Bebe and Lee.'

'Hi,' the two newcomers said in unison.

'Hello,' Alain responded, still somewhat dazed.

'Alain, why don't you and Lee grab the suitcases and take them upstairs? You can show Lee to your room and settle in, then I think I will make some hot chocolate. Bebe, I will just go and put the milk on, and after I will show you where you are to sleep.'

Alice followed Master Barwick into the kitchen, and Bebe trailed behind, but not before shooting a bemused look at her brother.

'I hope you do not mind sharing with me,' Alain said as he grabbed a suitcase and started up the stairs.

A grin split the boy's face. 'No, I'm sure it will be fun. I don't know anyone here, so it will be nice to have someone to talk to.'

Lee's strong resemblance to Stanislaus dispelled Alain's fears about bunking with a stranger. It could have been awkward, but at the moment it seemed more like he was sharing with an old friend.

'You know, I cannot help feeling like we have met somewhere before,' Lee said as they climbed the stairs.

'This is my first trip away from home,' Alain said. 'I live in the Hebrides—in Scotland.'

Lee shrugged. 'I've never been to Scotland, so I guess there is no way we could have.'

'No, I guess not ...' Alain said as he opened the door to their room. 'Here we are. Alice said you would need the bed, and I can see why.' The boy was well over six foot tall and moved confidently, like someone used to physical pursuits.

Lee dumped his case on the floor, turned around and grinned. 'Sometimes being this tall has its advantages, but we can chop and change if that bed is too uncomfortable.'

'No, it is not too bad,' Alain said, not wanting to lose his comfy bed to the other boy.

He popped Bebe's case outside the door to her room. As he returned, Lee was saying, 'I am not a big one for telly; do you mind if we put this in the wardrobe to make some room?'

'No, I'm fine with that. I had never seen one before today when I watched *Thomas the Tank Engine*, and I found it a little disturbing, so I think I'll stick to books from now on.'

Lee laughed. 'Well of course Thomas is weird—all those little talking engines. I could never understand why other kids didn't find it as scary as I did.'

He fiddled with some cords at the back of the telly, then carried it over to the wardrobe in the corner. 'Here, open this for me, would you?'

Alain held the door while Lee placed the telly on the ground in the closet, then closed it.

'So, is there anything much to do around here?' Lee asked.

'I only arrived this morning, but I was reading this good book ...'

'Did you say "book"?'

Alain laughed at the horror on the other boy's face. 'Yes—*Lord of the Rings*. Have you heard of it?'

'Who hasn't heard of it? One of the best movie trilogies ever.'

'Movie?'

'Oh man, your island must be very remote. Didn't you have a cinema, or a hall to watch movies in? I will see if Aunt Alice has a copy on DVD, but perhaps you should finish reading it first. Friends of mine say if you see the movie before you finish the book it spoils it.'

Although the conversation was mostly going over Alain's head, he felt more comfortable than he had since he arrived in this strange time. Like Stanislaus, Lee was open and friendly and easy to talk to.

Lee nudged his case under the bed with his foot, stretched and said, 'Come on. Aunt Alice mentioned hot chocolate, and although I think a coffee would help keep me awake for longer, I never turn down food. I wonder if we'll get cake to go with it?'

Yes, Alain thought. *This is exactly like being with Stanislaus.*

Alain was in heaven. He had not imagined anything could taste as delicious as hot chocolate. Then Bebe showed him how to add little fluffy balls called marshmallows, and he almost groaned in ecstasy. So intent was he on savouring his drink and consuming some of Alice's gingerbread loaf he was unable to concentrate on anything anyone said.

'You guys came all the way down here to study some rare disease affecting dogs?' Lee asked.

'And to check out a school for Alain,' Alice added.

'Yes, but my point is, don't they already have people in Hampshire investigating the outbreak?'

'Well, um, yes they do,' Master Barwick responded, looking a little like an animal caught in a trap.

Alice came to his rescue. 'Barnaby's unique skills give him a different perspective from the other scientists.'

Perhaps because he was hungry, or perhaps because he thought he should help Master Barwick out of a sticky situation, Trouble chose that moment to join them in the kitchen.

'Oh, what an adorable dog,' Bebe said as she left the table and crouched down to scratch Trouble behind his ears. Trouble moved his head to the side to allow her to give the other ear the same treatment, and leaned into her in apparent ecstasy.

'What's his name?' the girl asked.

'Trouble,' Alain said, suppressing a smirk.

'Oh, no! You named this beautiful boy Trouble. I bet you are no trouble at all,' she crooned.

Trouble's liquid brown eyes turned to Master Barwick, and he said, *See? Someone understands and appreciates me.*

'And you would be wrong,' Master Barwick mumbled under his breath as Trouble wagged his tail while continuing to stare balefully at the alchemist.

'When do you start investigating? Can we help?' Lee asked, leaning forward and resting his arms on the table.

'Well, I am not sure what you can do ...' Master Barwick started.

They are here to help, Barwick. I believe the old team will help us solve this more quickly, Trouble said.

But the old team isn't here; we're missing John, Alain told them, and he thought he heard Trouble say *yet* as he turned his attention back to the others.

'We could help you collect samples,' Bebe offered. 'It would be fun.'

'Fun?' Alain asked, unsure what was fun about running around in the middle of winter in a forest.

'And I can look things up on the internet,' Lee said.

Internet? Both Alain and Master Barwick thought together, but did not say anything as the others carried on sharing ideas. They were still in the dark as to what an internet was when a knock at the back door interrupted them.

Alice opened it to let in a girl about the same age as

the others. She removed the hood of her coat to reveal spiky brown hair and thoughtful chocolate eyes. After hanging the outer garment on a hook on the back of the door, she rubbed her hands up her arms encased in a black sweater and headed over to the Aga to warm up.

Her bright colourful skirt swished as she walked past, revealing to Alain what looked like black leather work boots. What drew his eye, though, was the line of rings this newcomer had all the way down one ear. Once he managed to get past her strange manner of dress, he studied her face as she warmed herself, and realised she looked familiar—very familiar.

John? Alain asked Trouble, and the dog nodded.

John had been pulled from outback Australia in the 1880's into Medieval England, and he had quickly adjusted to the situation he'd found himself in—better than Alain was adjusting to modern Hampshire. So he had high hopes that this reincarnation of his friend would display the same no-nonsense attitude that made him invaluable to their team when they'd saved King Henry.

'Hi Alice. Just dropping your keys back. I locked the float and the takings in the safe. It was a slow day, so there wasn't enough to warrant dropping at the bank.'

'Thank you, Jo. What shift is your mum on today?'

'Afternoons,' the girl answered.

'Do you want to join us for some dinner?'

'Um ...' She looked around the room as if she just noticed the other people. 'It looks like your hands are full already. I'll head off home.'

'I made a big pot of spaghetti Bolognese, so there is enough for everyone here with some spare. There is enough for you to take home for your mum too,' Alice informed her.

'Well ... I guess I can stay. It beats warming up a frozen dinner.'

Alice turned to the others. 'Jo works for me in the shop. Her mother is a nurse at the hospital in Southampton, and she often shares an evening meal with me when her mum isn't home.'

They all made room at the table for Jo. Alice poured her a hot chocolate while the others carried on as if there had been no interruption.

'I will be collecting samples tomorrow morning, bright and early,' Master Barwick told them. 'If you want to come you best be up and ready. I will not dilly-dally waiting for you.'

Alain got the impression Master Barwick was only offering because he thought the young people would not want to join him on an early morning stroll.

'Most mornings I get up for a run before sunrise, so I will be awake,' Lee said, preening a little and looking at Jo, who seemed not to notice his antics.

'Won't you have jet lag?' Jo asked.

Jet lag? Alain repeated.

Shh, I am trying to listen, Trouble said, placing his head on Master Barwick's knee.

'Mm, that is true, so I will probably be awake much earlier.' Lee smiled.

'Then you can wake me,' Bebe said.

'No grumbling if I do,' Lee responded. 'I don't want a pillow to the head because you forgot you asked me to do it.'

Bebe laughed, and the two turned expectantly to Alain. 'Hey. I was already going. After all, I usually help Uncle Barnaby with his experiments and studies.'

Jo looked quizzically at them all, and Alice said, 'The pasta should be about done. Come and help me dish up, and I will explain.'

With so many people sitting around the table talking and eating, Alain closed his eyes and was almost able to imagine himself back in the dining room at Winchester Castle. Well, until he took a mouthful of food. Although delicious, it was strange.

The long strands of spaghetti were difficult to wrangle into his mouth, even after Bebe had given him a demonstration. He gave his full attention to each spoonful and so, rather than joining in the conversation as he would have done at home, Alain found himself becoming quieter and quieter. In the end, he was content to just listen.

As the twins cleared the table, Alice offered some of her "world-famous" carrot cake for dessert. Bebe and Lee yawned.

'I couldn't eat another thing,' Bebe said, stretching like a cat.

'And I can barely keep my eyes open,' Lee added. 'I think it is bed for me. Barnaby, what time would you like us up in the morning?'

'Don't forget I have to open my shop at ten,' Alice said.

'Ah, well, shall we say seven?'

Alice shook her head. 'It will still be dark. What say

we get up at seven for breakfast and head out at first light?'

Having agreed upon a time, the twins rose to leave. As they did, Lee turned and said to Alain, 'Please try not to turn on the light when you come up. I'm a light sleeper.'

'I won't,' Alain quickly promised. There was no way he was going to touch the switch on the wall that made light appear using something called electricity—well, at least not until he figured out how it all worked anyway.

Alice told the others to make themselves comfortable in the living room and she would bring through coffee and cake. Alain warily followed Jo and Master Barwick into the other room, and sat on the sofa with Trouble half beside him and half in his lap. Patting the dog helped ground him, making this place seem less strange.

Are you all right, Alain? Perhaps my bringing you here was a little selfish. We could do with your help, but I think the stress of being in 2017 is getting to you, Trouble said as he dropped his head on Alain's knees.

'Who said that?' Jo looked at each of them in turn, then her eyes darted round the room.

'You heard that?' Master Barwick asked, head cocked to the side as he surveyed Alice's assistant, before turning to glare at Trouble. *You allowed her to hear you?*

The dog stared back, unperturbed.

'Yes, and obviously you did too. Is there some sort of speaker in here? And what did they mean about bringing Alain to this time?' Jo's eyes pierced Master Barwick's as if nailing him to a wall.

Please calm down, Jo. If you search your heart you will know who is speaking, Trouble said, his voice low and soothing.

Before Jo could respond, Master Barwick said, *Trouble ... umm ... Sigma, is it wise for you to be activating Jo's memories at this time? She is not quite ready for true understanding of the roles and responsibilities of a guardian, so awakening this part of her mind will serve no real purpose.*

She is close enough, Barwick, and it would help us to have one more person totally aware of what is going on. Once she fully understands the situation she will be able to help us, and especially Alain, while we are here.

Unaware of their private conversation, Jo pointed at Trouble. 'You ... you are talking into our minds. And ... we have met before, haven't we?' A frown drew her brows together. 'Not you and I, but ... Oh my, what did Alice do?'

'What did Alice tell you about us before?' Master Barwick asked, shooting a look at Trouble that screamed "don't interfere".

'Um, just that she called some friends to come and help with the dog problems around here. Oh, and that you came from somewhere far away, quite remote, in fact, and do not spend a lot of time with other people. She said I might find you both a bit odd.' Jo chewed on her lip for a moment before continuing. 'But I suspect you have come from quite far away—extremely far away.'

'Yes, we have, lass, from a time when our links to Mother Earth were much stronger than they are now. Being from the distant past, we bring unique skills to identify whether or not what is happening to the dogs is a natural occurrence, or something more sinister.'

Jo stared thoughtfully at the three of them. 'You're telling me you time travelled?'

'Yes, I am,' Master Barwick said.

Jo studied the three of them, and Alain squirmed under her scrutiny. She folded her arms. 'Can I assume that all dogs do not mind-speak in your time?'

'That is correct,' Master Barwick answered.

'Mm, so Trouble is not actually a dog.' The young woman's arms were still crossed as if they provided some sort of protection from this unusual situation. 'So ... who did Alice call to get you here? I thought she had phoned someone, but she didn't, did she? Ah, I know! She cast a spell from one of her books? One of the older ones? I found one on her desk.'

Phoned someone? Alain thought, then he remembered Alice talking to her friend before and he realised this must be quite a common activity in this time, and he chuckled at the thought of someone contacting the Guardians in that way.

Yes, she invoked an old spell asking the Time Guardians for assistance. It is an ancient spell, one not used in generations, Trouble answered.

Jo laughed. 'Oh my gosh ... for real? Time Guardians? My mum used to tell me stories about the Time Guardians, ones her great-great-grandad used to tell his kids and grandkids. Do you expect me to believe they are real?'

After our meeting, John Smith kept an eye out for events the Time Guardians might have had a hand in, and he wrote them down as stories and shared them with his family, Trouble explained to Barwick and Alain.

'John Smith. You met one of my ancestors? The one who wrote the book?' Jo was incredulous.

'Yes, we all did,' Alain said.

'All did what?' Alice asked as she entered the room with a jug, some mugs, and plates heaped with generous slices of cake.

'These are Time Guardians,' Jo said, almost as though she could not quite believe she was saying the words.

'I know. I called them,' Alice said as she placed the tray on the table under the window.

Master Barwick cleared his throat. 'Strictly speaking, Sigma, or Trouble, as we are calling him in this form, is the only Time Guardian in our group. I am still in training, and Alain is only an assistant on this mission—although we will certainly be making use of his chemistry skills.'

'Sigma?' Alice asked.

'The dog,' Jo offered.

'You're kidding me. You're saying that the dog is in charge, not you?' Alice turned to Master Barwick.

'He speaks into minds,' Jo said.

'Not into mine,' Alice responded.

I can if I choose to, as you have a small magical gift.

Alice spilt the coffee she was pouring. Placing the pot down until her hand stopped shaking, she frowned at the dog in front of her.

I would appreciate it if you all do not go 'round spreading the fact that I am a Time Guardian. It makes my job harder, the more people know who I am, Trouble told them. *Not to mention the fact most people will think you are crazy.*

Alice stared at Trouble, her face an unreadable mask, before disappearing, returning a moment later with a cloth to clean up the mess. As she cleaned, she muttered, 'Talking dogs, people from the past, all from a simple spell ... who would have thought?'

ALCHEMIST

With the mess tidied, and Alice's composure restored, they all settled down with their dessert and the room was quiet for a while until Alice broke the silence.

'Has Trouble only just started speaking to us?'

'No. Well I don't think so because I heard him.' Jo frowned and turned to Master Barwick.

'Um ... well ...'

'How come Jo could and I couldn't?' Alice shifted in her seat so she could also direct her question to the apothecary.

'Ah, now that is interesting,' Master Barwick started as Jo sat forward as if eager to hear the answer. 'I believe we need to open our thoughts specifically towards you for you to hear mind-speak. Jo though is almost ready to begin her training as a Time Guardian so is more likely to pick it up unless we specifically shield ourselves.

'I'm to be a Guardian?' A grin split Jo's face.

'Yes, of course. I would say one or two more reincarnations should do it?' Master Barwick looked at Trouble.

I would say that is about right.

'What? I am going to get a chance to time travel and save the world? How cool!'

'Perhaps not you, as such, although who knows?' Master Barwick laughed. 'In the meantime, though, we need your help with our current investigation.'

'I would have helped anyway, even without the promise of future adventures. I would do anything to stop more dogs getting sick,' Jo assured the group.

'Jo is on a gap year after finishing school. She is saving up to go to university to study to become a vet,' Alice informed them. 'Not only does she work in my shop for extra cash, but she helps out at the local veterinary practice to get some experience. She is the one who will take you in to see Pepe the dog tomorrow.'

'I popped in to see Pepe before going in to work today. They gave him a transfusion this morning, and he was looking a little perkier,' Jo informed them as Alain took his first bite of cake.

'Oh, this is amazing.' Alain took another mouthful. 'With this and hot chocolate, I may never want to go home.'

After picking up the drink Alice had told him was decaf coffee, he took a mouthful. Expecting something sweet and beautiful like hot chocolate, he had to stop himself from spitting the bitter liquid out. 'Argh. That is horrid though.'

'It is an acquired taste. Some people find a dash of milk and a little sugar help improve the flavour.' Jo sat forward and added milk to her own coffee to show him how it was done.

Following her actions, he tried the drink again, and found it more palatable. He ate a little cake, then drank some coffee. *Ah, apart one is too bitter and the other almost too sweet,* he marvelled, *but together they are perfect.*

Jo smiled at him. 'I think I am going to enjoy showing you around. Being with you is like learning about the world all over again.'

'Would you like some more?' Alice offered and Alain placed his plate on the table.

In spite of Master Barwick's disapproving stare, he accepted a second slice of cake and some more coffee. If he was going to be in this strange place for a while, at least he would eat well.

'Let him be,' Alice admonished Master Barwick as she returned to her seat beside him. 'I enjoy having someone with a healthy appetite in the house.'

'He won't be able to fit in to the house if he keeps eating like that,' Master Barwick said under his breath.

'Oh, there's Mum,' Jo said as a bright light penetrated a gap in the curtains. 'Thanks for the dinner, Alice.'

'Hold on a moment. I have some for your mother.' Alice disappeared into the kitchen.

Jo took the bag of food from Alice and waved goodbye to the others. 'I will see you at the vet tomorrow perhaps near the end of my shift—I finish around eleven. Come to the back door and I will let you in,' she threw back over her shoulder as she slipped outside.

Not long after Jo had left, Alice declared herself done in. Alain helped her take the dessert things back into the kitchen. After they had washed everything up, he followed her back out. While they were away, Master Barwick had made himself comfortable flicking through a history book.

'Are you not tired, Barnaby?' Alice asked, stifling a yawn.

'At my age, you do not need much sleep. Don't worry; I will lock up just as you showed me when I go to bed. And the key you gave me to let myself in tomorrow morning is quite safe,' he said as he patted a trouser pocket.

Creeping into the room he was to share with Lee, Alain stumbled over his bag and fell on the bed. Holding his breath, he waited for Lee to grumble his displeasure at being woken. His breathing remained steady and Alain could not help but smile. Just like Stanislaus, Lee slept like a log.

Changing into his pyjamas, Alain thought about the day. Rather than being excited by all he'd discovered, he found the strangeness of life here made him miss the comforts of home. Not even hot chocolate and Lee could make up for Barabal and Stanislaus not being here with him.

When he had decided to go on this adventure he had not considered how much he would miss them. It made it all the harder because his last conversation with Barabal had ended badly. Hands clasped behind his head, he stared at the ceiling as he relived the scene.

'All I said was I was thinking about going home to Winchester to visit my family and to help ensure the lands of the New Forest are given back to their rightful owners.'

Barabal continued tossing clothes into her travel bag. 'What about your apprenticeship with Master Barwick, and taking on his practice?'

When Alain did not respond, she carried on. 'And what about ...' She stopped mid-action as if unsure what to say next. 'I thought we had an understanding that we would both be staying on here at Westminster.'

Alain's stomach had knotted, torn between committing to Barabal or going home to have his father's lands restored.

'Alain. Alain! Are you even listening to me?' Barabal stood in front of him, hands on hips. 'Will you be here when I get back from escorting the princess to her wedding?' Barabal demanded an answer, but he caught a look of uncertainty in her eyes. 'I have to leave in a couple of hours so I don't have time to talk this through properly, but ...'

'I just need some time to think, Barabal. I will let

you know this evening before you leave—I promise.' Lala had assured Alain he would be home from the future before anyone noticed he was gone, so he should be back before dinner.

Lowering her troubled brown eyes, Barabal placed her chemise in the bag, then took her time doing up the straps. Meanwhile, Alain's stomach churned. He had not exactly declared his love for Barabal, and they were not betrothed, but the thought of hurting her made him feel ill.

'All right, I will see you before I leave. Best you go now. Master Barwick will be waiting for you.'

She would not look at him and he had departed, their unresolved issues lying heavy on his heart.

Unable to do anything about it now, Alain snuggled under the duvet and tried to clear his mind. Downstairs a door closed, followed by the crunching of gravel as Master Barwick retired to his room over the garage. A gust of wind caused a tree branch to scrape against the window and Alain rolled over, trying to get more comfortable.

Trying to relax, Alain found every time he closed his eyes his mind whirred with all the things he had seen, or some strange noise disturbed him. And Lee's snoring did nothing to help. It seemed like hours later his mind finally calmed down and he began to drift off to sleep.

CHAPTER THREE
ALABAMA ROT

A strange glow lit the room when Alain opened his eyes the next morning. The night sky though the gap in the curtains was still dark, so he rolled over to find out where the light was coming from.

Lee was sitting propped up in bed staring intently at a thin, square, book-looking thing leaning against his legs.

'Morning,' he said, his voice creating mist in the air, causing Alain to crawl farther under the covers.

From his snug bed, he asked, 'What time is it?'

'About five-ish.'

'That's early. Couldn't you sleep?'

'Sorry, this jet lag thing has me all over the place. I have been awake for hours.' Lee spoke without taking his eyes from whatever was in front of him.

'What are you doing?' Alain propped himself up on

his elbows.

'Searching Alabama Rot.'

'Alabama Rot?'

'Yeah, that's what they're calling what the dogs are getting.'

'And you are reading about it on that?'

'The Hebrides are the back of beyond, but you do have the internet, right?'

'Internet?'

'Yes, you know—a link from home to the network of computers all around the world,' Lee explained. 'Thank goodness Alice has decent Wi-Fi here. Life wouldn't be worth living if I couldn't plug in.'

The only word Alain recognised was the word plug, and he knew that meant something to do with electricity and stuff.

Not wanting to appear foolish, or give away their time travel secret, he attempted to be blasé and said, 'Actually, no. We didn't even have electricity, so what would make you think we had internet?'

'Come here and I will show you what I have been doing.'

Lee moved over on the bed, making room for Alain, who picked up his duvet and joined him. The thing in Lee's lap had a screen like a telly, but instead of pictures there were words, and he was using his finger to make the page move up and down.

'Okay, I swipe the screen like this, and it brings up a search engine—which is like a library catalogue. I type in what I want here—Alabama Rot—hit the search button, and it brings up everything it can find in books and articles all 'round the world.'

'Wow. You can get entire books on this thing? From anywhere you want?' Alain was impressed.

'And more—newspaper articles, blogs, scientific research papers. Most stuff has been made so you can access it on a tablet or iPad. It makes learning about things easier than going to a library.'

'That is amazing. What's this one here? "Man says Alabama Rot is God's Divine Curse".' Alain leaned over and pointed to the line that caught his eye. When he touched the screen it changed and went to another page, showing a picture of a man in front of a church with a grim, rather frightening face. Beside the picture was the headline again and some writing underneath.

'Ah, it didn't take you long to stumble on the curse of the internet. Anyone can write anything they want on whatever they want and publish it. That means every crackpot with a theory has a voice.'

'How do you sort what is real and what is not? It must be confusing,' Alain said.

'It can be.' Touching the top corner of the screen, Lee returned to the original page. 'See here? This one is like a sort of online encyclopaedia. It's updated by ordinary people and checked by them. You should always double check everything you find here, but it's not a bad place to start.'

'Sounds quite confusing. It would be nice to be presented with a single truth you could rely on,' Alain said, thinking back to the medical texts he had studied.

'Then you would not be able to form your own opinion. It's easy once you get used to it. You just need to make sure the authors or the publications have a reasonable reputation. If they don't, you pretty much discount them.'

'Still sounds confusing to me—almost like it shows you too much information to find out what is real,' Alain said.

Lee laughed. 'Sometimes, yes, but if you use your common sense you can find out almost anything. I like to be prepared, so I look heaps of things up.'

'Oh?' Alain did not quite know what to say.

'Bee …Bebe says it's because I can't think quickly on my feet, so I like to consider all options before I enter a situation. She may be right. I am not as smart as she is, but I am organised and I study hard.'

Not quite sure what to do with that revelation, Alain changed the subject. 'What did you find out on the internet about the disease affecting dogs?'

'Ah, well quite a lot actually.' Lee clicked a button and the screen went white, and Alain made out some scribbled lines of writing. Lee picked up a white pencil and pointed to a particular sentence. 'Alabama Rot has been found in a number of places around the world over the last few years. However, it appears that in spite of all the research carried out, and some promising initial findings, no one knows what is causing it or why some dogs become sick and others do not.'

'That is not very helpful,' Alain said.

'The recent outbreaks caused a flurry of new activity and some more research projects were set up. Quite a few people are interested because of the high level of activity around the New Forest recently—which we already knew—but it has scientists wondering if it has something to do with the waterways. Many of the dogs who have come down with the illness have been off-lead and enjoyed splashing in the streams.'

Alain nodded. 'I see the logic in that. We must make sure we get some water samples when we are out today. Did you find anything else useful?'

'I found a lot more, but I am not sure how useful it is seeing as I am not a scientist. Let's go downstairs and see if we can rustle up something to eat and I will show you the rest. Some of it is interesting.'

'Now you're talking,' Alain said as he rolled himself off the bed, stomach rumbling in anticipation of food.

They were finishing up their toast and jam when Master Barwick ambled in. Moments later, Alice and Bebe joined the group and the quiet kitchen became a bustle of activity. While the others ate, Lee left them to it and headed upstairs to grab his coat.

'Oh, Alain, one of my son's old jackets is hanging up in the hallway near the door. It's the green one with fur around the hood. There's a larger black one belonging to my husband; it should fit Barnaby. If you wouldn't mind picking that up as well please.'

As Alain left in search of the warm clothing, he heard Bebe ask, 'Where are your own coats? Surely no one travels in England without one at this time of year.'

'Some of their luggage was lost in transit, so they have to borrow a few things while they are here,' Alice deftly answered.

When Alain returned to the kitchen, he hung the coats over the door handle. Sitting back down, he found Trouble beside him. When he had Alain's attention, he stared mournfully at his bowl.

'Oh dear, we've not fed you this morning, have we,' Alice said. 'I'm not sure I have anything in the fridge suitable for a dog. I used the rest of the mincemeat last night, and everything else is frozen.'

'Did his food get lost as well?' Bebe asked mischievously.

'No, smarty pants. He has eaten all Barnaby had, and we have not had a chance to go to the shops to buy more,' Alice said.

Bebe leaned over the table and fed Trouble some crusts from her toast. 'This will do him for the moment.'

'Bebe, don't feed the dog food from the table!' Alice's shocked tone stopped Bebe immediately, and she dropped her head, appearing contrite, but Alain was sure she winked at Trouble.

Pulling on a jacket from the hook over the kitchen door, Alice said, 'I'll pop next door and ask if they have something they can spare for this morning. Their dog is around the same size as Trouble.'

She opened the door and a cold blast of air swept into the room, causing Alain to shiver. He was not looking forward to a morning walk in the forest.

Trouble watched Alice leave, then turned expectantly to Bebe, who obliged him with another sliver of toast. They both made sure to remove all evidence of their misdemeanour when Alice returned moments later with a bowl containing some small round things.

'Ellie said they have been tightening up the regulations about keeping dogs on leads since this latest outbreak of the rot. I know your dog is well-trained, but I think it best you keep Trouble on his lead this morning.'

Alain was about to say Trouble didn't have a lead when Alice held up a collar and some twisted rope with a link at one end and a handle at the other. The neighbour had obviously provided her with more than food.

After placing the lead over the back of the chair, she put the collar on Trouble, ignoring his sorrowful eyes. Finally, she put the food bowl on the floor and waited for Trouble to eat. He sniffed at the contents before raising his eyes, his expression even more doleful.

'This is not a restaurant,' Alice informed him. *You said we should treat you like any other dog in front of the others. Well, this is what dogs eat.*

Trouble huffed, then stuck his head in the bowl and began crunching through his biscuits.

'I am afraid we may have overindulged him by feeding him the same food as us.' Master Barwick raised his head from the book he was reading to explain the dog's behaviour before adding, 'He won't like using the lead either. He is very well-trained and we don't use one as a rule, but I guess if we must, we must.' A small smile played around his lips. 'If everyone is done we should be heading out.'

Picking up the lead, he attached it to the collar around Trouble's neck, then patted his head.

I hope you are enjoying yourself, Trouble said.

Immensely. Master Barwick chuckled as he left the lead on the floor. It snaked along behind Trouble as they headed for the door.

'You aren't taking him with us, are you?' Lee asked from halfway down the stairs.

'Yes,' Master Barwick informed him. 'I see no reason not to.'

'Should we really be taking him though?' Alain asked, suddenly worried for his friend.

'Yes. He could catch the disease,' Lee said. 'I mean, we are going to places where dogs have caught it before. It will be risky.'

'We will be careful with him. I promise,' Master Barwick said. 'We will keep him to the pathways and he should be fine.'

Trouble, you cannot catch this, can you? Alain thought to check with the dog.

No, I do not think so. I believe I am immune to viruses— one of the perks of the job. In fact, someone would have to inject me with something pretty toxic for it to affect me.

'Right, now that we have settled that, let's be off.' Master Barwick opened the front door and they all filed out after him into the chilly morning air.

Clomping through the damp grass in a sturdy pair of boots, and wrapped in a warm coat, Alain found himself enjoying this walk through the New Forest more than he had the day before. Trouble trotted beside him, the lead hanging loose as they drifted behind the others. Alice led them down a lane and through some fields before nipping through a copse of trees.

'This is the path my friend always takes with her dog, Pepe, and it is where I feel a wrongness in the forest,' she told them as they followed the muddy bridle path by the fast-running stream.

'I doubt very much it is something in the water, as some have suggested,' Master Barwick said as they walked.

'What makes you say that?' Alice asked.

'Nothing lasts long in running water, and that stream is running particularly fast,' he answered. 'Still, I had best take a sample.'

He pulled a glass vial from the pocket of his coat and carefully made his way down the shallow bank. As he leant over the water, he pulled the stopper from the bottle, scooped up some liquid, and placed the top back on. He proceeded to pull a pen from his pocket and write something on the glass, waited a few moments for the ink to dry, then placed the pen and vial in his other pocket.

Walking a little farther on, Master Barwick asked Alain to use his containers to gather some dirt from the track and from the pasture beside them. He set Bebe to pick samples of each of the plants she found, and Lee was asked to take some water from a selection of the puddles on the path and by the side of the road.

About half an hour later, the path began to loop back towards Burley. Bebe declared she had not seen any new plants for some time, and almost all their glass jars were filled with specimens. Master Barwick announced they were done for the day, and he suggested a fast walk home when Trouble, nose to the ground and tail in the air, began to tug at the lead.

'Trouble, no,' Alain said firmly, but the dog merely planted his feet and began pulling towards some trees a few paces from the path.

Trouble, what are you doing? Alain asked, but the dog

ignored him and continued his attempts to get to the trees.

'It is not a good idea for him to wander,' Lee reminded them. 'We don't want him to catch anything.'

'I am trying my best to make him stay on the path,' Alain said as Trouble almost wrenched the lead from his hand.

Alain, there is something under those trees, Trouble eventually managed to get out.

Well, why didn't you say? Alain asked.

I got caught up in the scent. I had to overcome my dog instincts.

Okay. If I go and look, will you stay here?

Trouble humphed and dropped to the ground—head on paws, eyes focussed on the trees. Placing the lead beside him on the path, Alain told the dog to stay. He traipsed through the wet grass to the spot by the trees where something definitely glistened with dew.

Crouching down, he found a collection of items that at first looked like rubbish someone had thrown away, but on closer inspection he realised what they were—an altar. There was; a small bag of salt for earth, a glass jar containing water, some burnt sticks—possibly to signify air and fire—and a piece of string with three knots.

A shadow fell across the ground as Master Barwick leaned over and said, 'Mm, interesting, a magical altar. Someone has been casting, and, from the looks of it, not a spell to do good.' He reached over and picked up the knotted thread, then placed it in his pocket.

'Are you sure? I mean, all the elements for a spell are here, but they're ... well ... different.'

'Young man, many of the things we take for granted

are not available to these people, so the elements to make a temporary altar to cast a spell may not appear as we would expect them to. Of course the magic created from these make-do items is not as strong as we are used to experiencing back home.'

'But ... if they have enough people casting a spell, they would increase the level of magic, wouldn't they?'

'They would indeed,' Master Barwick said. 'Perhaps you should have a scout around in the trees and see what you can find. I will search through the fields along the banks of the stream,' Master Barwick called back over his shoulder as he headed off by himself.

A few moments later, Alain joined the others on the path. He was in time to hear Bebe say, 'You cannot be serious ... magic? I am sorry, Aunt Alice. Magic is something you read about in books; it isn't real.'

'That may be what you believe, dear, but there are still people who practice casting spells. And if Master Barwick said he found evidence of a casting here then I am sure he is right. After all, he should know.'

Bebe snorted with laughter. 'When you said Barnaby was an expert, you didn't mean he was a scientist; you meant an expert in witchcraft.'

'Of course,' Master Barwick said, as if it was the most natural thing in the world.

Bebe's tone was so much like Barabal's, Alain's stomach clenched in a momentary pang of longing for his friend.

'Technically he is both,' Alice added.

Changing the subject, Alain announced, 'I found two more altars.'

'And I found an additional two. Interesting—enough

to form a pentagram. Someone was determined to ensure their spell was strong.' Master Barwick rubbed his chin thoughtfully, then abruptly turned on his heel. 'Well, there is nothing much more we can do around here. We may as well head back.'

Alain picked up Trouble's lead and they began walking behind the others. He asked, *How did you know?*

I didn't know exactly. I sensed something off in the air as we approached this field. A few moments ago, I caught a strong scent and, well, you saw the rest. Being a dog has its uses after all.

Are you sure this is related to what is going on? I mean, I cannot think of any magic able to do this type of thing. You know—cause a dog to get sick, Alain said.

Magic might not be the root cause, but if a person learnt the right spell they might help spread a disease. If that is what is happening, then this is far worse than the Council thought. I will wait until Barwick has a chance to look through what we found today, but I think I need to contact them. They may need to send in a more experienced team to deal with this.

As they plodded back towards Burley, Lee and Alain fell behind the others and walked in silence until Lee startled Alain by asking, 'Do you believe in all this magic being the cause of the illness in dogs? I mean, Barnaby does, but come on—supernatural powers? It's just stuff they put in movies.'

Alain took a moment to compose himself before answering. 'Those are two separate questions. Yes, I believe there are elements and forces that can be manipulated to affect our environment—call it magic, alchemy or science. Do I believe it is the cause of this disease in dogs? I'm not sure.'

'You're saying it is magic?' Lee pressed.

'Barnaby and I both believe strongly in having proof before jumping to conclusions, but I wouldn't rule it out.'

Lee's eyes were wide in surprise. 'That's crazy. I mean you believing in the same off-the-wall stuff my aunt does?'

'I believe not everything can be explained away scientifically.' Alain wasn't sure how much to share with this boy. He trusted him, but his view on life was clearly very different from Alain's own.

'I am yet to be convinced,' Lee responded, which caused Alain to smile. At least his mind was open to the possibility, unlike his sister.

They caught up with the others to find their path had been blocked by a rather haughty-looking woman with steel-grey hair, and even steelier grey eyes that looked down her nose in disdain at them. 'Good morning, Alice. Out for an early morning walk?'

'Good morning, Tabitha.' The tone of Alice's voice did not invite further conversation, and she made to walk around the woman.

'You should not have that dog out here,' the grey lady commented as she moved to stand in front of Alice while looking directly at Alain. 'Not if you want it to remain healthy.'

'Leave the boy alone, Tabitha. His dog is on a lead, and not wandering off the path. He should be fine. Now, I must be getting on. It is almost time for me to open my shop.' Alice sidestepped Tabitha, and the others followed.

Tabitha made no attempt to move, and as Alain passed her, he heard her mumble, 'There is something about that dog. I am not sure what. But I will find out.'

And there is something about that woman, Trouble sent. *She is conflicted, but it is more than that. I sense something: disharmony and a lot of anger.*

As they reached the outskirts of Burley, Alain caught up with Alice and Master Barwick.

'She was part of our coven up until about three months ago. She and four others broke away, saying we were not daring enough for them and they wanted to try something different.'

'That does not sound good. Do you have any idea what they wanted to try?' his master asked.

'Tabitha was angry about a small business that opened up near her farm. They process hides for a very exclusive market. She complained that whatever they were using to treat the skins was affecting her horses. She wanted us to work on a spell to bring ill luck to the business.

'As our coven's first rule is "do no harm"; we refused to help her. A couple of the newer members of the group agreed with her approach, and they broke away to set up their own community of witches.'

'Are they likely to do something like this though?' Master Barwick asked quietly, no doubt so Bebe and Lee, who had ranged ahead, would not hear.

'To be honest, although I never really liked the woman, I do not believe so. While she can be malicious to other people, she would never hurt a defenceless animal. Besides, not all of the attacks of Alabama Rot have been around the New Forest, so it is hard to imagine how they could be. Still, you never know ... she can be a little fanatical in her beliefs.'

Master Barwick rubbed his chin again. 'I agree it is unlikely someone who cared for animals would be a part of something like this. But if she were caught up with a larger group, she might be persuaded to do it. So, we cannot totally rule her out of the equation; nor can we ignore magical altars found in the area.'

Alice stopped dead in her tracks and Alain almost banged into her.

'A larger group? Do you believe this might be bigger than just a local break-out?' she asked.

'Um ... well ...'

Aware that Master Barwick was not at his best when confronted with emotional outbursts, Alain stepped around his hostess and said, 'I think what Uncle Barnaby was trying to say is, as a man of science he is not prepared to rule anything out. That does not mean he truly believes this might be part of a larger conspiracy. Right, Uncle?'

'Um, yes ... what the boy said,' Master Barwick muttered as he walked off.

You know there might well be others involved, Trouble said

If you mean who I think, there is no evidence they are involved in this. And until we have proof there is no point in worrying the others, Alain responded as he rushed to catch up with the rest of their group.

They reached the house, and the group prepared to split up. Bebe decided to go spend the morning with her aunt in the shop, while Lee had offered to drive Master Barwick

and Alain to the vet, which was in the neighbouring town.

Lee pulled some keys out of his pocket and headed towards Alice's horseless carriage, which he called a car. He pressed something; there was a beep and the rear lights flashed.

'Jump in,' he said as he walked round the car.

Alain hung back. It wasn't like he was scared …

All right, he was scared. His fear was partially due to the thought of travelling in this machine, but was mostly because he was not quite sure what to do when travelling in a car. Was it like being a passenger on a cart where you just sat there? Or was he expected to actually *do* something.

Master Barwick calmly walked forward and pulled the silver metal thing on the outside of the door, and it swung open. 'You had best take Trouble in the back,' he said as he slipped inside and closed the door behind him.

Suddenly wishing he had offered to go to the shop this morning instead, Alain walked tentatively towards the car. Pulling at the handle, he was pleased to find it opened for him just as it had done for his master.

Trouble appeared to have no fear of the vehicle. He jumped onto the seat and looked up at Alain as if to say, "What are you waiting for?" Taking a deep breath, Alain ducked down and joined the dog inside.

'Belt up,' Lee said as the car roared into life.

Lee pulled a long black piece of material out from the side of the car over his right shoulder, and a loud snick told Alain the metal end must have locked it into something. Master Barwick followed suit. Alain looked around and found an opening over his left shoulder and pulled at the silver metal. A belt sprung towards him. Placing it over his chest, he looked for where it was meant to go. Trouble discreetly put out a paw, showing Alain the opening the end would fit into.

Lee looked over his shoulder. 'All good? You had best hold on to Trouble. We don't want him falling off the seat, do we?'

Trouble obligingly draped himself over Alain's lap. Twining his fingers through the dog's hair helped soothe Alain's frayed nerves as they took off at speed out of Burley.

'Aunt Alice said we follow this road to the next town, and the vet is just as you go in. Should be a piece of cake.'

Lee might think the journey was simple, but after he had swerved to avoid a cyclist and had gone over yet another pothole at the side of the road, Alain realised that, like Stanislaus, he was not the best of drivers. In a horse and cart, ambling along like this was bad enough— but in a car that drove like the wind, it was terrifying.

Master Barwick looked around over the back of his seat. From the look of pure joy on his face, he was finding the experience exhilarating. 'This is fun, isn't it?' he asked, confirming Alain's suspicions.

Please stop. You're hurting me.

Alain looked down to find himself gripping Trouble's fur so tightly the dog was looking over his shoulder at Alain's fingers entwined in his hair.

Sorry. Alain released his hand just as Lee said, 'Here we are.'

Lee pulled into a driveway so fast Alain found himself sprawled over the back seat. Only the seat belt locking

up prevented him from squashing his travel companion.

Amazed they had not ended up in a ditch or a field, or driven another car off the road, Alain hauled himself upright, as did Trouble. He couldn't wait to open the door and let himself out. Trembling as he closed the door, leaving Trouble inside with Lee, he caught up with Master Barwick just as Jo appeared around the side of the building.

'This way. Jenna let the vet know she wanted you to examine Pepe, but the surgery opens soon so we don't have much time.' She led them around the side of the building and let them into a room lined with cages.

Though many of the inhabitants were cats and dogs, Alain was surprised to see a rabbit and a bright-feathered bird, and was that a ferret? Jo led them to the end-most cage and opened the door. The occupant was huddled in the back—a ball of white fur, its black button eyes widened in fear as Jo reached inside.

'Oh my lovely, no need to be scared.' Jo stood moments later cuddling the petrified animal in her arms. Placing him gently on a towel on the table in the middle of the room, the girl stroked the dog, all the while talking to him. 'You are a beautiful boy, aren't you? This man is just going to take a quick look at you.'

If Jo spoke to him that way Alain would just lie still and let her do anything she pleased. It had much the same effect on Pepe, who lay staring trustingly into her eyes. Master Barwick stepped forward and touched the dog's leg, carefully studying the angry-looking ulcer. The dog jerked away.

'You poor wee thing,' he said. He turned to Jo. 'I need to take a scraping from the wound, but I don't want to hurt him.'

'I thought you might need something to test, so I saved these.' Jo handed him a bag. 'We changed his bandages this morning, so the sample will be fresh.'

Master Barwick peeked into the bag, and nodded. 'These will do fine for what I have in mind.'

'Do you need anything else? A blood or urine sample?' Jo asked.

Master Barwick paused and stroked his beard before answering, 'Not with my current batch of tests. If they show nothing then I might have to reconsider.'

'All right. If you wouldn't mind helping me, I'll just put some more ointment on his sores then bandage him back up.'

Alain wasn't sure what help the girl needed as the dog just lay there while she dressed his wounds, and barely moved as she placed him back in his cage.

'Will he be all right?' Alain asked, worried that the animal did not have much life left in him. Tears welled in his eyes, and he brushed them away, knowing they would not change the dog's fate.

'The sores are healing, but it is his liver we are worried about,' Jo said. 'This disease causes liver collapse. Fortunately, Pepe is not at that stage yet. He had a blood transfusion yesterday and has perked up a little, but he is not out of the woods yet.'

Wow, if that is him looking better I hate to think what he was like before.

Jo continued, 'The vet will check him later and, if he is not improving, she may give him more blood. Apart from that and keeping him hydrated, there isn't much more we can do for him.'

Alain crouched and peered into Pepe's eyes. 'Hang in there, boy. We will help you if we can.'

'Thank you so much for this.' Master Barwick shook the bag. 'And for allowing us to study Pepe's wounds, but we should head back now so I can start my tests.'

'Actually, can I catch a lift to Burley with you? I'm finished here, and I'm supposed to be working a shift at the shop in half an hour.'

When Jo opened the door to the car, Lee blushed to the roots of his ginger-blond hair. Seemingly not noticing her new admirer, Jo jumped in on the other side of Trouble and put on her seat belt.

The ride home was less stressful, but was filled with chatter as Lee attempted to draw Jo out of herself. While the girl answered his questions, she asked none of her own, and it was clear to Alain she was being polite.

Back at Alice's place, Master Barwick gathered his samples and headed for the room over the garage, and Jo wandered off towards the centre of town to work.

As he locked up the car, Lee asked Alain, 'Do you think I have a chance with her?'

'I'm not sure.' How could he tell the boy Jo did not seem remotely interested in him in that way.

Trouble snorted. *He has no chance. Jo's heart belongs to another.*

As they headed inside, Alain asked Trouble, *How can you be so sure of that, you have only just met her?*

Destiny.

Shaking his head, Alain closed the door. Removing his coat, he asked Lee, 'Do you want to come over and help Uncle Barnaby and me set up?'

'Not really my thing—chemistry, that is. Besides I want to check my emails and chats to find out what's going on with my friends.'

Not completely understanding what Lee was going to do, Alain left him to it, eager to help his master find out what was causing this disease. Not only to be able to return home, but also because they might find something to help the poor dog he had just left.

CHAPTER FOUR
THE INVESTIGATION CONTINUES

Master Barwick placed glass squares, glass containers, eye droppers and some things Alain had never seen before on the bench when he arrived. Unsure of what Master Barwick would want him to do, Alain leaned against the cupboards behind the workspace and watched before asking, 'If the scientists from this age cannot find a cure for Alabama Rot, how will you be able to?'

'Alain, remember we are not here to find a cure. Our job is to make sure this is a naturally occurring disease, not something caused by the Time Wreckers to serve their own ends. Once we confirm that, we can go home.'

'So we will not be helping Pepe?'

'Not as such. If we find something that might be useful we can tell Jo where to look, and that might save the dog from further discomfort. Here—can you mix this for me?

The instructions are on the back.'

He handed Alain a bag. It appeared the powder inside would provide the perfect conditions to allow bacteria to grow. While he mixed the powder with water to create something called agar, he carefully considered his master's words.

'I don't believe the Time Wreckers would do something like this,' he said. 'I mean, don't they tend to concentrate on large-scale historic change?'

'Yes. They focus on bending major events to their own end, so this does seem a little small-scale for them. Which is good for us as it means we should be able to leave soon.'

While Alain wanted to get back home as soon as possible, something nagged at him. 'Master Barwick, Alice asked us here to help her sort out the problem in the New Forest. If we just leave, what will happen to the dogs? Will they still get sick and die?'

The elderly man stopped what he was doing and looked at Alain. 'Perhaps. If we find events are happening as they are meant to, we will leave and allow things to take their natural course.'

'Can't we ...?'

'Time Guardians are not allowed to directly act to change history. Even if we find Time Wreckers are influencing this, we still cannot take direct action to stop them. We would merely be able to encourage and advise people living in this time on how they might counter the Wreckers' actions.'

'But ...'

Master Barwick held up his hand to silence any protests. 'It is the hardest part of our job, but it is an

important rule for us—it is the thing that makes us different from the Time Wreckers. While they feel it is their duty to change history to make a better world, we believe the timeline must be kept intact. However, that does not mean we can't do a little research and find out if we can offer anything new to the situation without becoming hands-on.'

Painting the agar gloop on the bottom of the flat, sterilised, round glass containers Master Barwick had set out, Alain said, 'It will be hard explaining that to Alice.'

His master was silent for a moment as he placed a small sample on the agar, then put the lid securely on top. He wrote on the container in pen, and moved on to the next sample before answering. 'Yes, it will be. We can only hope she will understand.'

For the first time since they had arrived, Alain hoped that something untoward was going on. Then there would be a reason for them to help Alice ... and Pepe.

When he'd finished putting agar in all the dishes set out on the bench, Alain washed his equipment and leaned his elbows on the counter. 'Master, how is it you know how to use all this equipment?'

'I told you how I travelled with Sigma a few times before. On one of those journeys I spent some time with a doctor in Scotland. He was an advanced thinker for his time and studied what are called micro-organisms— things like bacteria.'

Alain nodded his understanding and Master Barwick continued, 'Although all this stuff is quite a bit more advanced, the principles are the same. Also, I spent part of last night reading the instruction manuals.' Tapping the book on the end of the counter, he said, 'And I read this text book to bring myself up to speed.'

After carefully adding the last sample to its own dish and closing the lid, Master Barwick stood and stretched his back. 'Right, over there are some glass slides and a bottle. If you could use the brush attached inside the lid to wipe some of the liquid on each of the slides, and place them along the counter, I will just put these Petri dishes away.'

Alain did as his master asked, setting up four slides ready for him to use. His teacher returned with the container of water they'd collected that morning and used a dropper to place a little on each of the slides. He reached under the bench and pulled out a tray of brown bottles with droppers for tops. He picked a few up and read their labels before selecting four and placing them on the counter.

With intense concentration, he added one drop from each of the bottles on one of the slides. Finally, he placed another glass slide over the top and put the bottles away. He turned to wash his hands in the sink before declaring that set of experiments done.

'What are they for?' Alain asked, curiosity getting the better of him.

Master Barwick sighed. Reaching under the counter once again, Master Barwick emerged with a strange-looking piece of equipment. 'This is a microscope. It is able to magnify things by an alarming amount. With this, I can identify any bacterial activity in the water.'

'And the stuff we put on the glass?' Alain chanced his luck, hoping the master was in a good mood.

'It fixes things to the glass. The liquid in the bottles helps identify certain micro-organisms.' Flicking through the book on the edge of the counter, Barwick found the spot he was looking for and turned it to face Alain. 'This explains it much better than I could.'

Alain took the book over to the couch and curled up with the tome in his lap. It was all so interesting, but he much preferred it when Master Barwick explained things to him. While he studied, his teacher labelled the slides.

He read the chapter as quickly as he could, then returned the book to the counter. As he placed it down, he noticed a clean notebook had appeared from one of the numerous drawers and cupboards. Master Barwick wrote notes on each of his experiments before storing them in a cupboard under the bench.

'Ah, you are finished,' Master Barwick said. 'How about you head over to the house and get some food?'

The mention of eating pushed all other thoughts from Alain's mind. Not even pausing to ask Trouble if he wanted to join him, he dashed out of the room.

The door had barely closed when the old man slumped on the sofa beside the dog. 'This is not looking good, Sigma. There is more going on here than meets the eye.'

There was an odd feeling in that field today. I felt strong magic—too strong for this day and age. And it had an oily taint to it.

'No doubt we will learn a bit more once I finish these tests. The raw samples showed nothing obvious wrong, so all we can do is wait for the cultures to grow.'

When do you think you will have the preliminary results?

'This evening possibly ... definitely by tomorrow. Alice's husband has an incubator, which should speed up the process a little given this cold weather.'

Trouble's head dropped on to his paws. *I can't wait until then to make my report.*

'I am going to study the water samples in more detail before I eat. Maybe I will find something, but it is unlikely as the stream was quite fast-running.'

I have been thinking on those altars and what about them smelled so off. I believe they reek of old magic, and that worries me. I think it might be best to contact the Council now.

Trouble took himself over to the blanket placed under the window by the radiator and curled up. He relaxed and closed his eyes, but the buzzing in his head told Master Barwick that rather than taking a nap, the Time Guardian was consulting his Council.

Turning back to his work, Master Barwick became so engrossed in the water samples and the superpowered microscope that it was a moment before he realised the dog had re-joined him.

I spoke briefly with Beta, Trouble said. *Something else has come up with this case and he was called to an emergency Council meeting. He will present our concerns and will tell us the outcome, hopefully sometime tonight. I get the sense our time here will soon be over.*

'What a shame. There is so much I would like to see and learn. Before you say it, I understand I cannot use any of it when I return to my own time, but still—there are so many new inventions here. It boggles the mind.'

Then you'd better make the most of the little time we have.

Trouble wandered back to the electric heater, leaving the alchemist to his experiments. Left to himself, Master Barwick picked up the first slide, noted its details in his notebook, then placed it under the microscope. He twisted knobs, looked through the viewer, then twisted the knobs again until what was on the slide came into focus.

'Mm, interesting.' He adjusted the microscope again to confirm what he saw.

He repeated the process with the other three slides, talking to himself as he did. 'Now, I did not expect that. Let me think.' He opened the text book and flicked through the pages until he found what he was looking for. He took some more notes. 'How curious ...'

Taking another couple of slides, he put a drop of water from the stream on one with nothing else on it, pressed the other slide on top, and put it under the microscope. He studied it intently. The only sound was the ticking of the minute hand in the clock on the wall beside him.

'Ah, I found you,' he whispered to the slide, nodding in satisfaction. 'You are a wily wee thing, but you cannot escape me.'

He searched through the book again. Nothing quite matched the organism under the microscope. Shutting the book in frustration, he walked over to the bookshelf. Running his finger along the titles, he soon found what he was looking for—*Mutations of Common Organisms*. He took the volume back to the bench and continued reading and writing.

Sometime later, he shut another book with a thwack, rubbed his forehead and glanced around the room. It had turned dark outside, and the large hole in the bookshelf where he'd removed books during the afternoon stood testament to his hard work. He stared at the dog by the heater. Trouble raised his head sleepily.

Is that tantrum because you found something and are not happy? Or because you have not found anything and are unhappy?

'Humph.'

So, it is the latter, Trouble said as he dropped his head back on his paws.

Ignoring the Time Guardian, Barwick opened another book and flicked through the pages. 'Ah, well that is interesting.'

He turned back a few pages before slamming that book shut as well. 'But not quite right either.' He added the discarded volume to the growing pile beside him, closed his notebook and leaned his arms on the counter.

'This is so frustrating. I found something in the water. It is not like anything I have ever seen before, so I thought it might be something discovered since my last visit forward in time. Only, just when I think I have found out what it is, I find a little detail that is not quite right.'

It must be frustrating, but not unexpected. Scientists have been working on this little problem for a couple of years now and have not found an answer.

'Nice to know you have so much faith in me, Sigma,' Master Barwick grumbled.

Barwick, if I didn't think you were up to the task you would not be here with me. But even you cannot expect to sort this out on your first day.

'Well, I didn't expect to,' he conceded. 'But when I found the organisms ... well, I hoped ...' Master Barwick stretched out his back and closed the other books on the bench.

'I am done for the day. Let's go and find the others,' he said to Trouble.

The dog stood, shook himself, stretched, then followed Master Barwick to the kitchen, wandering onto the lawn for a pit stop on the way.

Bebe was not sure what to make of her aunt's shop. Its mixture of touristy kitsch with *Harry Potter* wands, birthstones and charms was everything you would expect from a store attempting to fleece the tourists of a buck by making the most of the magical history of the area.

However, around the back Alice stocked serious books on the history of witchcraft and the practice of modern magic, along with pots and bottles full of all the accoutrements—everything the modern magical practitioner would ever need, or so Bebe imagined.

She spent the next hour unloading stock while her aunt served the few customers who wandered in. When the shop had been empty for a while, Alice checked outside to gauge the likelihood of potential customers before nipping out the back to make them a cup of tea.

Having told her aunt she took hers white with no sugar, Bebe idly cleared down the counter and tidied displays while she waited for her drink. The shop bell rang, and she popped her head around a display stand to find Jo had turned up.

With a quick 'hi', Jo slipped her backpack off her shoulders and headed out the back. She returned moments later backpack free, but with two steaming mugs of tea.

'Here, this is yours.' She handed Bebe a cup. 'Your aunt just left for the post office with the internet orders I packed yesterday. They are mostly in pre-paid bags, but as all the town gossip filters through the post shop, she won't be hurrying back and time soon.'

How many modern witches could there be? And how many ordered supplies from the shop? 'I knew Aunt Alice sold stuff online, but does she truly sell that much?'

'About twenty-five percent of our sales come through online. We are a little out of the way here, and most of our foot traffic is from tourists. So many of our less touristy items are mostly internet sales. Funnily enough, some of our best customers are from overseas. We even have one regular buyer from Salem in America.'

Jo laughed, seeming more amused than insulted by Bebe's questions. As they sipped their drinks, Jo leaned forward to better see the well-dressed, middle-aged woman entering the shop across the road. 'It's unlike Gladys to be arriving this late in the day. I wonder if her assistant opened for her.'

'Mm.' Bebe frowned and started over her cup at Jo. Why would she even be interested in what went on across the road, much less comment on it?

'They are our rivals. Well, not actual rivals. Gladys and Alice's friendship goes back years, back to when Alice first moved here with Donald. Although she sells some magical items in her store, Gladys sticks to local, handcrafted things whereas we do the touristy and the imported items. And, of course, all the local witches come here for their supplies.'

'Surely you do not believe in all that stuff? I mean, you're going to be a woman of science, a vet.' Bebe's tone invited Jo to agree with her.

'Actually, I do believe in it. I come from a long line of witches. I am part of the local coven. I also cast spells, most of which are successful.'

'What sort of spells? Love potions and things?' Bebe joked. She did not wish to offend Jo, but she couldn't get her head around all this nonsense about magic.

'Spells of protection and spells of remembering. Spells for a good harvest, or good health.' Although Jo did not appear to be upset by her questions, her voice had an edge to it as she took pains to add, 'I believe in science, but I also believe natural energies surround us that science cannot explain, and I am happy to call on them to help myself and others.'

'Barnaby said something similar today when Lee found out he is not a man of science, but someone who studies and practices magic.'

Bebe had expected Jo to laugh, but she merely nodded before saying, 'Although Barnaby calls himself an apothecary, someone who deals in herbal medicines, I think you will find he is also an alchemist.'

'An alchemist? Do they really exist? Outside of fantasy novels, I mean.'

Jo laughed and explained, 'Alchemy is a term for anyone who mixes science with magic. In fact, I can probably find you a book on all the different types of magical practices if you like.'

'No, no, you're all right. I admit I don't know what I am talking about.' Bebe tried to laugh off her unease as she sipped her tea.

Placing her cup on the counter, Jo said, 'Alchemists were, and are, very real—as are witches. How come the subject of magic came up on your walk this morning? I thought you were just collecting specimens for Barnaby.'

'We found some weird things. Alain and Barnaby said they were altars for casting spells and were surprised to find five of them.'

Jo blanched. 'Five altars—the points of a pentagram. They meant business, whoever set them up. Can you tell me any of the other things found with the altars?'

Bebe frowned, trying to remember if she saw the men pick anything up. 'I am not sure I can. You should come 'round after work though. I am sure Barnaby will tell you everything. We found them just before heading home, and I was too busy at the time trying to stay warm to listen to what they were saying about them. Then one of Aunt Alice's friends arrived. She blocked our path and began acting kind of strange.'

'Oh? Who?' Jo asked.

'Some snooty woman named Tabitha. She was quite rude and, come to think of it, she didn't look dressed for a morning walk in the forest. I am sure her coat covered a suit, and she wore heels. Perhaps she was driving somewhere, saw us, and detoured to find out what we were doing.'

With her lip curling distastefully, Jo sneered. 'Nothing

would surprise me with that woman.'

'You don't like her?'

'No, I do not, and I can honestly say, you should keep away from her.' Jo's aggressive tone took Bebe by surprise.

'I hope that is not me you are talking about.'

They looked around to find an attractive girl with wavy black hair and the most startling blue eyes Bebe had ever seen standing in the doorway. Strange, Bebe thought. I didn't hear the shop bell. The girl's lips curled into a supercilious smile. If Bebe had been a cat, her hackles would have risen, so intense was her dislike of this interloper, but for the life of her she could not tell why.

Jo, on the other hand, blushed, and the usually confident girl appeared nervous. 'Hi, Izzy. What can I do for you?'

The stranger's eyes twinkled with mischief. 'I can think of many things but, unfortunately, I've come across to beg some roll for the till from you. Gladys has run out.'

'Yeah, sure,' Jo said, knocking items off the shelf under the counter as she searched for the rolls.

'Here.' Bebe picked one up off the floor. 'Here you go.'

Izzy did not take her eyes off Jo as she took the item from Bebe's hand. 'Thanks. Perhaps I'll see you at the pub later.' She winked as she closed the door behind her.

Bebe turned to Jo. 'Who was that?'

'Gladys' new assistant. She isn't local. She arrived about ten or so weeks ago.' Jo started clearing up the things on the floor, and Bebe couldn't see her face.

'And you and she have a thing?' Bebe teased.

'What? No! I mean, I might have, but Gladys is a member of Tabitha's coven, and Izzy joined up soon after she started working in the shop. They are into some weird stuff—stuff most of us witches stay away from. So I'm steering well clear of her.'

'Still …' Bebe let the thought trail off.

'Mm,' Jo said. 'Still …'

Just as the conversation was getting interesting, the bell interrupted them and a couple of customers entered. While Jo helped one of the ladies select some tarot cards, Bebe assisted the other one in choosing a wand for her grandchild. She surprised herself by being able to remember the *Harry Potter* characters well enough to sell a wand belonging to the woman's granddaughter's favourite witch.

Thanking the shop assistants, the two women exited with beaming smiles just as Alice returned from the post office.

'Long queue, was there?' Jo smirked at her boss.

'You know full well there wasn't, you cheeky minx.' Alice took the ribbing in good heart. 'Now if you two are all right here, I think I will go out back and catch up on my ordering.'

'We'll be fine. It isn't very busy. Oh, don't forget to put the new stock up on the website. With all of yesterday's orders I didn't get a chance,' Jo reminded her.

A steady trickle of customers visited throughout the rest of day. Around four it turned dark, and the small town was soon deserted. Alice popped her head out and said, 'Not much is going to happen now. You can begin packing up. Jo, would you mind doing the till while I finish off here?'

As Jo ran off the till totals and began counting out the float, Bebe tidied the shelves. The girls chatted, finding out a little more about each other.

Then Jo asked the dreaded question. 'So, now high school's over, what are your plans?'

Bebe's stomach clenched, and she attempted to sound nonchalant as she answered, 'I'm not quite sure yet.'

Jo's life was pretty much planned out, so Bebe tensed for a lecture on the importance of preparing for the future, but Jo surprised her by saying, 'That must be tough for you, especially with your brother having his next few years all sorted.'

'It is. I know what I'm interested in, but finding somewhere to channel it has been difficult.'

'Not so long ago I was in the same boat,' Jo said, and Bebe stopped what she was doing and reassessed the confident person she'd met only a day before. 'I can tell you're sceptical, but don't be fooled by what you see now. A couple of years ago, after my dad walked out, I was a mess. I was on the verge of being thrown out of school and was causing my mother all sorts of pain.'

Walking around the shelf she had been tidying, Bebe started sorting through the knick-knacks on the counter so she could watch Jo's face as she spoke. 'What changed?' she asked.

'The children's court sent me to a councillor. Ruth was amazing, although I didn't think so at first. I talked and she listened, and I told her of my passion—animals—and she arranged for me to spend some time at the local vet.'

'She sounds smart.'

Jo smiled. 'Yes, she is. My counsellor at school always spoke about my "feelings" and my "anger issues".' Jo used her fingers to make air quotes around the words to emphasise her disdain. 'Ruth found something I loved, and in turn talked me through what I would need to do if I wanted a future as a vet. After a while, the vet offered me some shifts. It didn't pay enough for me to be able to consider university. Then Mum told me Alice needed help, so I started working for her as well.'

'Wow. You must have been busy.'

'Yes, with the extra work I took on at school, and with two jobs, I was soon too busy to be angry. After a while I started looking forward and not back, and the pain of my father leaving was no longer the driving force in my life,' Jo said as she closed the till and began putting the cash in a money bag.

'Do you ever catch up with your dad?'

Jo paused. 'This last year he got in touch again. He lost his job just before he left us, and things weren't great between him and Mum—hadn't been for a while. But he has sorted himself out now. It is hard, but maybe soon we can be friends again.'

Jo took the money out back while Bebe locked the door and pulled down the window blinds, before meeting the others by the back door.

During the walk home, Jo and Alice chatted but Bebe couldn't say about what. Her attention was on her conversation with Jo. Not on her story, but on the woman Ruth. She had helped Jo turn her life around, and the spark of an idea began to form.

'Bebe? Were you listening?' Jo's impatient tone interrupted her thoughts. 'What did you say about Tabitha today?'

'That she was rather snooty?' Bebe offered.

'No, the rest of it,' Jo prompted.

'Um, that she wasn't dressed for walking in the forest; it seemed more like she was heading somewhere else and came over to find out what we were doing.'

Alice paused for a moment. 'You're right. I was so annoyed at seeing her there, and with her arrogant behaviour I didn't even notice. How clever of you to work that out. I wonder what piqued her interest?'

As they continued their walk home, the other two chattered about what Tabitha's motivations might have been, while Bebe drifted back into her own thoughts. How was she ever going to flesh out what she wanted to do with her life in this backwater town where they believed magic was real?

Curled up on the sofa, Alain once again lost himself in *The Lord of the Rings*. Seated in a chair by the fire, Lee was "looking things up on his tablet". The fire crackled and the wind whipped around the windows as if trying to gain entry, but Alain hardly noticed, so caught up was he in his book.

'How can you read something that long and boring?' Lee peered over the top of his tablet at Alain.

'Huh?'

'I said ... how can ... oh, never mind.'

Holding his finger inside the book so he did not lose his place, Alain looked over and asked, 'What are you looking up now?'

'I am researching alchemists.'

Alain placed a slip of paper from the coffee table into the book and put it on the sofa beside him. 'Why didn't you just ask me?'

'What? You mean you're an alchemist too?' Lee swung his legs around so he was sitting properly in the chair, a glint in his eye.

'Almost. I'm an apprentice alchemist. Well, if I am honest, I am more of an apprentice apothecary,' Alain admitted. 'But Barnaby started to teach me alchemy so I can better treat my patients.'

'Alchemy has not been taught as a meaningful line of study for centuries, so I assume it's more of a hobby sort of thing?'

Alain's brow furrowed, suddenly wary of the boy in front of him. He came across as happy-go-lucky so it was easy to forget he was quite smart.

'In fact, it says here alchemy died out in and around the time of the Renaissance, when science took over,' Lee continued. He raised his eyes and pinned Alain with his steady gaze.

Shifting uncomfortably, Alain realised he may have given too much away. This version of Stanislaus was much more perceptive than the one he knew.

'Well, Barnaby is a bit old-fashioned ...'

'Yes, but Medieval old-fashioned?' Lee pressed. Alain could not meet the other boy's eyes, and Lee smiled. 'I knew there was something odd about you two. It's all right. I won't tell anyone your secret.'

'What secret?' Alain asked in a last-ditch effort to throw Lee off the scent.

'That you two are not only not from around here, but

not from this time at all.'

'Um, I am not sure I understand what you mean.' Alain fumbled for a plausible explanation.

'Come on. You two practice alchemy and magic. Then the way you behaved in the car today—it was as if you had never been in one before.'

'Your driving would do that to anyone who wanted to live,' Alain countered.

'Your reactions were too extreme for that. No, somehow you guys travelled through time to be here.' Having presented his case, Lee sat back in the chair.

'Don't be ridiculous. Time travel isn't a real thing.'

'I think your being here is proof it is. Add that to the fact that some pretty knowledgeable scientists agree that in theory, travelling through time is possible, and —'

'Please, you cannot tell anyone. Master Barwick will be so disappointed in me for giving the game away,' Alain pleaded.

'I will make you a deal. If you tell me about some of your cool experiments, I promise not to let on I know anything.'

Alain pondered the proposal for a moment. Deciding it was the lesser of two evils, he reluctantly agreed.

He spent the next hour recounting some of his past antics: the experiments gone wrong, the diseases he'd cured and the tricks he'd played on others. Lee insisted on checking everything out on the internet.

When Lee showed him the screen, Alain was fascinated to find how things in the fields of chemistry and medicine had moved on from his time. Not so academically inclined, Lee showed more interest in the stories and the mayhem than letting Alain study drawings of the body, or allowing him time to read up on the details of new discoveries.

Saving the best for last, Alain told Lee about using Greek fire to blow up a door to break a friend out of a dungeon. The other boy was suitably impressed and they spent a little time researching Greek fire online. Lee then showed him how easy it was to make an explosion from everyday household items.

At the sound of footsteps in the hall, Lee turned his screen off, and the two tried to look innocent of any wrongdoing. Clearly, they were not successful, as Bebe stood in the doorway, hands on hips, and asked, 'What have you two been up to?'

'Nothing.' Alain's cheeks heated, finding it as hard to lie to Bebe as it was to keep the truth from Barabal.

'Mm.' She pursed her lips. 'Alice just put the kettle on and is warming some cottage pie for dinner if you would like to join the rest of us in the kitchen.' She turned on her heel and left the room.

'Remember, you promised,' Alain said as they followed her out.

'And I keep my promises,' the other boy responded. Then, under his breath, he said, 'Even though it might be impossible to keep this from Bebe. She always figures out when I am hiding something.'

'You've got to try,' Alain insisted.

'What did you promise?' The question came from behind, causing Alain to jump.

'Ah, Barnaby. I didn't see you come in,' Lee answered. 'I was just saying I promised Alain he and I would try the local ale one night soon—maybe tonight. Bebe and I

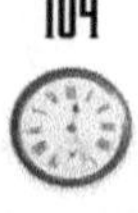

turned eighteen yesterday and, because we were travelling, we still haven't had our first legal drink. He said you would probably not let him go, and I said I would speak to you about it. Would you let him come out with me? In fact, do you want to come along with us? We can make it a boys' night.'

Stopping in his tracks, the elderly man frowned. 'Why, thank you for asking, young man, but I am afraid my tavern days are long over. Besides, I want to spend some time checking my samples this evening. But you young ones go out and enjoy yourselves.' As he shuffled past them, Trouble in his wake, Lee winked at Alain. Just when he thought they had got away with it, Trouble turned and stared at him.

We will talk about what Lee found out later.

How did you know? Can you read minds? Alain asked, but the dog did not answer. He simply wandered into the kitchen, turned around a couple of times and flopped down in his place by the Aga.

CHAPTER FIVE
NIGH-TIME ANTICS

s Alice bustled around busily preparing a meal, the others chatted happily drinking tea and spoiling their dinner by munching their way through a plate of home baked biscuits in the cosy warmth of the kitchen.

Alice placed a pie in the oven and started preparing vegetables. She paused mid-chop and turned around. 'Did you find out anything useful today, Barnaby?'

'Humph, not really. It was most frustrating. I did find some odd organisms in the water. They are not like anything I have seen before. If they are also in the soil or the puddles, we may have found our culprit.'

Alice paused for a moment. 'That's great, so why the long face?'

'Try as I might, Alice, I was unable to find any clues as to what it is. If Alain can help me go through some of your husband's books tomorrow, hopefully two eyes will be better than my poor old ones and we will find a name for it.'

'Of course,' Alain said. 'I am all yours.'

'Are you crazy?' Lee asked. 'It will take you hours to find something by going through books. I'll bring over my computer and we shall find it much quicker.'

Master Barwick raised one sceptical eyebrow.

'He is not joking, Barnaby. You should see the amount of information he can access on his tablet. If he helps I am sure our search will go more quickly,' Alain confirmed.

'I guess it is worth a try,' Master Barwick conceded reluctantly. 'We may also be able to narrow down the search parameters if our samples grow overnight.'

'My computer can deal with an awful lot of information, so don't worry too much about that,' Lee said.

'And we can still take a quick look through your books if you like,' Alain offered in an attempt to reassure his mentor.

'So we haven't moved any further ahead,' Alice said as she took a seat at the head of the table.

'Well, Barnaby hasn't, but I think Bebe may be on to something with her comment about Tabitha,' Jo said.

Bebe shrugged. 'You think that's important?'

'Yes, of course.' Jo turned to face Bebe.

'All I said was, don't you think it odd she came to talk to you all when she wasn't dressed for a walk in the forest? I mean, what would make a person stop their car and traipse across the wet grass just to speak with you?'

'You raise an interesting point. Why would she do that? Probably to find out what we were up to ...' Barnaby

mused, then nodded. 'Maybe she knew about the altars and wanted to know if we found them?'

'Of course,' said Jo, banging her hand on the table. 'And the only way she would know they were there was if she and her new coven of witches were responsible for putting them there in the first place. They are probably up to their necks in this.'

'Hold on a minute.' Master Barwick help up his hand. 'Let's not get carried away here. It doesn't necessarily follow that those altars have anything to do with the disease affecting the dog community—the spell cast using them need not have been malignant.'

'There is only one way to find out,' Lee said. 'We need to break into Tabitha's house and see if we can find any evidence one way or the other.'

As Alain murmured his agreement, Alice exclaimed, 'You will do no such thing! Not only is breaking and entering illegal, but what would your parents say if they found out I let you do something so dangerous?'

'And stupid,' Bebe added.

'We will be in and out so quick it will be like we were never there—and our parents need not be any the wiser,' Lee said.

'No, and that is my final word on the matter. Let Barnaby finish his tests and things, then, if they prove those altars are somehow involved, we can discuss how to approach Tabitha.'

Seeing Lee about to object, Alain touched his arm and shook his head. He had a better idea. 'Listen to your aunt, Lee. Besides you promised me a trip to the local pub tonight.'

Lee nodded, 'I did, didn't I. Is that all right with you, Alice?'

'Mm, I am not sure. You and Bebe have only just turned eighteen ... how old are you, Alain?'

'I am eighteen,' the lie rolled easily off his lips and he prayed Master Barwick did not rat him out. He was not eighteen for a couple of months yet, but it was clear that for his plan to work he needed to pretend to be a few months older than his actual age.

'Well ...' Alice started.

'We will come with you,' Bebe jumped in. Lee opened his mouth to say something, but before he did, she carried on. 'Jo, you want to catch up with Izzy, and I would not mind meeting some of the locals.' Her eyes twinkled mischievously as she poked her new friend.

Lee winked at Alain.

Folding her arms and tutting, Alice said, 'You should keep away from that Izzy, Jo. She is bad news; I feel it in my bones.'

'You're worried because she's joined Tabitha's coven, but she's okay.' Jo defended herself.

Jo really seemed to like Izzy. Understanding washed over him, and he knew now what Trouble had meant by Lee not being Jo's "type".

'It's not just that ... I mean, something about Tabitha's new coven is definitely odd. I guess you are old enough to make your own mistakes though. Just be careful; that is all I ask,' Alice said as the oven beeped and she rose to finish preparing the meal.

'Shall we head down to the pub too, Barnaby?' Alice took a steaming pie from the oven as she asked the question, and so missed the worried glance Lee shot at Alain. In turn, Alain nearly cursed out loud. It would be difficult enough to lose the girls, but if the adults came too, a detour to Tabitha's wouldn't be possible.

'Uh, I guess we could, but I was planning to check on my experiments, and a couple of your husband's books looked very interesting. I want to flick through some more of them and maybe spark a new line of enquiry,' Master Barwick said.

Alice placed the meal on the table. 'Well, I am just as happy to curl up by the fire with a good book for the night,' she said, before serving the rest of the food.

The room fell into silence as they turned their attention to filling their stomachs.

Barwick, don't forget I want to meet with our friends tonight too. Do you want to join me?

What meeting was Trouble talking about? Alain glanced towards the dog, who appeared to be sleeping and did not even stir.

Is this something I should stay around for? he asked.

No, it is important, but we can update you on the outcome tomorrow. You go and enjoy yourself, but be careful.

Careful? Why would you say that?

You know why. The dog closed his eyes, ending the conversation.

As his attention returned to the meal, he found Jo staring thoughtfully at Trouble. Had she heard the whole conversation? Alain was pretty sure she had.

After the meal, the boys cleared down the table while Bebe and Jo washed the dishes. The two girls laughed and whispered as they worked.

Looking up from his phone, Lee asked, 'What's so funny?'

'Wouldn't you like to know,' Bebe tossed over her shoulder, causing another round of giggles.

Once the kitchen was cleaned and the dishes put away, they headed out to the living room. Alice and Master Barwick had settled in around the fire and were both engrossed in books. On the table between them sat a pot of tea and some of Alice's carrot cake.

Alice rose to escort them out, and as Alain passed by her she placed a hand on his arm. 'Here, you will need this if you are to buy some drinks. Although it might be best of you let the others buy them for you as you might need ID to prove your age.' She slipped some paper into his hand, which he assumed was what passed for local currency.

'ID?' Alain frowned.

'Yes. Something like a driver's licence or student card. You need it to prove you are old enough to purchase alcohol.'

Grateful for her generosity and advice, he bent down and gave her a quick peck on the cheek, and she rewarded him with a blush and a smile as she closed the door.

Now they were free how they were going to give the girls the slip, and how were they going to find out where Tabitha lived? He need not have worried. No sooner had the door closed than Jo said, 'C'mon, this way.'

'The pub is this way, isn't it?' Lee pointed in the opposite direction.

'But my mum's car is parked over here.'

Jo turned her head and motioned towards a dark green car parked a little way down the street.

Bebe laughed. 'A blind man could see you guys intended

III

to drop us at the pub and disappear off to spy on Tabitha.'

'My mum sometimes gets a lift in to work and leaves her car here for me to drive home,' Jo said. 'We can all drive to Tabitha's, find out if we can get inside, rummage around quickly, and still have time for a pint in the pub before closing.'

'You are not coming with us,' Lee told them. 'It might be dangerous.'

Oh no, Alain thought. How could Lee be so clever about some things, and so dumb about others?

'All right, smart arse, how do you plan to get to Tabitha's?' Bebe glared at them, hands on hips, her face a mask of defiance.

'Come to think of it, do you even know where she lives?' Jo stood shoulder to shoulder with Bebe.

'And if it's too dangerous for us to go, the same could be said of the both of you.' Bebe leaned forward as she spoke, as if daring them to disagree with her.

Now they were playing tag team, and Lee simply crossed his arms over his chest and said, 'You're not coming.'

Sighing, Alain knew he was beaten even if Lee didn't. 'They're right, you know. We have no idea where we are going, and if Tabitha's place is not in walking distance ...'

'... I thought we would take Alice's car,' Lee answered.

'If we sneaked the keys she would hear us leave, and if we asked she would want an explanation as to why we need to drive the short distance to the pub.'

Even in the face of such blinding logic, Lee would not budge.

Shrugging, Jo said, 'We don't need your permission to do anything and, unlike you two, I at least know where to go.' She turned and walked down the street. Alain and Bebe followed.

Glancing over his shoulder at Lee, who had not moved an inch, he said the words he knew would goad the other boy into joining them, 'Come on. You don't want to miss all the fun, do you?'

The look he got in return screamed "traitor", but Lee had caught them up by the time they had reached the car.

With Lee safely in the back seat, his rigid stance emanating waves of disapproval, Jo pulled away from the curb. In spite of the tense atmosphere, Alain did not find the short drive to Tabitha's property too disturbing. It may have been that he was getting used to travelling in cars, or perhaps it was because Jo was a better driver than Lee. She didn't launch them around corners at speed and when she parked the car a little way up a lane near their destination, she did not stop suddenly, flinging everyone forward in their seats.

They all piled out of the vehicle and milled around. Even from where they had parked they were able to see a light on at the back of the house.

'Looks like someone is in the kitchen,' Jo said.

'What makes you say that?' Lee moved beside her and peered over her shoulder.

'We used to come here a lot for coven meetings before ... you know ... she and the others broke away. The kitchen is at the back. It has French doors leading out to the back lawn.'

That wandered back to the corner, then turned down the road Tabitha's house was on. They kept to the shadows as they drew near to their destination, using the hedges lining the country lane as cover.

'I only saw one car in the driveway when we drove past, so there's a decent chance she's alone,' Bebe said.

'I would not be so sure of that,' Jo responded. 'Just over a month or two ago, not long after Izzy arrived, an American friend came to stay with Tabitha. It was the talk of the town, how this handsome, younger man came to live in her house, and with her husband working in London during the weeks. You know how gossip runs riot in small communities.'

'You say this happened about two months ago?' Alain asked. 'Around the same time the recent Alabama Rot outbreak started to get bad?'

'When you put it like that, it sounds suspicious,' Jo said.

'And that was around the same time Izzy showed up.' Bebe tapped her index finger on her lips, then raised her eyebrows.

'I am sure that is not related.' In the darkness, Jo's voice sounded unconvincing even to Alain's ears.

'So, let's just confirm the timeline here.' Bebe pressed her point. 'Tabitha left your coven, some guy shows up, then Izzy arrives and the Alabama Rot gets worse.'

'No,' Jo mumbled.

Wanting to soften his next words so Jo did not feel under attack, Alain placed a comforting hand on her arm before he spoke. 'Why don't you tell us what order things happened in?'

'Tabitha got angry and split the coven. Soon after,

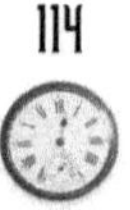

Izzy showed up. Gavin, the guy staying with Tabitha, came a week or so later.' Jo stopped, and was silent for a moment. 'We've had a few cases of the rot over the last couple of years, but this bout started ... um ... when the weather turned ... around the beginning of September, I guess. But the cases started becoming more frequent later on that month.'

Aligning the times in his head, Alain figured out the likely chain of events, but wanted to double check. 'So, you had your first cases just before Izzy showed up. You think they got worse still later in the month ... Do you have any idea who this Gavin chap is? Because it appears the cases got worse after he arrived.'

As if he wanted to spare Jo any discomfort, Lee said, 'This is all very interesting, but it is only speculation. What we need is evidence. So, if we are going to check out the house we should do it now.'

'Oh, you're actually coming with us, are you?' Bebe teased.

Lee continued, 'I suggest you two girls take the front. Alain and I will head 'round the back and see if we can get a peek at what's going on in the kitchen.'

'Why do you guys get to go where all the action is? Is it because you are all manly and it's too dangerous for us mere females?' Bebe's lips curled into a sneer.

'No, my angry little sister. Because if someone catches us they won't know who we are or why we are snooping. We've a good chance of making up some story and getting away with it.'

'With Tabitha knowing Jo, it would be more risky for the two of you given she is more likely to be at the back of the house.' This time, Alain was able to support Lee.

'Oh ... right. That makes sense,' Bebe admitted. 'And I'm only five minutes younger than you, you know.' She punched Lee on arm.

'If that's all the questions, shall we go now?' When no one objected, Lee clambered over the fence, using the hedge bordering the property to cover his movements.

Alain followed him. Moving as silently as possible, he just made out the crunching of gravel as Bebe and Jo ran across the driveway. At the edge of the hedgerow, Lee found a wooden picket gate. He opened it quietly and held it for Alain to slip through before pulling it to. 'In case we need to escape quickly,' he whispered.

Keeping as much to the shadows as possible, they shimmied underneath the kitchen window, backs to the wall, then stopped short. Light spilled across the lawn from French doors leading to a deck and, worse still, the doors were open. Sitting at an outdoor table was a woman gazing out into the backyard as she sipped intermittently from a glass of wine. She was so deep in conversation with the man in front of her, she had not noticed them.

'Drop,' Lee whispered, as he sunk to the ground, trying to make his form as small as possible.

Alain was too slow. Before he could react, the woman looked up and stared him straight in the eyes.

'Who have we here?' she asked, rising to her feet. The man with her moved his chair to get a better view of what was going on, but his face remained in the shadows.

Alain decided the best defence was offence as he stepped into the light. 'Good evening, ma'am.' Politeness usually worked with strangers. However, Tabitha's steely grey eyes did not soften one iota.

'What are you doing skulking around in my garden?' After moving around the table to stand by her companion, Tabitha leaned forward, frowning slightly. 'Hey, aren't you one of the kids I met in the New Forest this morning with Alice?'

His brain felt sluggish as he searched for a plausible answer to both questions. Ignoring the first, he went straight to the second. 'Alice? Yes, my uncle and I are renting the room above her garage for a few weeks. She offered to show us a few of the local sites. Was that you she stopped and talked to?' He peered into the darkness as if trying to get a better look at her. 'Yes, it was. Hello again.'

The man beside Tabitha shifted in his seat, allowing Alain to see Jo had been right—he was about ten to fifteen years younger than Tabitha. An amused smile played around his lips, and eyebrows raised in query over his pale blue eyes. Rather than appearing amused by the situation, though, the play of shadows and light turned his chiselled face angular and sinister.

'You still have not answered my first question. What are you doing here?' Tabitha's impatient voice drew Alain's attention back to her.

'Well ... it's a bit embarrassing ...' He stopped and looked around, hoping some excuse might present itself, then divine inspiration struck and he allowed tears to form in his eyes. 'I was out walking my dog in the lanes. He caught a scent of something and took off. I lost him in the dark and I've been looking everywhere. I'm sorry. I don't know this place and I stumbled into your backyard.'

'Yes, yes,' Tabitha said, turning her wine glass in her

fingers. 'But that does not explain why you were walking a dog out here at night, or why you were lurking in the shadows.'

'Well ... when I arrived, you were having a private conversation, and my dog obviously isn't here—there's no way he would have been able to resist coming up for a pat, and I didn't want to interrupt, so I was just going to sneak past ...' He trailed off when he realised Tabitha was glaring at him.

'Where is your lead?'

'Lead?' Alain had no idea what she was talking about.

'Yes, your dog lead,' she said each word slowly as if talking to a young child.

'Oh, that is the embarrassing part. I was daydreaming a bit and when Trouble bolted the lead slipped out of my hand. I was not quite quick enough to grab it.' He dropped his head as if trying to hide his shame.

'You call your dog Trouble?' The man laughed a great belly laugh, which sounded odd coming from such an ominous-looking individual. 'Seems like it is a very apt name for him. Come on, Tabitha, no harm done. Let the boy go find his dog. We should finish up inside anyway.' He stood and moved to go indoors.

Tabitha paused, tapping her wine glass as if considering what to do next, her eyes locked with Alain's. A crash from the back of the house drew her attention, and Alain took the opportunity to dart off towards the gate they had left open, then ran full tilt all the way back to the car.

Jo and Bebe were inside when he arrived, with the engine running and seat belts on. He opened the door, and moments later Lee pushed him from behind and he found himself sprawled across the seat, Lee on top of him yelling, 'Go!'

'Door,' Jo said.

Alain flinched as Lee's elbow pushed into the soft flesh of his stomach as he reached to comply.

Jo slowly accelerated and the boys scrambled to upright positions and belted themselves in. They crawled along the lane, lights off, until they reached the end of the road. Lee turned to check out the back window and confirmed they were not being followed.

The car filled with nervous laughter as Jo turned on the lights and sped up to the speed limit. Turning the car back towards Burley, Jo asked, 'Anyone else need a drink?'

They all agreed a trip to the pub was in order. As they pulled into the parking lot a few minutes later, Lee said, 'Did you recognise the man she was with? I would never have expected him to be that Gavin—not in a million years.'

CHAPTER SIX
ANOTHER PIECE OF THE PUZZLE

'Are you sure it was Gavin Vaughn?' Bebe asked.

'I said it was him a hundred times already.' Although Alain was unable to see Lee's face in the darkness, his frustration rang clear in the tone of his voice as it filled the pub car park.

Was he the only person who did not know who Gavin Vaughn was?

'Who?' Jo said.

Apparently not.

'You have no idea who Gavin Vaughn is? For real? He's only one of the world's most famous eco-terrorists,' Lee said.

'Otherwise known as Lee's hero.' Bebe feigned a swoon to add emphasis to her words.

'He is not,' Lee protested as Jo moved between them,

120

pushing Bebe towards the pub door.

'What has he done that is so great?' Jo asked as Bebe reached for the handle.

As warm air carrying a hint of stale beer hit them, Lee answered. 'He started off with Whale Watch, interfering with whale-hunting. Then governments agreed to tighten regulations and he risked going to prison if he continued, so he moved to South America. He began sabotaging big corporations involved in deforestation for profit. To keep big business happy, some governments put a price on his head, forcing him to flee. It looks like he ended up here.'

As they walked past Jo into the pub, Lee pulled his phone out of his pocket and showed Alain a picture. 'This was the man you spoke to, right?'

The man in the image had a beard, but the eyes were unmistakable. 'Yep, that's him.'

'What do you want to drink?' Jo caught them up as they searched the crowded bar for a free table.

Lee pushed past them and wiggled in between two guys leaning on the bar. 'Four pints of lager,' he demanded.

'Three and a bitters lime and lemonade, thanks Peter,' Jo called over his shoulder.

'What?' Lee turned to ask Jo.

'I still need to drive home, plus I start work early tomorrow morning, so I need a clear head.'

Lee shrugged. 'Okay, you guys find somewhere to sit and I'll bring them over.'

Alain and Bebe followed Jo to an empty table they spotted in the far corner. Used to the rather basic taverns in his time with sawdust on the floor and serviceable wooden furniture, Alain was pleasantly surprised by the modern equivalent.

Brightly coloured carpet covered the floor and a fire blazed in the open fireplace. Although the furniture was wooden, someone had spent time polishing it, and it was of a much better quality than those in the taverns he frequented. The only thing the same was the smell. The underlying hint of stale hops, smoke and unwashed bodies made him feel right at home.

Alain took a seat beside Bebe, leaving a space in between him and Jo for Lee. Putting the drinks down on the table moments later, Lee took his place and said, 'So, it is likely Tabitha is working hand-in-hand with an eco-terrorist. But why?'

Jo and Bebe shared a supercilious smile, before Bebe said, 'We may have the answer to that.'

'What did you …?' Lee started, but Jo spoke over him.

'Before we explain, let me tell you a little about Tabitha Synden-Moore.' Jo placed her drink on the cardboard coaster, then straightened it in line with the table before proceeding. 'She has been heavily involved in protecting the New Forest for years. From protesting against potential oil exploration, to lobbying against conifer tress being introduced, she is a strong advocate for leaving the forest as it has always been.'

'That may explain how she met this eco-terrorist,' Alain said as he tried to piece all the bits of information together. 'I mean, his being here now may just be coincidence. They do have common interests after all.'

'A nice thought, but Gavin Vaughn's tactics have become increasingly extreme over the past few years,' Bebe said, and Lee glared at his sister. 'Well, they have, Lee, and you know it. If he is here, something big is on the cards.'

'Anyway, there is more.' Jo intervened before a sibling squabble took over the conversation. 'Tabitha used to be an elected member of The New Forest Association, a group that basically runs the forest and surrounding area. It has a balanced government and elected officials. In the last round of elections hardly anyone voted for her.'

'I bet she was annoyed by that.' Bebe smirked before asking, 'Is there any particular issue or reason people stopped voting for her?'

'I believe so. She wanted to open the forest up to the public for only one month a year because she believes tourism is killing it.'

'Would that be so bad?' Alain asked. 'After all, perhaps the New Forest should be protected for those who live and work here, and for the future.'

Jo's hand stopped midway to her mouth and she glared at him. 'How can you agree with her? Many of the people who live in this area rely on tourist dollars to make a living. With fewer people coming in, many people would be forced to close their businesses and move away.'

'And there are other options. Something like turning the area into an environmental haven would achieve the same end, as well as teaching people how to respect the land,' Lee said.

Jo and Alain turned, surprised at his input. 'What? I am a great believer in saving our environment. Why do you think I even know who Gavin Vaughn is?'

'While this is all very interesting, can we just focus on the problem at hand?' Bebe pointed to Jo's phone as she spoke.

'So ...' Jo picked up where she'd left off. 'After she lost her position, Tabitha became more extreme in her ideas. She wanted our coven to not only cast protection spells for the forest, but to actually perform castings that might backfire and actually hurt people who did harm. That is not what we are about, so she took some of her cronies and left our group.'

'Do you really think the altars we found this morning might be theirs?' Alain asked, finally seeing the bigger picture she was painting.

Jo nodded, so he continued.

'You think they were casting a malicious spell?'

'I do, but I don't believe they have anything to do with the rot showing up in dogs. Tabitha loves animals. She would think nothing about hurting humans, but hurting dogs is a completely different matter.'

'But there is still more,' Bebe said as she took her phone from her pocket. Turning it on, she brought up images of typewritten documents interspersed with handwritten notes and drawings of buildings, as well maps. Placing the phone so Lee and Alain could see, she scrolled through the photos.

'Where did you get these?' Lee asked.

'We found an open window ...' Bebe started.

'You snuck inside? That was you making the noise that distracted Tabitha?' Lee clenched his fists. 'You fools. What if they'd caught you in the house? What if they had called the police? We wouldn't have been able to rescue you.'

'Keep your hair on,' Jo said. 'My foot knocked a book on the edge of a dresser as we climbed back through the window.'

'We didn't move anything else, and we left everything exactly as we found it,' Bebe added.

'And we hid behind the front hedge when the lights came on inside. Your friend Gavin rushed out the front door, and as he turned on the outside light, a cat took off from behind a bush. He cursed at it and went back inside. We waited a moment to make sure he wasn't returning before we ran back to the car,' Jo told them.

'Besides, it was worth the risk to take these.' Bebe raised her chin defiantly.

'What are they?' Although Alain could still understand everyone, his ability to read had left him. Trouble must be involved in something else, or perhaps Alain was too far away to benefit from the Guardian's full magical ability.

'They are planning documents from a local council.' Lee picked up his phone, typed into the screen, waited a few moments, then entered a number from one of the images. 'That is a planning application reference, and from what I can tell from the local council website, they haven't been made public. I'm guessing they are probably stolen.' Lee flicked through some more of the photos before saying, 'Did you read any of this?'

'Yes. I scrolled though a few of the documents while we waited for the two of you,' Jo answered. 'They propose ten thousand new houses be built in the New Forest over the next five years. This here is an impact assessment, and this one details new facilities that will need to be developed to support the population growth. This one in particular worries me—it is an impact assessment on the forest itself,' Jo said as she passed the phone back to Lee. 'The handwritten notes talk about how to "handle" the release of the details to prevent locals opposing the plan. The environmental impact will be devastating, and will change this part of the New Forest forever.' Jo's hand shook as she took her phone back.

'We should tell Alice and Barnaby about this,' Bebe said. 'It may not be related to what Barnaby is doing, but it is important. Though we can't say how we found it. Alice expressly forbade us from going to Tabitha's tonight.'

Used to getting himself out of tight situations, Alain's response was swift. 'We don't tell them … well, at least not yet. They are concerned about saving the dogs and what we found tonight isn't linked to that. I see no need to risk getting ourselves in trouble.'

As the others nodded their agreement, Lee said, 'That doesn't stop us from following up and seeing if we can find out some more about what is going on. I mean, this is so wrong. We can't just let the development go ahead.'

'Hello Jo. Don't you all look serious?' The voice coming from behind Alain sounded familiar, but he couldn't exactly place it, even though he had only spoken to a few people in this time. 'May I join you?'

Not waiting for an answer, the girl pushed past him and he caught a glimpse of dark hair and a leather jacket as she placed a chair between Lee and Jo and proceeded to sit. Lee went to object, looked at Jo then stopped and shuffled over closer to Alain.

'I never stood a chance,' he muttered under his breath, 'I'm not her type at all.' Lee stared morosely into his beer as Bebe looked on sympathetically.

'Are you here to catch up with me?' Placing her body to exclude the others, the newcomer was clearly speaking to Jo.

'Actually, I came here with my friends, Izzy,' Jo said, a blush rising from the neck of her T-shirt.

The dark-haired girl turned to study the group as if she'd just realised they were there, and Alain's breath caught in his throat as her violet-blue eyes slid past him, then back again. For a fraction of a second, Izzy looked at him as if trying to place his face before returning her attention to Jo, ignoring the rest of their party once more.

He'd come across Izzy before—only then, she'd called herself Isolde. *I must warn Trouble of this.*

Later, when Alain rose to replenish their drinks, Izzy followed him over to the bar to help. As they waited for the barman to fill their order, she leaned in close so no one else was able to hear what she said.

'What are you doing here?' she hissed.

'I could ask the same of you.' Alain attempted to calm his voice while his stomach clenched in dread.

'You aren't here by yourself. Where is your guardian?'

Picking up the tray of drinks, he turned to face her, and with more confidence than he felt, he said, 'We beat you last time, and will do so this time as well, whatever you are up to.'

A smirk hovered around the corners of her mouth.

Damn, I gave too much away. Now she knows I have no idea what her plan is.

Then she frowned and looked back at the table. 'We? Jo is another John. That girl in the shop today ... she couldn't be ... so ... he is ...'

Ignoring her, he walked back to the table, not caring whether or not she followed.

Around nine thirty Alice excused herself, saying she normally talked to her husband around this time every night. When Sigma heard the door close upstairs, he turned to Barwick.

I have been trying to get hold of Beta all night, but not a single one of my contacts is able to reach him.

Do you want me to stay up with you while you keep trying? Barwick asked as he stretched and yawned.

It's all right; no sense both of us losing sleep. Though I may come over and stay with you tonight just in case I need you.

Barwick mumbled his agreement, and Sigma followed him outside and up to his room above the garage. He waited patiently for the old man to pull out the sofa bed and make it. As soon as the bed was ready he jumped up, turned round a couple of times then flopped down.

He then proceeded to watch Barwick check all the cultures he and Alain had set up that afternoon. The alchemist nodded as he looked at each container, then smiled as he shut the incubator door before walking back to the bed. He undressed and crawled under the covers as Sigma settled beside him.

Sigma attempted to contact Beta a few more times before the warmth of the room, combined with a comfortable bed and an active day, caused his eyes to close. Soon he had joined Barwick, the two of them snoring soundly.

At some time during the night, the temperature dropped. Trouble rose, stretched and moved closer to the warm sleeping form of Barwick. As he did, the door handle rattled.

He jumped down from the bed and padded over to the room's entrance. Sniffing the air, he then cocked an ear, trying to figure out what was going on. A scraping noise sounded. Was someone trying to pick the lock?

A growl formed in his throat, and he let it out. The scratching stopped, and a moment later there were footsteps on the stairs. Placing his nose to the floor again, Trouble had a good, long sniff and barked quietly as he placed the scent—she was here, in this time. Had she followed them, or had she come for her own reasons? His tail swished in irritation; either way, it was not a good sign. He humphed. There was nothing he could do about it in the middle of the night.

Confident they would now be left alone, he returned to bed but was unable to sleep. He was still awake when car engines started as Burley began to raise itself for the new day. He contemplated waking Barwick and asking to be let out into the garden when finally he felt the familiar tingle alerting him—someone from home was trying to contact him.

Sigma.

He relaxed. It was his mentor, Beta. If he was to be recalled, he would prefer the message to be passed on by a friendly face who would not rub his nose in the fact he had not been up to the job.

Yes, Beta, I am here.

Sorry to take so long to answer your calls. Things have been ... well, let us just say they are not good.

They are not good here either. Not only are there likely to be magical implications, but I think the Time Wreckers are here as well. One of them tried to break in last night, Trouble informed Beta.

I can confirm Time Wreckers are nearby, and are a part of what is happening. In fact, reports of their activity in your time are coming in thick and fast. We have had to send a couple of teams to other incidents. From what we can make out, something big is planned, and they are trying to divert our attention by causing as much noise as possible.

That does not sound good at all. Trouble sat up on the bed, trying to focus his sleepy brain.

Unfortunately we cannot tell whether your situation is a diversion, or the main event, Beta told him.

You are not calling us back, are you? Before this conversation started Sigma would have welcomed this news, seeing it as the council reaffirming their trust in him. Now, he was not so sure. *Beta, this is only my second solo mission. I am not ready to lead an assault against a full-blown Time Wrecker attack. Besides, I need to make sure Barwick and Alain return home.*

I understand all that, Sigma. Not only is there no one available to replace you, but we believe Barwick's skill as an apothecary and alchemist will be needed in Burley.

But what about Alain? Sigma asked. *We might be placing him in grave danger.*

We cannot help that, I am afraid. Besides, I believe Alain's magic is stronger than Barwick's, and you will most certainly need him in the days to come.

Still ...

Tell me, did you get a sight of the Wrecker they sent to Burley? Beta changed the subject, and Trouble was sure

it was a ploy to forestall any further arguments.

Realising he was not going to change his mentor's mind, Trouble sighed, then answered, *Not a look as such. More of a scent.*

See? I knew your penchant for taking animal rather than human form would come in handy. Who is it?

Isolde.

That news is not totally bad. She is a relatively new recruit, so if they sent her to Burley to disrupt the timeline then it is most likely a diversion.

Sigma considered his mentor's words, and he had to admit, he agreed. *She might only be a minor player, Beta, but Isolde does go off-script, sometimes in the most dangerous way. She might turn this little fiasco into a major incident whether the Wreckers intended it to be or not.*

Beta did not answer, and Trouble was about to close the connection when his mentor spoke again.

I agree. You need to be careful. This mission is no longer about fact finding. Your new instructions are to stop whatever Isolde is up to—no matter the cost. Good luck.

Before Trouble was able to answer, he sensed Beta drop their link. Although in dog form, the sinking of his stomach was no less disconcerting. He had some planning to do. First things first, though—he had more pressing needs. Stretching, he leaned over and licked Barwick's face.

'Leave me alone, you mutt,' the man grumbled and rolled away.

Deliberately targeting his bladder, Trouble climbed over the half-awake man and licked his face again. Barwick cursed and sat up as Trouble walked over to the door, making his intentions clear.

CHAPTER SEVEN
THE PLAN

Snuggling under the duvet, Alain imagined himself back home in his own bed. The thoughts comforted him until he noticed the mattress was too soft to be his. Concentrating on returning to his half-dream, he was unable to completely submerge himself as Lee's snores kept interrupting. They were loud enough to wake the dead. Unable to stand the noise any longer, Alain got up to use the toilet.

Heading back to his room, he banged into Alice—literally. As he attempted to sidestep around her, she moved in the same direction. He tripped, grabbed hold of the bannister, then righted himself.

Alice pulled the towel from in front of her face as she said, 'Sorry, Alain. I shouldn't be wandering around towelling my hair with others in the house. I am so used to being here by myself ... Were you wanting to use the bathroom? There is plenty of wat ...' Alice stopped midway through wrapping the towel around her shoulders. 'Oh my goodness, I have just realised ... I can't believe you have stayed two nights and I haven't ...'

'At home I only bathe once a week,' Alain assured her. 'But if it's okay with you I would like to clean up a bit.'

'Have you used a shower before?' Alice had regained her composure and was back to her businesslike self.

'Is a shower something like a bath?'

'Ah, no, nothing like a bath. Here let me show you how to work it.' She led him into the bathroom and moments later Alain stood under a glorious stream of hot water, lathered in something called shower gel. As he washed, he attempted to figure out how this magnificent invention worked.

He could have stayed under the water for hours. Mindful of the fact others might want to use the facilities, he dragged himself out, dried himself off, and wrapped a towel around his waist. Opening the door he found himself face to face with Bebe, and automatically took a step back. Aware of his almost complete lack of clothing, his cheeks burned with heat as the girl stared at him, wide-eyed.

'Um, excuse me. I must, um ...'

Bebe was quick to compose herself. 'Ah, Alain, good thing I caught you. Jo texted me a couple of minutes ago. She wants to meet around ten in the cafe near Alice's shop to discuss our next moves. Can you tell Lee please?'

Not understanding why this news couldn't wait until he had dressed, Alain mumbled, 'Okay.' He slipped past the pyjama-clad girl, and almost ran to his bedroom. Shutting the door firmly behind himself, he leaned back against the wood.

'Wha …?' Lee spoke blearily from under the blankets. 'What happened?' Lee pushed himself upright. 'You look like you've seen a ghost.'

'Ah, I ran into Bebe in the hall. We are to catch up with Jo at ten for a planning session—at the café.'

As he spoke, Lee studied him carefully before chuckling to himself as he threw a shirt to Alain. 'You haven't got a chance with her, mate. Many a better man than you has tried and failed.'

'I wasn't … I'm not … I have a …'

'Come on, get yourself dressed and let's get some breakfast while she's in the shower. Then we can get Barnaby's search set up before we need to get to the cafe.'

They rushed through their meal and had just finished washing up when Bebe joined them. Feeling his cheeks flush, Alain dropped his head as opened the outside door before stepping outside.

'We are going to help Barnaby with his research,' Lee told his sister as Alain beat his hasty retreat.

'Don't forget the cafe at ten,' she responded. 'We have some planning to do.'

Lee picked up the rectangular item he had brought downstairs and joined him.

'What's that?' Alain asked to distract Lee from mentioning his hasty departure.

'My laptop. It's like my tablet, only on steroids.'

Alain nodded knowingly, not wishing to admit he had no idea what steroids were.

Alain froze as the door to Master Barwick's room swung open when he raised his hand to knock. Tentatively, he stuck his head through the gap and found complete disarray. Lee pushed past him and surveyed the devastation.

'What happened here?' he asked. 'Where are Trouble and Barnaby?'

'Right here,' a voice came from below, followed by heavy footsteps on the wooden stairs.

'What ...?' Barwick halted when he spied the state of his room over Alain's shoulder.

He pushed the boy out of the way and rushed to the bed. Leaning over, he pulled something out from underneath and heaved a sigh of relief. Alain frowned, unable to comprehend why the dog bed Alice had borrowed for Trouble was so important.

As Master Barwick lifted the cushion out of the bed, Trouble said, *We had a visitor last night, so when we went for a walk after breakfast we hid the samples.*

In the dog bed? Alain shook his head in wonder.

It was all we were able to think of at the time. You couldn't tell anything was in there once we put the pillow back on top.

'Who did this?' Alain had forgotten Lee was with them. 'We should tell Aunt Alice and call the police.'

'There's no harm done,' said Master Barwick. 'No use getting the authorities involved. Give us a minute to clean up and it will be like nothing ever happened.'

'Are you completely mad? We need to catch whoever

broke in.' Lee swept out an arm to indicate the mess. He pulled out his phone. 'What do you call for the police here? Nine nine nine?'

'We already know who it was.' Alain grabbed Lee's phone as he moved into the room. After placing the mobile on the bench, he began cleaning up.

How do you know? Trouble and Master Barwick asked together.

I met Isolde at the pub last night. Turns out she is Jo's friend, Izzy, Alain explained.

Lee had made his way to the bench and picked up his phone. 'What is going on here? Who broke in? And Why? What's more, why do I keep hearing a buzzing in my ears? And why do you keep looking at the dog as though you're expecting him to answer?'

Alain took the phone and placed it back on the counter. 'We believe it is Izzy because we foiled her plot to kill King Henry. She was definitely working against us then, and I believe she is now as well. And I keep looking at Trouble because, believe it or not, he is the brains of this outfit.'

Alain! Master Barwick and Trouble both shouted in his head as Lee burst out laughing.

'You've all lost your minds.' He grabbed for his phone again, but Alain beat him to it. 'Give that back. I am calling the police.'

Holding the phone away from Lee's grasping hand, Alain appealed to the others. 'Guys, Lee already worked out we came from another time. He can almost hear mind-speak, and maybe he would be better able to help us if he knew the whole story.'

Sigma? It's your call. After all, you are the brains of

the operation. Master Barwick's mouth twisted into a wry grin.

Thanks for that. Trouble turned to Lee. *I am a member of an organisation called the Time Guardians. We are tasked with ensuring history unfolds as it should.*

'What? For real? Why are you here?' Lee asked.

Your aunt called us here to investigate whether or not other forces were at work in the New Forest causing dogs to become ill.

'What sort of forces?'

Unnatural forces, or perhaps mystical ones.

'And you all think there are? Don't you?'

Yes. Isolde, Izzy, works for an organisation called the Time Wreckers. Their agenda is different to ours. They seek to cause chaos and confusion. It was she who broke in here last night. I can smell her scent all over the place.

When the dog finished, Lee sank onto the bed and still did not speak. The others watched him for a moment, but as his silence continued for a number of minutes, they returned to tidying the room. When Master Barwick needed to fold up the bed, Lee stood as instructed then sank back down on the sofa.

About half an hour later, once Master Barwick returned to fiddling with his experiments, Alain and Trouble wandered over to Lee and sat down beside him.

'The dog spoke to me in my mind,' Lee whispered.

'Yes, he did.'

'We had a conversation about weird organisations, like one good and one evil.'

Alain tried to lighten the mood. 'Yes, he did—although why your mind is sticking on that and not the time travel bit I will never understand.'

'And they are here in Burley?' Lee continued as if Alain had not spoken.

'Yes.'

'And someone sent you to fight them?'

'Yes, and I believe it is likely you are here for that reason too.'

'What?' The glazed look left Lee's eyes and he turned his startled gaze to Alain. 'You can't be serious.'

'Okay, let me ask you a question. When did you make plans to come here and visit your aunt? I mean, was it planned a long time ago, or did something come up suddenly?' Alain asked.

'We booked our flights last week after Dad got a last-minute job offer. Dad had to use his influence to get our seats.'

'So ... it probably isn't a coincidence that you are here now with us.'

If I may? Trouble butted in. *Lee, this is not your first time confronting the Time Wreckers. An earlier incarnation of you and Bebe worked with Alain and Jo to defeat a plot to stop Prince Henry becoming King Henry the First.*

'Trouble, did you have to tell him that? He was barely coping with talking dogs and secret organisations—now you've thrown reincarnation at him.' Alain worried for his friend, but he need not have bothered.

'Funnily enough, reincarnation is the one thing that is not odd about this. I always believed our spirits would be reborn into another body after we die. I also kinda thought we would keep meeting up with the same people. Time travel is also logical. Well, it's based on pseudo-science.

It's the talking dog and the good-versus-evil thing. I feel like I am in a Marvel-*Secret Life of Pets* mash-up.'

'Marvel? *Secret Life of Pets*? Mash-up? What on earth are you on about?'

Lee laughed out loud, and it seemed to dispel all the tension in the room. 'If you are truly from the time of Henry the First, then being here must be weirder for you than me getting my head around this. If you can put that aside and get on with the job, I guess I should step up and do the same.'

Picking up his laptop, Lee walked over to Master Barwick. 'Okay, Barnaby, let's see if we can't find this organism you've been talking about.'

Lee and Trouble wandered over behind him. Barnaby pointed to the four slides he had prepared for the microscope the day before.

'I have chosen samples of the same life form in four different stages of development.' He pointed to the slides. 'What I am not sure of is how your computer can help identify them. I spent hours looking through your uncle's books, and I cannot find anything useful at all.'

'Fortunately for you, I was talking to my uncle a couple of weeks ago about his new piece of equipment, and I did some research online about,' Lee said as he pressed the power button on his laptop.

While the screen flickered away, Lee pulled a plug out of his back pocket and connected it to a point in the back of the microscope. He plugged the other end into a hole in his laptop. He turned the microscope on, then fiddled around with something on his computer.

'All right, we are ready.' He placed one of the slides

under the microscope, adjusted the lens, pressed some keys on the keyboard, and adjusted the lens again. 'Ta-dah.' He held his hands out in a flourish.

They others shuffled around behind and looked at the screen. In front of them, in glorious detail, was the image of the organism on the slide.

'Amazing though that is, I do not see how that helps us identify it,' Master Barwick said.

'Watch and learn.' Lee touched a couple of buttons on the keyboard and the computer made a *snick* sound. He followed the same process with the other three slides. When he had finished, he played around on the keyboard again, and the others crowded closer to see what he was doing.

'Right, I saved the images to the hard drive.' He showed them the pictures from the slides on his laptop. 'This programme here will search all the images on the internet and find any that are similar. I just need to load our pictures into the programme and start it up.'

He pressed a few more keys, checked the screen, and finally looked up. 'There, done. Now, I am setting the parameters to find an eighty percent match, or greater. That way we should be able to find any similar organisms and that may give you some idea on how to deal with this disease.'

Master Barwick leaned over Lee's shoulder. 'And this, um, programme, looks through hundreds of images to find a match?'

'Hundreds of hundreds of thousands,' Lee said.

'How long will all this searching take?' Master Barwick asked.

'Well, I am running four images against the billions

and trillions of images available on the internet looking for a near-perfect match. So about four—'

A grin split Master Barwick's face. 'Four days! That is faster than I imagined. Still, it will give me some time to run other tests to see if I can identify ways of slowing the growth down, or perhaps killing it.'

'I was going to say four hours, give or take an hour.' Lee laughed.

'Oh.' Master Barwick froze mid-movement, and turned back around and stared at the laptop and nodded. 'I shall wait then.' Master Barwick settled with his elbows on the counter, watching the screen displaying the number of images checked.

'You won't be able to see much until the process is finished,' Lee said. 'There is still plenty of time for you to do some tests or check on your other samples.'

'Yes, true. I might try and work some more on a cure.' The older man stood and began clearing the bench, stopping every now and then to check progress on the screen.

'Will you be using magic?' Lee turned as he spoke, his eyes following the alchemist's movements. 'Can I watch?'

Master Barwick chuckled. 'Lee, I am first and foremost a man of science and healing, so I will be trying standard tests first. If that yields nothing, only then will I turn my focus to magic. All I will do after is test whether or not the elements were manipulated by magic to alter what is found in the natural world.'

'Cool, so you can do alchemy and magic?' Lee's eyes widened in fascination.

'I am not sure whether or not I will actually be able

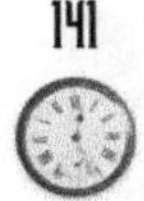

to do much in this time. Humans' link with the natural world has grown weak as they moved to cities and stopped tilling and caring for the land. Magical power is so weak here, so the tasks I am able to perform are severely limited,' Master Barwick said.

Deciding now was the best time to interrupt and ask a question that had been on his mind since last night, Alain said, 'Master Barwick, is it possible for the other coven to have had something to do with the development of this organism?'

'I spent hours teaching you the basics of alchemy, so you obviously realise a large part of it is the practice of transmuting elements into something else by combining them, or using heat, cold and the energy of the world to alter it. If you consider it in those terms, how do you think the coven might be involved?'

Alain disliked it when Master Barwick turned questions into teaching moments. It slowed everything down while he considered his answers, which in turn impaired his ability to take action.

Sighing, he sorted through the little he had learned about alchemy as opposed to his trade as an apothecary before he responded. 'Well, I guess if they found an element to alter bacteria or a virus they could make it more lethal, but you would not really need magic to do that.' Master Barwick nodded encouragingly, and Alain thought about the first lesson he had in basic alchemy, helping plants to grow. It was as though a light had come on in his head. 'Some growth spells might be able to be applied to a virus or an organism to speed up its development.'

'Yes, that is a definite possibility. But there is no evidence to say whether or not that has been done—yet. Now, do you want to stay and help me, or have you two got other plans?'

'If it is all right with you, we arranged to meet the girls for tea at the cafe, but I can stay if you need me to,' Alain added, hoping Master Barwick had not planned this morning's work as a lesson for him.

'No, no, you run along. I need to make sure I have all the things I need for my tests. When I'm finished, I'm going to do some more study and it may throw up some more things we can test later.'

'You really don't need us?' Lee was partway to the door as he spoke.

'No, but if you can arrange to be back here later this afternoon when the results come in—both of you? I will need some help with this computer thing.'

Alain headed for the door, and Trouble made as if to follow.

'Sorry, Trouble. Dogs are not allowed in cafes here.' Alain stood in the doorway, preventing the canine from joining them.

Trouble sat and cocked his head to the side as if pondering something.

And why do I think that is precisely why you are all meeting in a cafe? What do you not want us to find out? Maybe something to do with what you uncovered on your nocturnal activities? Trouble raised his eyebrows.

Um …

Don't bother making up a lie. Simply promise me you will think before you act, and be careful.

The cafe was buzzing with people when Lee and Alain arrived. It seemed the cold weather had encouraged most of Burley into the warmth of the local meeting place. Jo waved them over to a table near the window, miming she had organised drinks for them all.

After they peeled off coats, scarves and hats, the boys sat down in the two vacant seats. Alain took a sip of his warm, milky tea. It was just as he liked it, and he looked over the rim of his mug to find Bebe smiling at him. It warmed his heart that she had remembered what he liked, and he immediately felt disloyal to Barabal, even though they had no formal arrangement. Feeling heat rising from his collar, he dipped his head and took another sip of his drink before asking, 'What is so important that we had to meet here today?'

Jo grinned. 'I spoke with Mum last night and she let slip Tabitha invited her to a coven meeting tonight, hoping to poach her.'

'You talk as though she is being asked to turn to the dark side.' Lee snorted.

Jo flashed him a disdainful look before continuing, 'Of course, Mum is not going, but she did say she regretted missing out on Tabitha's carrot cake, which means the meeting will be at her place.'

'How did you come to that conclusion?' Alain tilted his head to the side as he tried to follow the logic.

'Tabitha only goes to the trouble of making her famous carrot cake—which she swears is far better than Alice's—when the meetings are at her's.'

'You think we should go and spy?' Lee's cheeky grin was replaced with a glint of anticipation.

'Goodness no. I was thinking I might talk Izzy into taking me along. Make out I am getting a bit bored with the inactivity of my coven. I could be our insider, so to speak.'

Bebe's eyes widened in surprise. 'Jo, I really do not think that's such a great idea. If they are trying to stop the development, with Gavin involved, it might be quite dangerous.'

With Isolde involved, and with her knowing who they all were, Alain was not keen for them to do anything that would be seen as confrontational either. 'There must be another way—one that doesn't put you at risk.'

'If we skulk under windows again and listen, we might pick up something. But I don't think we will find out as much as we would if I attended the meeting,' Jo said.

Alain had to admit her idea had merit. Attending the meeting was a great opportunity to find out if Tabitha's actions to stop the New Forest development were connected to the outbreak of Alabama Rot. Hopefully, though, it would be a typical coven gathering and they would be able to discount the coven's involvement.

Lee, who had started scrolling through things on his phone when he realised they were not going to plan another group spy mission, now leaned forward. 'What about a compromise? How about Jo does what she proposed, but we also go along and wait outside. One of us can act as a watcher, and two of us can be prepared to create a diversion should Jo need to escape.'

The determined set of Jo's jaw told Alain trying to talk

her out of going would be a waste of time. Perhaps they should explore Lee's compromise. 'What sort of diversion did you have in mind?'

'One of the stories you told me yesterday has given me an idea. We might need to rummage around in Alice's garage to find what we need, and we still have to meet with Barnaby and help him interpret the data from the search, but there should be time to build the diversion I have in mind before tonight's meeting.'

'Lee, what are you up to?' Bebe stared intently at her brother.

'Never you mind,' he said, tapping the side of his nose.

Jo said, 'Look, I'm sure this is going overboard. I know these women. Even if there is something going on, none of them would ever hurt me. But I guess if I do not go along with it you will just turn up anyway.'

'Yep,' Lee agreed.

Sighing, Jo stood. 'All right then. The meeting is set for seven. You guys will need to be in place well before the start. Do you remember the way?'

'Yes,' Lee and Bebe said together.

'And we will be in place early—you won't even notice we're there,' Lee told her.

'You don't want to tell me what the diversion will be?'

'No, you need to be as surprised as everyone else. Otherwise they will suspect you are a part of it.' The grin on Lee's face as he said this worried Alain, especially as he had an idea of what his friend had in mind.

Jo tilted her head to the side and frowned at Lee. 'I thought the diversion's purpose was to give me a way out should I get into trouble.'

'This is even better. It not only gives you an escape, but because you will also be surprised by what I have planned, they won't link you to it. Just be ready to leave when something unexpected happens.'

Alain was sceptical, and Jo's frown had not disappeared—in fact, if anything, it had deepened. Even so, the girl pulled on her coat and said, 'Well, I hope I don't see you tonight.'

Lee and Bebe laughed, but unease churned in Alain's stomach. Any way he looked at it, this was a bad idea.

CHAPTER EIGHT
A STEP FORWARD

'So, what exactly are we looking for?' Alain's voice echoed in the empty garage as Lee turned on the light.

'Here.' Lee passed over his tablet.

Alain studied the screen and a grin spread across his face. 'Oh, I like it.'

They spent half an hour or so finding what they needed, then another hour assembling the items in a container.

Lee stood back and admired their work. 'Right. We just need to put on some twine.'

'Shall we tie it on?' It was not the best option given the shape of their creation, but Alain saw no other way to attach the string.

'No. We glue it.'

'Glue? We don't have time to make it. Besides, it wouldn't have time to set by tonight.'

148

ALCHEMIST

'Surely you've heard of super glue? No, of course not.'

Lee opened a drawer and rummaged around, eventually pulling out a tube about the length of a finger. After removing the top, he placed a small amount of clear liquid on the container and pressed the twine on a spot near the bottom. Alain noticed he took care not to get his hands anywhere near the glue. A minute or so later, he announced, 'There, it's done.'

Alain didn't believe any glue was able to dry that quickly, or that such a small amount would hold the twine in place. But he gave the thin rope a tug and almost fell backwards when the container slipped off the workbench to hang from his hand.

'Amazing.' A smile worked its way to his face as he considered all the possible uses for a fast -acting glue. As Lee tidied up, Alain palmed the small tube of super glue, knowing exactly how he would use it later.

Hiding their efforts under a cardboard box, they grabbed a quick sandwich for lunch before heading up to Master Barwick's room.

The alchemist mumbled to himself as he peered into the microscope and scribbled notes.

'You can record what you are doing on the computer and attach it to images and the like,' Lee said.

Master Barwick glanced up, blinked rapidly a couple of times, then focussed on the boys. He frowned as he said, 'No, no. That would not be useful at all. Writing things down helps me think. Besides, your computer has been making funny noises—beeping and such. I think it might be broken.'

'Excellent. That means the search is complete.' Lee picked up his laptop and sat on the sofa. Alain joined him, glancing over his shoulder at the results on the screen.

'Oh, this is interesting,' Lee said, his eyes glued to the computer.

'What did you find?' Alain looked at the information. 'It says you did not get a one hundred percent match on any of the images. How is that interesting?'

'It is because it tells us something very important.' Lee paused while Alain considered the data.

'It does tell us something quite important.' Master Barwick sat on the other side of Lee so he too was able to see the result. 'It tells us that although there are other cases of this disease around the world, our current outbreak does not match any samples taken in those investigations. That is, if I understand Lee correctly, and his programme checked images taken from all those outbreaks.'

'You are correct,' Lee said. 'They don't even match previous instances in the New Forest itself. We found some similar-looking organisms though, which may help you.'

'Are you not going to give us an analysis of those results?' Alain teased, and Lee tensed beside him.

'I know I'm not the sharpest tool in the toolbox, but you don't have to point it out all the time.'

Alain frowned, unsure where the comment had come from. 'Hey, I didn't mean that—I think you're smart. I ... I don't know what to say.'

Lee coloured. 'Sorry, sore point. I'm not as quick as Bebe and a lot of our friends, and they tease me about being a dumb grunt because I'm joining the army—even though it is officer training. I like the idea of structure and knowing what is expected of you, as well as being able to help people, of course. They still think it is a cop-out though.'

'From what your aunt tells me you're attending a very prestigious army college and will be taking a degree in Computer Science,' Master Barwick added.

Lee shrugged. 'I am good with computers and better with math. My brain seems to be able to put those things together easily enough. I struggle with any other subjects though, and I'm very good with abstract ideas. I am also bad at adapting to new situations, so I like to prepare.'

'You seem perfectly fine to me,' Alain said. 'You accepted us, and you have been a great help finding information on the internet—you always manage to come up with what we need. I'm not sure how well I would have survived here without you.'

Again, Lee coloured. 'I spend a lot of energy and time learning to cope with change, and to hide my nerves. Now I research and find things out so no one realises I see things differently to them.'

'That in itself is a type of smart,' Alain said, admiration welling for Lee. Perhaps he could learn something from the way his friend studied and planned before he acted.

'Maybe it's best if you look at the full results. Here. You use this to change screens or to move the information up and down.' Lee handed the laptop to Alain, and sat on the floor beside Trouble, running his fingers through the dog's hair.

It takes a very evolved person to appreciate their own

limitations and work with them, Trouble told Lee, bringing a wan smile to the boy's face.

Alain scrolled through the pictures and the information in the image-matching programme, clicking on links like he had seen Lee do, and reading everything there before returning to the initial report. After about half an hour, he had pulled together some sort of a potted outline not only about Alabama Rot but their localised version of the disease as well.

'Do you want to read this, Master Barwick?'

'No, no, you summarise it for me and I will follow up on anything I find interesting.'

'All right. Firstly, Alabama Rot is more accurately known as Cutaneous and Renal Glomerular Vasculopathy—or CRGV for short. The closest thing the search showed to its makeup is E. coli, like you find with food poisoning, or aeromonas hydrophilia, a bacteria found in fish. The current belief is it is a form of bacteria found in water or mud.'

'Mm, that is interesting,' Master Barwick said. 'It's a bacteria rather than a virus, which at least tells me I was heading in the right direction. My research this morning led me to believe this was bacterial as the cells changed when I added certain oils like garlic, cloves and oregano. If I added some goldenseal or echinacea, the change was more marked.'

As Master Barwick spoke, Lee pulled out his phone and began tapping away. 'That is interesting. The internet said both garlic and cloves are used in fighting E. coli-type diseases.'

'Yes, they can be most effective in helping bacterial infection. It also explains why blood transfusions help some animals. It breaks the bacterial growth cycle and allows antibiotics and such to work,' Master Barwick said.

'Antibiotics?' Alain asked.

'Ah, yes, of course. They are a fantastic invention,' Master Barwick started but Lee interrupted, handing his phone to Alain so he could read up on the drugs.

'Wow, that is amazing,' he said handing the phone back before continuing. 'Another important fact is the bacteria is only found in dogs. It has not evolved or mutated enough to be able to spread to humans or other animals.'

'That at least is a blessing,' Master Barwick said. 'What I find more interesting though, is my attempts at finding a cure would get to a certain point, then either fail completely or make no further progress. I managed to interrupt the growth cycle. I mean, the disease stopped replicating, but I was unable to find a way to break down the bacteria and clear it up. This seems to be the point where other researchers have failed as well.'

'Don't lose hope Barnaby. Our samples are slightly different to the other images of CRGV, so maybe you can find something they haven't,' Alain said.

'What do you mean?' Master Barwick leaned forward.

'I mean, this programme says the fully developed bacteria is only a ninety percent match. If a sample had been brought over from, say, America, and the coven had done something like accelerated its growth using magic, that could alter the bacteria or how it grows,' Alain said.

He looked through the images again, finding the closest match for each one. 'Look at this.'

Alain swivelled the laptop around to show everyone the screen. 'This shows our first slide has a ninety-seven percent match with early CRGV; our second is only ninety-five percent compatible, and the third drops to ninety-three. As our version of the bacteria grows it gets further away from the parent sample. If someone altered it magically early on to grow faster it would stand to reason the difference would accelerate.' Alain presented his case.

Master Barwick smiled. 'I knew there was a reason I took you on as an apprentice. I believe you are quite correct in your assumptions.'

But as an investigator you need to come up with evidence. We need to find out who is doing this and why.

Lee physically jumped as Trouble entered the conversation. 'I had almost forgotten you could do that,' he said, laughing.

'Well, we know Tabitha and her coven are up to something; I reckon it's them,' Alain said.

Master Barwick's eyebrows rose. 'And just how do you know that?'

Realising he had let something slip, Alain looked to Lee to bail him out.

'We may have found some evidence last night,' the boy said.

'At the pub?' Master Barwick pressed.

'Um, well ...' Lee stuttered.

'No, we took a bit of a diversion on the way there,' Alain admitted.

'What sort of a diversion?' Master Barwick held up his hand. 'No, don't tell me. I don't want to know. I only came here to work on the infection. I have no interest in becoming involved in anything else.'

154

ALCHEMIST

Given our new orders are to stop the Time Wreckers, I am happy for you to follow up your lines of enquiry, Alain, Trouble said. *So long as you share everything with us, and, it goes without saying, you will be careful, won't you?*

'Of course we will be careful,' Lee said.

And one more thing. You found something at Tabitha's place and you are all excited about it, but she is not the only person who has an axe to grind around here. You might need to cast your net wider.

There was a moment's silence while Alain thought through the pros and cons of telling Trouble about the information they had picked up. Finally, common sense won.

'At the moment, I believe she is our strongest lead, even if she is not the only suspect. We found out Tabitha is working with an international eco-terrorist, and they are doing something about a planned housing development in The New Forest.'

Trouble cocked his head to the side as though thinking about the implication of this new information. *Is Isolde working through Tabitha or this terrorist?*

'What do you mean by working through?' Lee asked.

'Oh, Time Wreckers cannot directly involve themselves in events; they can only encourage people to act. If they act themselves, time will find a way to balance things back to the way they were. We operate under the same constraint,' Alain explained.

'Oh,' Lee said. 'This is beginning to sound like a *Doctor Who* episode. How does Master Barwick coming up with some sort of a cure fit into the balance? Might he not just cause a rip in time?'

'*Dr Who?* Is he someone who might help us?' Master Barwick asked.

Lee chuckled, 'He is a character, like in a play, Barnaby.'

'Um … yes …well as to your question about my potential cure poses an interesting question. How does that fit in with the rules?' Master Barwick looked to Trouble for an answer.

Normally it would not. You would need to have someone like Jo find the information to create a cure. Then it would be up to her to actually work on producing it, Trouble said.

'Perhaps Lee using the computer programme to find the mutation has been enough to meet our requirement not to interfere in events so far,' Alain said.

'You may be right.' Master Barwick nodded, then ran his hand through his already messy hair. 'I am a little worried about how close we will be coming to breaking the rules if we use that information and succeed in making a cure—then if we use it on an animal ...'

Mmm, we would be walking a fine line. I think if this form of bacteria was the result of Time Wrecker interference, we should be all right identifying something that will help with the New Forest cases only, Trouble offered.

'Or I might be able to come up with something to slow the mutation down enough to allow the current treatments to work.' Stroking his beard, Master Barwick wandered back over to his workstation.

'Do you need any help?' As silence followed his question, Alain assumed Master Barwick was deep in thought, and he turned to Lee. 'What's is our plan for the rest of the afternoon?'

'I think we should get some more food in our stomachs

if we are going to be out before dinner,' Lee said, his mind, as ever, turning to eating.

I shall come with you tonight, Trouble announced, following them out the door. *I want to see what is going on myself.*

'Are you sure?' Alain asked. 'We shall be doing a lot of hiding. It is only Jo who will be in amongst the action.'

Then you shall take me to Alice's shop and I will go with Jo tonight.

Trouble would not be talked out of his plan, so Alain reluctantly set off to The Witch's Hat, with Trouble walking jauntily beside him, while Lee went to organise their food.

Alice had taken a little convincing to loan them her car when they asked at afternoon teatime. At first, her main concern was their driving in the dark in a strange place. Then she said the pub they were going to for dinner was not really a place for teenagers.

'The crowd who hang out there are known to be a bit rough.' Alice's brows drew together in a frown.

'But Jo recommended it because the food is meant to be fantastic,' Bebe said. 'She told us we would not get a better beef and Yorkshire pudding anywhere.'

'If you are worried, perhaps you and Barnaby should come with us,' Lee said, and Alain threw him a worried glance—what happened if they said yes?

Master Barwick hastily declined. 'There's some more work I want to do on my experiments; I am at a crucial stage.'

Perhaps his mentor had declined because he knew full well they were not going to the pub at all, but Alain thought it more likely he was just so engrossed in his work he could not even contemplate a night off.

'What about you, Alice?' Bebe asked

'Well, much as I would like to, tomorrow is a work day. Besides, I don't want to miss my call with Donald. But you go and enjoy yourselves.'

Having gained the permission they required, the three went upstairs to dress for the evening. 'What were you thinking?' Alain asked Lee. 'What if they had said yes?'

Lee stopped outside their room and smiled. 'Why, I would have had Jo text us to cancel the pub meal and invite us 'round to her place instead.'

Bebe punched Lee playfully on the arm. 'That is a tactic worthy of me, bro.'

'It so could have backfired,' Alain grumbled as he followed Lee through the door.

When they returned downstairs, all three of them dressed in black, Alice tutted disapprovingly. 'I appreciate it is the fashion, but I don't like all this dressing in dark colours,' she told them. 'It makes you all look so old.'

'I guess that is somewhat the point,' Master Barwick said from his chair by the fire.

'Perhaps you're right. Still ...' Alice said as she handed over the keys to Bebe, who had offered to be the sober driver. 'Behave yourself while you are there please. I don't want to be called to come and get you—well, I wouldn't be able to come anyway because you will have my car. And don't be too late home.'

'We promise to behave ourselves.' Bebe smiled.

'And don't forget to swing by Jo's and pick up Trouble on the way back. The goddess only knows what those two have been up to today, but I think it would be best for him to come home tonight as Jo's vet shift begins early in the morning.'

Alain started—it was odd to hear the goddess spoken of in modern times, even though he knew witches still revered her now as they had in the past.

'We won't forget him,' he promised as he closed the door.

Although only just past six o'clock, it was dark outside and the street was deserted, as was the village they drove through. Jo had suggested they drive a little beyond where they'd parked the night before and head a little way up the side road. Waiting there would mean they would not be seen by anyone arriving at Tabitha's, no matter which direction they were coming from.

Lee and Alain headed back along the hedgerows until they reached Tabitha's house. Once they arrived, Lee leaned out to make sure no one was about, then they crossed the driveway to hide behind the hedge on the other side of the drive.

They crouched and listened before moving again. Certain the only sound in the night was their own breathing, Alain stood lookout while Lee placed their device in the letterbox. He then gently closed the door, leaving a thin piece of twine hanging out.

A few paces beyond the property line, they both stood and started walking back to the car as though they were two people out for an evening stroll.

As they walked, Alain's stomach dropped and he grabbed his companion's arm. 'Lee, we need to go back.

We forgot the matches.'

'No we didn't.' The other boy's teeth flashed white as he grinned. 'I have a lighter.'

'A lighter?'

'Here. I'll show you.' Lee pulled something out of his pocket. There was a snick in the darkness and a small flame appeared in his hand.

'That is amazing.' Alain grinned.

'That is our own brand of modern magic.' A mocking tone coloured Lee's voice.

As they reached the corner to return to their car, they just made out the silhouette of another vehicle coming along the road. Once it passed them they turned in time to see the brake lights go on—the first person was arriving at Tabitha's.

As they walked, another vehicle's lights swept along the road. They waited in the shadows of the hedge, eyes following the car as it turned into the driveway, before they continued back the way they had come.

'We cut that a bit fine.' Lee laughed and Alain joined him, releasing some of the tension in his body.

The boys met Bebe back at the car, where they waited until about ten past seven. Jo had informed them one of the coven members always arrived around five minutes late, so they gave her a bit more time before they headed back and took up their positions.

The boys kept to the shadows along the road while Bebe cut across the fields. At Tabitha's house, they took their positions: Alain behind the hedge on the far side of the driveway, Lee on the nearside, and Bebe at the corner of the house under a window, listening so she could signal the boys if they needed to activate their diversion.

'I really hope we didn't go to all that trouble today for nothing,' Lee whispered.

Alain's agreement was blocked out by the sound of a car speeding along the lane. A screech of breaks sounded followed by the crunch of tyres on gave. The offending car came to an abrupt stop not far from their hiding place.

'We're only late because you felt it necessary to convince me not to come,' Jo said as a door slammed.

'Our coven really isn't your sort of thing. You should just wait in the car.' Izzy's weary voice was less clear than Jo's in the night air.

Alain peeked around the hedge just in time to see Trouble's rear end as he followed Jo and Izzy inside. Crouching back down, he made himself comfortable, preparing for a long wait.

The freezing air fingered its way through Alain's clothing, and he shivered as he watched and sat tight. His mind drifted and he shook his head, trying to keep his focus. Why they had ever thought waiting outside for an indeterminate amount of time in the middle of winter had been such a good idea, he would never know. Oh yeah—something odd was going on, dogs were getting sick, perhaps because of magical spells, and they were the only ones who knew. Alain's body trembled, and this time it wasn't from the cold.

CHAPTER NINE
FOLLOWED BY A LEAP BACK

The warmth of Trouble lying on her feet comforted her as Jo sat back and observed the other members of Tabitha's coven. At first, they'd been suspicious about her presence, which she fully expected because in the past she had spoken out against their extreme ideas on magic.

They believed she was now doing a complete about-face. They were sceptical of her motivation, not fully buying her speech about not being sure where her heart lay after talking things through with Izzy.

'Like you all, I am worried about what is happening in the New Forest. At the vet, we treat many of the dogs who are getting sick and it breaks my heart. I believe we must do something more to protect our heritage and our animals. I'm not sure my coven will be able to do that. Besides, I would like to be with a group closer to my own age.' She smiled coyly at Izzy, hoping they might believe she'd come to the meeting because of their obvious feelings towards each other.

After about twenty minutes, the other members relaxed and appeared to accept her presence, although every now and then she would raise her head to find someone glancing surreptitiously at her, as if gauging her reaction to one comment or another.

'As there has been no change in public opinion since we started our last campaign, I suggest we move to phase two.' Tabitha's announcement brought Jo's attention back to the meeting.

The stricken looks on the faces around her had Jo thinking they did not feel the same way as their hostess. Even Izzy wriggled uncomfortably in her chair.

'It's a little soon to take such a drastic step,' Ruth said as she reached for her cup of tea. 'After all, we only set our plan in motion a month ago when we cursed the first site. And we only cast our second spell last weekend. We should give everything a little more time to work.'

Tabitha's lip curled in distaste. At Alice's coven meetings, the woman had not taken kindly to anyone who disagreed with her. The chilly look she threw at Ruth caused the other women to shuffle nervously in their seats, and told Jo she was still the same old tyrant.

'Well R-u-th,' she drew out the annunciation of the protestor's name in a patronising way. 'That would be an option, except I found people rummaging around near the site of our last working. I haven't had an opportunity to go back and check if our altars are in place. If someone moved them, that means the magic we invoked will not be as strong as we expected, and it will not last nearly as long.'

Ruth was not daunted but rather took Tabitha's words as a challenge. 'That may be so, but let us not throw out the baby with the bath water. We can reinforce that casting, or we can recast the spell in a new part of the forest—perhaps somewhere with more foot traffic to see if it will have more effect.'

Tabitha and Ruth glared at each other from opposite sides of the room. Izzy winked at Jo, obviously enjoying the battle, and the other three found themselves suddenly very interested in the plates of carrot cake they held.

'Yeee-ss, that is an option … but why do that when we can move forward.' Tabitha's tone sounded reasonable, but past experience told Jo she was preparing to strike.

'Why take a leap forward when we haven't exhausted all our options with this spell?' Ruth countered,

'It is that sort of talk that led us all to leave our old coven. Our new, brave group of talented witches is prepared to take on the world to save our New Forest.' Tabitha's oily smile did not reach her eyes, causing a shiver to run down Jo's spine.

'You are proposing an extreme move here, Tabitha,' Izzy intervened, and all heads in the room swivelled to watch her. 'Do you not want to perhaps continue our current work in and around the forest, expand it to more areas, and monitor the effect on public opinion before you take such a drastic step?'

Trouble believed Izzy was the brains behind Tabitha's plan. Yet here she was, if not quite counselling caution, at least getting Tabitha to think about how she moved forward. *Is this some sort of reverse psychology, do you think?* Jo asked Trouble.

Shh, I am listening, the dog replied.

Out of the corner of her eye, Jo caught Izzy's questioning glance before the girl turned her gaze to Trouble and tapped her chin thoughtfully. Oops, she must not speak to Trouble or she would give his identity away, Jo thought as she caught the end of Tabitha's response to Izzy's comments.

'... besides, Gavin and I discussed our situation, and we believe only a much bigger threat will force people to appreciate that overdeveloping our natural environment places the whole world in danger,' Tabitha argued.

Ruth placed her teacup on the table, only the rattle of the china giving away her anger. She stood and held Tabitha's gaze as she spoke. 'Are we a coven of witches, or the puppets of some smooth-talking man? Are we saving our forest or supporting the agenda of a foreign interloper?'

'How dare you!' Tabitha glared over the table at Ruth.

Izzy swiftly stood and moved between the two women. 'Come now, ladies, we are a coven, and we make up our own minds. I am sure Tabitha was just voicing an opinion. Shall we sit down and take a vote on the matter?'

The two women sat, although they did not break eye contact. Izzy remained standing. 'Shall I do the honours and outline the motion?' When no one spoke, she continued, 'The decision each of you must make is whether or not to continue spreading our little concoction through the New Forest to force a change in decisions relating to increased use of the land, or whether to ...'

'They are spreading Alabama Rot. Wait until the others find out,' Jo muttered under her breath. The room went quiet. Everyone had heard her. She froze, unable to move as her mind went blank.

I see some things never change. You open your mouth before thinking even in this reincarnation. Trouble rose to his feet, readying to leave.

'I knew you were not to be trusted.' Tabitha turned her anger towards Jo. 'You are here to spy for the others, you traitor.'

'She's heard too much. We cannot let her leave.'

Almost every head in the room swivelled towards the doorway where Gavin leaned casually, staring intently at Jo—everyone except Izzy. She looked at Trouble, a finger thoughtfully tapping her lips.

Jo's stomach dropped, and she felt sick. How could she have been so stupid? Not only had she not heard Plan B, but because of her words, Trouble had mind-spoken again. Now Izzy's earlier suspicions had been confirmed and she knew Trouble was a Time Guardian. And if all that wasn't bad enough, Jo's mind was still not working. She had no idea how to extricate them from the mess she'd created.

Tabitha smiled at her, and Jo felt like a fish caught on a hook. Ruth moved in front of a snarling Gavin, her eyes filled with concern. No one else moved; it was as if time had stopped for them.

BOOM!

Everything in the room shook.

Run, a voice said in her head—and it was definitely not Trouble's.

ALCHEMIST

Pieces of letterbox exploded into the air around him, and Alain's face broke into a grin. His and Lee's handiwork had performed beautifully. As he stood watching the devastation an outside light flicked on, just catching Lee and Bebe as they sped up the road, followed by angry shouts and footsteps across the gravel. Trapped, Alain wiggled backwards into the hedge, hoping no one would look his way as they chased his two friends.

Luck was with him, or so he thought until a voice came close to his ear, 'Shall I call my coven members back?'

His heart sunk. 'Izzy, you found me. Are you going to turn me in?'

He couldn't make out her expression in the shadows, but he hoped the fact they were talking meant he still had a chance to escape unnoticed.

'I should do, but no, I won't. But only if you promise me you will not let Jo do anything that stupid again.'

'Huh?' Alain wasn't sure he understood. 'Do you mean spying on the coven, or giving herself away?'

'I assume you all got together and cooked up the plan for her to attend the meeting tonight, to find out what was going on?'

'Uh, no, that was all her own idea. Besides, you could've stopped her when she asked to come with you. You can't tell me you believed she wanted to join the coven.'

A low chuckle escaped from beside him. 'I tried to talk her out of going, but you know Jo—or, should I say, you knew John. Once they set their mind to something, stopping them is impossible.' Izzy sounded almost as though she was as attracted to Jo as the other girl was to her.

Shaking his head, Alain attempted to focus. 'You're right; there is no arguing with Jo. So I could promise to keep her away from danger, but you and I both know that would be a lie—as if she would listen to me.'

Izzy sighed. 'Look, you clearly think I'm the bad guy here, but I'm not—I only want what is best for humanity, and Jo. To demonstrate this, I'm going to tell you something I shouldn't. I am not in control of this pony show.'

Alain snorted his disbelief.

'I mean, I was. I had Tabitha right where I wanted her. All up in arms about developments in the New Forest with a plan on how to spread a disease amongst dogs to cause outrage and stop the travesty of overdeveloping a natural resource—something I think you would be able to get on board with, given your connection to the area. Didn't your father once own land around here?'

'He did, and I am passionate about the New Forest. But supporting anything that would harm animals goes against everything I believe in.'

'We will have to agree to disagree on that point then.'

'So what went wrong?' Alain asked, changing the subject.

'That American showed up, licking his wounds from a fight in South America somewhere. Tabitha thinks the sun shines ... well, let's just say she admires him. She rebuilt his ego, and now he feels like he has to prove something, and he wants to hit back at the world for mistreating him.'

'So how is he planning to do that?' Icy fingers of fear worked their way down Alain's back, and he shivered. Izzy sounded scared, and anything that scared the girl who'd attempted to kill a king at his coronation had to be bad.

'He and Tabitha found a way to modify the CRGV bacteria so it can jump species.' She paused for a moment.

Her words slowly sank in and Alain froze, almost too scared to say the words. 'To humans?'

'Yes, to humans,' Izzy confirmed his fears.

'Isn't there anything you can do to stop it?'

'It is almost done.'

'What do you mean?' Alain clutched her arm, digging his fingers in so hard, she groaned and pulled away.

'They tested a small sample on an elderly aunt of Tabitha's yesterday. The woman had spent the last few years in a coma. She died suddenly this morning—everyone else believes from natural causes—but I know better.'

'But ... that's murder.' Alain's voice was not much more than a whisper.

'And that's not the worst of it. Tonight they will take a vote on whether or not to cast the spell that will spread the new bacteria in one of the busier tourist spots in the forest. Then all they will need to do is wait until the next full moon to say the spell that will cause untold devastation.'

Initially, Alain was speechless, then he latched onto his one remaining hope. 'Perhaps they won't agree to do it.'

Izzy snorted. 'Oh, the coven is against it, but I am sure Tabitha will convince them over the next day or so, if not tonight. They will all turn up on Saturday night to do her bidding.'

'Hold on, Saturday night? That's only two days away.' Alain swallowed the fear threatening to choke him.

'I know, so you had better hurry and find out a way to stop them, or chaos will be released into the world.'

'Hold on, aren't you Time Wreckers supposed to foster chaos?'

Alain waited while the silence drew out. He thought she wasn't going to answer, but it seemed she was merely choosing her words carefully. 'That is not all we are. We intervene in different eras for different reasons.'

'Why in Henry's coronation then?'

'Because the Norman system of government was stifling the people. We believed if we brought chaos to England, the common man would throw off the yoke of Norman control and live free thereafter.'

Alain considered her words and strangely saw sense in them, but her explanation left out one important detail. 'But at what cost?'

'You cannot make an omelette without breaking an egg,' she replied. 'Besides, Henry was no saint. I can personally attest to that.'

He shook his head, unable to reconcile the way she casually spoke about death with her desire to save the world. 'And why are you here now? What do you hope to achieve?'

'I am sure your guardian told you we are targeting this time to bring about massive changes. We have co-ordinated a number of activities aimed at highlighting how greed and avarice is killing the planet—and people are not slowing their consumption in spite of the warning signs.'

'If I take that explanation at face value, then why are

you against having CRGV move to humans? Surely that would be a much stronger message than killing pets.'

'You must really think me evil.' Izzy's voice carried a sadness as she said the words. 'Truth be told, I was not happy about hurting animals, but I saw it as the lesser of two evils. Though I am against allowing the bacteria to move to humans because if you introduce a new organism to the world, you cannot control it. If it sets off a worldwide epidemic, millions might die—it may even wipe out most of the human race.'

'They could simply start again—make a better world. Isn't that what you want?'

'I don't want humanity to end, and I don't want them so caught up in fighting an epidemic they forget the issues we are trying to highlight,' Izzy said.

'If you feel so strongly about it, why don't you just stop them yourself?'

'I can't. Not only would history find a way to counterbalance my actions, I would also be expelled from the Time Wreckers. Where would I go then? Even talking to you like this will earn me a sanction.'

'Why are you doing it then? Talking to me, I mean.'

'Because I started this.' She spoke the words so softly he almost did not catch them.

'What do you mean?'

'I showed Tabitha the spell to mutate bacteria to make it grow faster. She then added that to another spell, which mutated the cells again, enabling them to infect humans.'

'How could you do something so stupid?' Alain clenched his fists to stop himself from reaching out and shaking the girl. Was she mad?

'I wanted to save the New Forest, save the world. I acted without thinking. Can you not see how someone might do something in the heat of the moment then regret it later?'

'Yes,' Alain said; he could see exactly how it might happen. However, not wanting to let Izzy off the hook that easily, he asked, 'What, and now you want to roll back time?'

'Yes, I do, or at least try to undo a little of what I set in motion. Will you help?'

Alain didn't know what to say. He was so angry with Izzy he wasn't thinking straight. Besides, he had no idea whether or not it was against the rules to work with a Time Wrecker or not.

Luckily, the sound of footsteps on gravel saved him from answering—the coven members had returned. Izzy stood and strode away.

'Where were you?' Tabitha spoke brusquely.

'I went 'round the other side of the house to check,' Izzy glibly explained herself.

'Good thinking. Look at my poor letterbox,' Tabitha complained. 'It was a one-off I had commissioned for the house. They destroyed a work of art.'

'Do you think it was pranksters?' One woman's plaintive tones irritated Alain.

'Or do you think someone suspects what we have been doing?' Another frightened woman voiced her concerns.

'Oh, quit it, Beth. I put up with these things all the time. It is the result of being outspoken. It was just a prank. Did anyone see what happened to Jo?'

'Oh, she took off when we all rushed outside. Her dog

tried to escape too, but I gave him a little dose of something special to warn her to keep quiet.' A male voice sounded sinister in the darkness.

There was a yelp and a crunching of gravel, and Trouble's nose peeked around the hedge, but he stopped, making no move towards Alain.

'How will it get home?' Beth asked.

'I don't care,' the man answered. 'Come on inside, ladies. Now the interloper has gone I am sure you will want to finish your meeting. You have a vote to take, after all.'

The front door closed, plunging Alain into darkness. He reached for Trouble. *I am here*, he sent

I know. I can smell you. Trouble moved closer and leaned against Alain's leg.

Are you all right?

No, not really. The dog settled more closely against him.

What did they do to you?

That man, Gavin I believe, grabbed me as Jo and I tried to escape. I told Jo to run on. When we were alone, Gavin took me into the laundry and injected me with something. He told me this would teach Jo a lesson she would never forget. He laughed, saying I would be gone soon and there was nothing she could do to stop it.

I thought you said you couldn't contract the disease. Alain tried to soothe the shaking Time Guardian.

True, but I think what they did to the original bacterial infection to change it allowed it to attack me—that and the

fact he injected it directly into my bloodstream. I feel kind of odd, as though something is moving through my veins.

Do you hear that? It is a car, I think. Maybe we can catch a lift back to Alice's and let Barwick take a look at you.

As the light shone on his crouched figure, Alain shaded his eyes. It looked like Alice's vehicle, but he was not totally sure when he waved it over. His stomach clenched as it pulled up behind them. What if it was one of Tabitha's coven? Then the door opened and Jo leaned out, Alain sagged with relief. She signalled for them to climb in as she scooted across the other side of the seat.

As Lee pulled the car away, Jo made sure Trouble was comfy, while Bebe turned in her seat to find out what all the fuss was about in the back.

Once they were underway, in the lights from the dashboard Alain noticed Trouble's breathing was laboured. Placing his hand on the dog's chest, he found his heartbeat was faster than normal. Alain's hand trembled and Jo reached across and took hold of it.

'It will be all right,' she said, but he wasn't sure it would be.

'They did something to him, didn't they? I will kill them all if they have hurt Trouble,' Bebe threatened.

'I think they injected him with the disease, from what I overheard,' Alain said to explain how he knew for Bebe's sake.

'All right. Lee, turn here, then take the first left. We're taking him to the vets.' Jo dialled a number on her phone and spoke to someone on the other end, asking them to meet her at the surgery.

'Wait. We should take him to Uncle Barnaby,' Alain

protested.

'He needs a vet,' Jo said. 'She can stabilise him, then we can get Barnaby involved.'

The others agreed with her, and Alain was too worried to argue. He gently stroked Trouble, trying to calm them both. When they pulled up outside, Alain went to pick up the dog, only to have his arm pushed out of the way by Jo.

'Leave him to us. We will work more quickly if we don't have to worry about you. I promise we will do the best we can for him. You will be more help going back to Alice's and finding out if Master Barwick has come up with a cure yet.'

Alain grabbed her hand as she reached for Trouble. 'Will he be safe here? I mean, what if they come for him again?'

'The building is secure, and Susan, the vet, will be here soon. Besides, I think they have done their worst; they are unlikely to give him a second thought.'

'I can't leave him alone with you,' Alain insisted, tears welling in his eyes.

She bent her head close to him and whispered, 'Yes, you can. Master Barwick may need you to help with developing a cure. You do realise if something happens to Trouble you may be stuck here for a while. He is the Time Guardian, after all, so I suspect he is the only one who can take you home.'

Alain's heart nearly leapt out of his chest at Jo's words. She was almost right. Although Trouble's body could die, the Guardian would not. But it would be some time before his spirit was recharged enough to take another form and return to them. Meanwhile, he and Master Barwick would be stuck here not understanding a word anyone said. How would they survive, let alone deal with the threat they faced?

He let go of Jo's arm and watched as she carried the dog to the surgery. The door opened and she disappeared inside. He told Lee to drive, and for once was grateful the boy saw speed limits more as a suggestion than a rule.

CHAPTER TEN
A TESTING TIME

Alain flung open the door and jumped out before the car came to a complete stop. After running up the stairs to the room above the garage, he flung open the door only to find Master Barwick wasn't there. As he descended the stairs, the back door to the kitchen opened, flooding the backyard with light.

'What is all the noise about?' Alice asked.

'Where is Master Bar ... Barnaby?' Alain spoke so fast his tongue stumbled over the words.

'I am here.' The master's voice came from behind Alice. 'What is so urgent you had to call me away from my dinner?'

'It's Trouble. He has the disease ... and it's bad.'

'I thought he said he was immune,' Alice said.

'What do you mean "he said"?' Bebe joined them by the open door.

'I mean, well, I just assumed he wouldn't catch it, otherwise Barnaby wouldn't have taken him into the forest the way he did.' Alice recovered herself.

'Gavin injected him with the bacteria,' Alain explained. 'So not only does he have it, but it's working faster than it does in other dogs.'

'How did he get injected? Was it at Jo's, or did you take him to the pub with you?' Alice's eyes narrowed with suspicion.

'No time to discuss this now.' Master Barwick pushed past Alice and headed towards the stairs. 'Alain, we need to get to work. I am so close, but perhaps with two minds working together ... well, we might be able to produce something in time to help Trouble.'

'What do you want us to do?' Lee's hand rested on Alain's arm, causing him to pause.

'You won't be much help with our work. I suggest you eat and be ready to take Alain where he needs to go when we are done.' Master Barwick spoke as he ascended the stairs, bundling Alain in front of him.

As they climbed, Alain heard Alice say, 'But I thought you went out for dinner. Why would you need more food now?'

Shutting the door behind them, Master Barwick started firing off questions. 'Tell me exactly what happened tonight, and don't leave any detail out.'

Alain sunk down on the sofa, and dropped his head into his hands. 'Bebe signalled Jo was in trouble, so we blew up Tabitha's letterbox.'

'How did Trouble get hurt?'

'In the confusion, the eco-terrorist grabbed him and

decided to teach Jo a lesson for spying. He injected Trouble with a fast-acting high dose of the bacteria.' Telling the story to Master Barwick caused Alain's stomach to clench all over again, and he wrapped his arms around himself.

Master Barwick took a seat beside him and patted him on the shoulder. 'And how is Trouble now?'

'By the time we dropped him off at the vet he was not in a good way.'

'I am sure we can ... hold on a minute, you blew up a letterbox?'

Alain glanced sideways at Master Barwick. 'That's what you are focussing on?'

'Greek fire? That's some dangerous stuff. It can't have been easy to get.'

Alain sighed. 'We didn't. Use Greek fire, I mean. Lee and I found a recipe to make a homemade bomb on the internet, and we whipped one up this afternoon. It worked amazingly well. I think I might be able to replicate it when we return home.'

'Excellent.' The older man's eyes sparkled in anticipation.

Not willing to allow him to be further distracted, Alain held off telling Master Barwick about the wonders of super glue.

'Right, let's get moving.' Master Barwick took charge. 'I know Sigma cannot die, and he would return to us as soon as possible. However, with everything that is going on I would not like to be long without his skills, and particularly his link to the Council.'

'Me neither,' Alain agreed.

'Now, the good thing is I think I've almost found a cure. It's a combination of the natural extracts I spoke of earlier.

I used a little magic to make their molecules resonate faster and it began reversing the effects of the infection. If it were to be combined with the treatments the vets have been giving the animals, I think it gives the dogs enough of a chance to fight off the infection and make a full recovery.'

'But Gavin seemed certain that what he injected Trouble with would act faster than the other one—what if it was a super-charged version? Would your cure still work?' Alain asked.

'Let's be clear. I am not one hundred percent sure it will work at all—it hasn't fully eradicated the bacteria in any of my tests, and it hasn't been tried on an animal yet. However, I am thinking that with two of us working on a growth spell we might double the effectiveness, and it might work well enough.'

'Really?' Alain was too scared to be too hopeful.

'I said think, young man. As an apothecary, there are no guarantees a cure will be successful. There are fewer when we are forced to rely on our alchemical skills as well.'

'I guess we can only try,' said Alain. 'The alternative is to do nothing, and that would be worse.'

'Right. If you're ready, let's go. You read through my notes while I assemble everything we need.'

Deciphering Master Barwick's handwriting was difficult at the best of times. Reading it when upset was almost impossible. Seeing his master had started measuring ingredients into a beaker placed over a single-flame burner, Alain skipped the section on how to concoct the potion and went straight to the spell.

Having memorised it, he moved on to the potion itself. Reading the alchemist's handwritten recipe, Alain was surprised at the quantities. 'Will that be enough?'

'Of course, it expands a little when heated, and a little more with the spell.'

Once all the ingredients had been added, Master Barwick stirred them together before holding the beaker up and assessing the murky brown liquid. Shaking his head, he swirled the contents, then checked again. It was now a lighter brown.

Seeming satisfied with the results, he returned the beaker to the rack over the flame, and the two of them stood and watched as the liquid came to a simmer.

Using tongs to remove the glass container, Master Barwick placed the potion on a wooden board before turning off the burner.

'We need to let it cool for about ten minutes before we cast the spell,' he said.

'But we may not have much time,' Alain protested, anxiety causing his voice to rise a little.

'If we do not allow it to cool a little and we apply magic the liquid grows too fast and explodes, along with the beaker.' Gesturing to the almost overflowing rubbish bin in the corner, Barwick said, 'Believe me, this is truly the least amount of time we can wait without having to potentially start again.'

Alain huffed, then busied himself cleaning up. Every couple of minutes, Master Barwick touched the outside of the glass and shook his head. Full of pent-up energy, Alain tidied the bookshelf and made his master's bed. He was just reaching for the bin to take it outside to empty when Master Barwick said, 'It is time.'

Joining his master, Alain started the routine he had

been taught to follow before using magic. He closed his eyes and cleared his mind. Then he reached out until he found the gentle hum of magic present in all living things. It was not strong in this world, but if he supplemented it with a little of his own life force he might be able to gather enough to cast the spell.

'I am ready,' he said, placing his hand over the beaker.

Master Barwick wrapped his fingers around Alain's. 'Remember, this spell not only requires the words to be spoken, but also for you to visualise the elements in the potion working together to grow in strength and size.'

'Right,' Alain said, and he imagined how the liquid would change as he and Master Barwick recited the words of the spell:

'In my mind thee doth see,
hastily grow at a rate extreme.
Bring my thought-form to life this night,
and fight evildoing with all thy might.'

Opening his eyes, Alain found the liquid was now inky black and appeared to be moving in the container. At fist the movement was gentle, but it sped up until the potion was sloshing up the sides.

'We are done.' Master Barwick sighed as he opened a drawer. After removing two glass vials, he decanted half the liquid into each one. 'Now all we can do is pray to the goddess.'

Carrying one dose of the new potion and another of Master Barwick's original formula, each vial wrapped in its own handkerchief and stowed safely in his jacket pockets, Alain returned to the kitchen. He opened the door to find Lee asleep, head resting on his arms on the table, and Bebe staring at something on her phone.

She raised her head when Alain entered. 'Have you done it? Have you and Barnaby come up with something we can try?' she asked, unable to keep the hope from her voice. Her phone pinged. 'Oops, let me just say goodnight to Mum, then I'm all yours.' Her fingers began moving over the screen as she spoke to him.

Alain smiled. She reminded him so much of Barabal, and in the midst of tonight's trauma he missed his friend so much he ached. 'Yes. One for Trouble and, if that works, one to try for Pepe.'

'Excellent. Come on.' She finished typing then she stood, sweeping the keys up from the table.

'What about Lee?' Alain asked, and a look of fierce determination appeared on Bebe's face.

'I am just as capable as he is,' Bebe huffed as she pulled on her coat. 'Are you coming or not?'

Alain followed her out the door. 'I didn't mean anything by what I said. I just thought Lee might like to come with us.'

'He'd be grumpy if we woke him. It's better for all of us if we leave him be.'

He opened the door and slipped into the front passenger seat, escaping the chilly night air. Bebe started the car. She didn't speak and the silence was uncomfortable. He began to wonder if she expected him to say something, and he was trying to decide what when she spoke.

'Sorry for jumping down your throat. It's not anything you said—it's me. Lee is so focussed and organised, and everyone loves that about him. Adults always ask him to do things because he is so dependable.'

When Alain didn't respond, she continued. 'Me? Well, I don't know what I want. I don't even know where I'll be living in a month's time. People never ask me to do anything. They always assume I will muck it up—as if not planning my future makes me incompetent in some way.'

Bebe paused, one hand on the steering wheel and the other covering her mouth. 'Goodness, I did not mean for all that to come out.'

The silence lengthened as she concentrated on the road. Alain tried to think of something to say. The atmosphere in the car was becoming more unbearable the longer he didn't say anything at all.

'I'm sorry if you thought I didn't trust you. I didn't mean it that way.' The air in the car lightened.

'It's okay. I guess it was on my mind because Mum just asked if I'd had any more thoughts on my future.' Bebe chewed on her lip. 'I had to tell her no. I mean, we've all been caught up with what is going on ... I need time to prepare what I'm going to say.'

In the couple of days since they'd met, Alain had grown to like Bebe. He felt closer to her knowing she'd offered to drive him tonight in spite of her own troubles. Perhaps it was only because she was so like Barabal he felt compelled help her—but what advice could he offer?

Alain smiled to himself—of course. Bebe was like Barabal—perhaps he did know a way to help her out.

184

'I have a friend. She's a lot like you. Her options for the future are more limited than yours, and most of them revolve around making the right marriage. She also finds it frustrating trying to carve out a place where her talents can be used.'

'That does sound familiar,' Bebe acknowledged. 'Well, except for the marriage thing.'

'I think that may have more to do with where she lives than what we are discussing. Anyway, one of the things she is passionate about, is finding ways to make it easier for other girls to contribute more by being a role model, and by pushing at the boundaries of what is considered acceptable. She believes everyone has something unique they can contribute to the world—they just need to find it.'

Bebe chuckled. 'I think I would like your friend. I understand what she's saying. It's easy to do what others expect of you, and do it in the same way women have done for centuries. When I look around, there are so many options to choose from, but there's a lot of pressure to meet everyone's expectations as well.'

'She may have fewer choices than you do, but she doesn't let that stop her. She excels at finding workarounds.'

'My father would like nothing better than for me to follow in his footsteps and join the army like Lee. He tells me a brain like mine can be put to good use in the military, but women in the army are still treated differently, no matter how much he wants to deny it.'

'I can't imagine you being good at following orders.' Alain laughed at the thought, and Bebe joined him.

'Me neither. I think I would hate being told what to do

and how to do it. My mother, on the other hand, thinks my empathy would be best utilised following her into psychology.'

Alain had no idea what psychology was, but he didn't want to let on to Bebe so he nodded, hoping she wouldn't catch on.

'I want to help others, but I am not sure that is the way for me to go. The thought of delving into people's deepest emotions makes me ... well, to put it bluntly, it sounds boring. Please don't tell my mother I said that.'

'I'm hardly likely to ever meet her, so I don't think that will be a problem.' Alain laughed. 'But seriously, I can see you helping others. Are you sure psychology can be ruled out?'

'Yes. I want to do something that is a little more proactive and practical.'

'What about becoming a healer, or a teacher ...?' Alain trailed off, not knowing what other options were available for women in this day and age.

While he waited for Bebe to answer, he remembered his own parents' reactions to his wanting to become an apothecary. Although they didn't understand why he'd wanted to do it, they had been nothing but supportive, urging him to follow his heart. Then again, they'd been landless after William the Conqueror had dispossessed them, and were grateful their son had found a future for himself.

'In my experience, parents just want their kids to be happy. Perhaps yours are happy in their work, so they are offering their jobs as examples for you,' Alain finally said.

'I'm sure you are right and Mum and Dad are just

trying to help. Ignore me. I'm only taking advantage of this journey to have a whinge.'

Alain chuckled. 'We all need to do that sometimes. But do you have to make your mind up now?'

'No, I guess not. Mum and Dad would be happy enough if I took a year off to decide what to do, just as long as I can support myself.' Bebe was quick to defend them.

'So, what's the rush?'

Bebe chewed a little on her bottom lip. 'I guess, when you put it like that, the pressure is coming mainly from me. Taking a year off to make a decision is such a waste of time.'

'All right, if that's how you feel, perhaps we should make a start in the few minutes before we get to the vet. What do you like to do?'

'Read—but you cannot make a career from that. I like sports and I really enjoyed coaching a junior netball team this year.'

Alain wanted to ask what on earth netball was, but he forced himself to stick to the point. 'What was it you enjoyed about working with teams?'

Bebe didn't answer immediately. She gnawed on her lip for some time before answering. 'I like finding the best position for each girl, developing their skills, and helping them work as a team.'

'See? Just like my friend, you want to find out how to bring the best out in people,' Alain said.

'But I can't be a professional mentor or netball coach. I'm not good enough for that.'

'You are a smart girl, Barabal ... sorry ... Bebe. Those are not the only options open to you.' Alain hoped he had

covered his slip.

'Is that your friend's name? How pretty. You must miss her a lot.'

'I do, but don't change the subject. There must be other things you can do.'

'Yes, of course. I looked into teaching, but I don't think it is for me.' She opened her mouth as if to say something, then shut it again, before pressed her lips together and focussing on the road.

'Go on. What is it?' Alain prompted.

'Well, Jo talked yesterday about a time when she was younger. After her dad died, she got into a bit of trouble and turned quite wild by all accounts. Her mother tried everything to help. Eventually, the courts sent her to a counsellor who worked with her to target her energies towards something she loved. She always felt comfortable with animals, so they found a vet who would let her help out after school. That was when she decided what she wanted to become, and she knuckled down and started studying for her future.'

Alain waited for Bebe to continue, but she remained silent. 'And ...'

'Well, last night I looked up some courses on the internet. The University of Southampton offers one that leads to that sort of a counselling position.'

'There you go. You do have some idea of what you want to do next year. Why didn't you tell your mum?'

'Because I need to wait until my exam results come in before I apply. Also, it is a popular course and rejection rates are quite high, and they show a preference towards candidates who can demonstrate experience working with children. And I also need some endorsements from someone who already works in the field.'

'That doesn't sound too bad to me,' Alain said.

'Perhaps not, but the course doesn't start until the new university year in the United Kingdom, which is September—almost a whole year away.'

'That sounds like ...'

'... excuses. I know. Alice would put me up, and help me find a part-time job, and might also have some people for me to contact about volunteer work with children. And I can work on everything I need to do to apply while waiting for my results.'

'Mmm, and you said Lee was the planner in the family. Still, why didn't you tell your mum when you were texting her?'

Bebe sighed. 'I guess because I want everything in place before I can prove I can do this by myself. And with everything going on, I haven't had a chance to talk to Alice, let alone follow up any other leads.'

Bebe slowed the car and pulled up in front of the vet. 'Here we are. Thank you for being my sounding board. Especially when you have so much on your mind with Trouble being sick.'

Alain opened the door and turned to look at his driver. 'No, thank you for taking my mind off my worries, and for reminding me there is more to life than this crazy situation we've found ourselves in. Are you coming inside with me?'

'Thanks, but I think I will wait here. Maybe do a little more research on my phone and finish off talking with my mum.'

Alain rushed to the door Jo had taken Trouble through and knocked. He waited, stamping his feet to keep warm, then knocked again. His stomach clenched as all his fears about Trouble returned. As the wait lengthened, he imagined all the reasons why Jo had not answered immediately—the foremost being they were trying to revive Trouble after some seizure or other.

Just as he raised his fist to knock again, the door opened and Jo's annoyed face confronted him.

'Are you trying to wake the whole neighbourhood?' she whispered furiously.

'Um, ah ... when you didn't answer the first time I got worried.'

'I was in the toilet.'

'Oh.' Suddenly, Alain had nothing more to say.

'Well, come in.' Jo held the door open to allow him past. 'Bebe not coming in?' she asked as she waved to the girl in the car.

'No, she is talking to her mum. She seems to want some privacy.'

Jo closed the door behind them and led him through to the room containing the crates for animals staying overnight.

In a panic, Alain looked around for Trouble and found him lying on his side in a cage. Rushing over, he opened the door and patted his head. The dog looked up with liquid brown eyes clouded with pain. Jo leaned in beside him and gave Trouble a gentle pat.

'Are you here alone?' Alain looked around for signs of anyone else.

'Yes. When it was clear I was going to be here for a while, Susan, the vet, went home for some dinner. She'll be back in about half an hour though.'

'Why? Is something wrong?'

'No, nothing's wrong as such. We stabilised him, but Susan is worried because he should be improving by now. She is coming back to give him a blood transfusion and some intravenous antibiotics.'

'Oh, that is good.' Alain wasn't sure it actually was, but he felt obliged to say something.

Not so good for you, I am afraid, Trouble's voice was a mere whisper in his head. *I heard them talking, and they are going to give me anaesthetic while they do the blood transfusion so I do not move about.*

That is good. You won't be in pain anymore.

Trouble looked at him, as if the effort to talk was too much.

Jo touched his arm. 'What he is trying to say is, he provides some services for you and Barnaby while you are here. I've allowed him to continue to do so until now, but he won't be able to translate for you once he is under anaesthetic. I also advised him to stop until he is well on the road to recovery. He needs all his energy to beat this.'

Alain opened his mouth to object, then paused. His main concern about the guardian's death was being stranded here and not being able to communicate with people. Having that situation come about while Trouble was being treated highlighted how unworkable his death would have been, especially when they still had to stop

Tabitha and her coven. Still, it was more important for Trouble to rest and fight the organism invading his body than to support them.

'Don't worry. It's night-time. Go straight to bed when you get home, and do not get up until I come for you in the morning. Hopefully no one will notice anything is wrong before then, and you and I can concoct a story as to why you can't speak—a sore throat, perhaps. All you need to so is smile and nod at anything I say.'

'Um, okay.' Alain was still a little in shock. 'He will be all right though, won't he? Is he in any pain?'

They gave me lovely painkillers ... and ...

'... and they are making him a little spaced out. As to whether he will pull through, a lot will depend on how he reacts to this treatment and, of course, whether or not Barnaby was able to come up with something to help fight the infection.'

When Alain did not respond, Jo held out her hand. 'Do you have anything for me?'

Alain shook his head and concentrated on what Jo was saying. 'Oh, yes. Of course. That's why I'm here.' Alain reached into his pocket and handed the vials to Jo. 'This is the best we could do on short notice. Master Barwick believes in conjunction with the other treatments, this should wipe out the infection. The blue label is a stronger one for Trouble, and this is for Pepe.'

As Alain handed over the second vial, Jo's face fell. 'Poor Pepe passed away this afternoon.' Her eyes welled with tears and Alain was suddenly hit with the realisation that Trouble was in real danger, and that what happened in the next twelve hours would affect them all.

ALCHEMIST

As he patted the dog, the silence lengthened. How would they get by without him? 'If something happens to Trouble, Barnaby and I will be left facing this threat to the world on our own—our link to the Time Guardians would be severed and with it, all our support.'

'Then you best let us get on with it.' Jo's matter-of-fact approach was reassuring.

She allowed Alain to pat Trouble one last time before closing the crate. As she opened the door to let him out, she placed a hand on his arm and said, 'I will not let anything happen to him. I promise.'

Alain looked back over his shoulder at his sick friend. *Take care, Trouble. You have to recover from this. Not just because I will miss you, but also because we all really need you.*

Trouble raised his head slightly, and Alain left, brushing unshed tears from his eyes.

When Alain returned to the car, he found Bebe dozing, her head leaning against the window. She awoke as he slammed the door shut.

'How is Trouble?' she asked dozily.

'How quickly can you drive us home? I need to talk to Master Barwick.'

Alain was so focussed on his need to talk to his mentor before the vet began Trouble's procedure, he did not realise he was being rude until he saw the hurt look on Bebe's face as she did as he requested.

'I am sorry, Bebe. I know it's no excuse, but I am

worried about Trouble, and I need to check something with Master Barwick for Jo. It may be important to the procedure Trouble is to undergo soon.' He didn't like lying to her, but he was unable to tell her the truth.

Bebe glanced at him out of the corner of her eye, and sighed. 'You are right; it is no excuse, but I can understand how worried you are. So I will forgive you ... this time.' She smiled, and when he didn't smile back, her face transformed with a worried frown. 'Is Trouble worse?'

Pain radiated through Alain's hands, and he looked down to find them clasped together so tightly the knuckles had turned white. He shook his head slowly. When did I do that? Unclasping them, he turned and tried to focus on Bebe.

'He's not in a good way. The vet managed to stabilise him and are going to give him a blood transfusion this evening. We hope that the cleaning of his blood, combined with the antibiotics and Master Barwick's tonic, should start to reverse the effects of the bacteria. In order to help that happen, they are going to put Trouble to sleep for a while.'

'Oh Alain, I am so sorry. You must be devastated.'

Bebe's empathy opened the floodgates, and Alain let the tears roll down his cheeks unchecked. He had been so intent on doing something—anything—to save Trouble that he'd held his emotions in check. Now there was nothing to do but wait, and worry overwhelmed him.

How would they cope with the threat to humankind without Trouble's guidance? Did the Council know about this turn of events? Alain looked down to find his fingers once again had wound around each other, and he concentrated on stretching his hands to release the tension.

As they pulled into the driveway minutes later, Bebe said, 'You go talk to Master Barwick. I will update the others so you don't have to. I'll leave you a chamomile tea on the table for when you come in. It might help you sleep. Would you like my phone so Jo can send you updates?'

Although heartened by Bebe's support, he answered, 'No', knowing that in a few minutes he wouldn't be able to understand anything. 'If you do not mind, I would rather hear any news, especially if it is bad, from an actual person.'

Bebe placed a comforting hand on his arm. 'Sure, I understand. Now go and see Barnaby.'

She left him to climb the stairs as she headed into the kitchen.

Before he reached the top, he noticed the light was off. Either Master Barwick was asleep or he was in the house. Turning, he saw Master Barwick exiting via the kitchen door and hurried to meet him in the middle of the lawn. In hushed tones he gave the older man his update.

'I know in my heart this will not kill Sigma, but I do hate for my friend to suffer so.' The older man tugged at his beard.

'He has the very best care, and Jo said she will stay with him tonight,' Alain attempted to console his master.

'He will also be worried about us. I wonder if he managed to speak to the Time Guardian Council and warn them? He might not have been able to; they are extremely busy with all that is going on at the moment. They have been out of contact a bit.'

'All that is going on?' Alain's head jerked up at the comment. 'Izzy mentioned a few Wreckers are here. What do you know about it?'

Master Barwick ran a hand through his hair, causing it to stand up more than it normally did. 'Only a little. Trouble has not told me all the details—only that a number of Time Wrecker attacks are planned. Most are diversions, but one of them is going to have a massive impact. The Council is spread pretty thin covering everything, and they instructed us to get on with the job here by ourselves.'

Alain had thought this night couldn't be any worse, but he had been wrong. 'So we have to assume the Council don't know the coven are planning to release the infection on humans?'

Master Barwick's hand stopped mid-run through his hair. 'I am sorry. What did you say?'

'I said Izzy told me the coven—well, Tabitha and Gavin really—developed a strain of the virus for humans, and they were taking a vote to decide whether or not to release it in two days' time.'

'The night of the full moon,' Master Barwick said distractedly.

'Yes, and I'm not sure we can handle this ourselves.'

'You're right.' His hand moved from his hair to tug at his beard, and his eyes unfocussed. Then he took a deep breath. 'This is way worse than Sigma and I thought—an attack on humans with a new form of bacteria ... I do not even know where to start.' He stood staring into the night as his hand again worked through his hair. 'It is late; there's not much more we can do now. Let's sleep on it, and regroup in the morning.'

Frowning, Alain said, 'You are to be a Time Guardian— can't you speak to the Council? You need to warn them of the danger.'

'Only one initiated as a Guardian can make the connection, and I am a little way off from that. They can contact me if they cannot reach Sigma, and we must hope that will happen sooner rather than later so we can pass on your news.'

Still not ready to let it go, Alain persisted. 'If we wait until tomorrow we will not be able to speak with anyone here, except in a limited fashion. We will be completely isolated.'

Placing his hand on Alain's shoulder, the older man stared deep into his eyes. 'We can spend all night worrying about what might happen tomorrow, but these things are now out of our control. It is time to get some sleep so we can keep up our energy. Worrying about things we cannot control does no one any good. In the meantime, perhaps a prayer to the goddess, or even the god of this time, will help.'

When Alain did not move, Master Barwick pulled him into a gruff hug. 'We have each other, and Jo and Alice, and the Time Guardians will not abandon us, no matter what. Now, would you like to sleep upstairs with me tonight?'

Alain shook his head, and his mentor released him. 'I will be okay. And you are right; we should worry about tomorrow when it comes.'

Turning away, Alain let himself into the kitchen and

smiled at Bebe's thoughtfulness when he saw a cup of camomile tea sitting on the table. He carried it upstairs and found Lee asleep in his bed, the light of the reading lamp he had left on for Alain casting him into the shadows.

Relieved he didn't have to try and talk to his roommate, Alain quickly changed into his nightclothes before propping himself up with pillows and sipping his tea. Picking up his copy of *The Lord of The Rings*, he found his ability to read was already gone.

He attempted to pick up some words from chapters he had read before, hoping to improve his grasp of modern English. However, the words appeared to be swimming across the page, so he put the book on the floor before reaching over to turn off the light. As he snuggled down under the duvet, waves of homesickness washed over him and he wished with all his might to be somewhere—anywhere else.

CHAPTER ELEVEN
FIGHTING BACK

Strange noises woke Alain early the next morning. Hiding under his covers he listened, trying to work out what had awoken him. When he did, he gulped in a snort of laughter lest Lee realise he was awake and try to talk to him.

His roommate crept around in the dark, searching for something and cursing under his breath when he couldn't find them. In his attempt to be considerate, he managed to make twice his normal noise.

As Lee pulled on his jeans, he lost his balance and banged into Alain's bed. Alain considered sitting up and putting him out of his misery, but it was too entertaining. Finally, his roommate closed the door behind himself and Alain relaxed, happy to be left alone.

Leaning over, he picked up *The Lord of the Rings*, immediately confirming his worst fear from listening to Lee—it was gibberish. Trouble was not yet awake and back to normal. Dropping the book to the floor, he rolled to his back and stared at the ceiling, hands clasped behind his head.

The overwhelming despair from the night before had morphed into resolve. Trouble's absence did not mean work had stopped. They still needed to move forward. Shaking the sleep from his head, he focussed on coming up with a plan of action.

Firstly, they needed to find out the results of last night's coven vote. If they'd voted yes to distributing the bacteria tomorrow, he and Master Barwick needed to find a way to stop them. If they'd voted not to, there was time to work with Jo, Lee and Bebe to find a way to destroy the new people-friendly bacteria.

Right, time to visit Master Barwick and find out where they stood. He swung his legs out of bed and started to push himself up when a noise on the stairs stopped him. Rolling back over on his side, he pulled the duvet up so it covered his face. In his hiding place, he froze as the door creaked open, admitting Lee and Bebe in the midst of an argument.

'See? He is still asleep,' Bebe whispered. 'Just leave the food, Lee.'

'It's late. He can't sleep all day. Besides, I want to find out what happened last night, and he might enjoy some company.'

'If he wanted company he would be downstairs already. Jo hasn't called, so we've nothing new to tell him. Just put the food down and leave him be.' Bebe's tone was insistent.

Well, that was what he imagined they were saying from the fragments of words he understood. There was a clatter of dishes and the click of a door closing.

All right, perhaps finding out about the coven was not the first thing he needed to sort; his inability to understand

what anyone was saying was far more pressing. Leaning over, he saw a plate of toast and a cup of tea on the dresser and his stomach grumbled, reminding him he was ravenously hungry.

After wolfing down the food, he felt a little better. Once again, he studied the ceiling as he wondered how Master Barwick was doing. Had he ventured into the kitchen or was he avoiding everyone as well? Closing his eyes, Alain attempted to mind-speak with the other man. Either the distance between them was too far or Trouble had been assisting them with their usual connection because he got nothing.

Whether from boredom or stress, Alain dozed off again. When he opened his eyes he found light streaming into the room from the window. Someone had opened the curtains and taken his empty dishes away. The position of the sun told him there was little left of the morning.

Come on, sleepy head. Get yourself dressed and come down here. There are things we need to discuss.

He sat bolt upright, suddenly wide awake. *Jo? But how ...*

Yes, it's me. I am about to call Barnaby. Get yourself down here.

But... but I cannot understand the others. They will notice, he said.

I found a solution for that. Please trust me and come down. The voice in his head was impatient, and it left as abruptly as it had entered.

Standing in the shower a few moments later, he realised he had not asked Jo about Trouble. He sent his mind out to her, but she was no longer there. Then he laughed;

there was only one way Jo would be able to talk to him mind-to-mind like that. *Trouble? Trouble? Are you there?*

Still, nothing.

Somewhat bewildered, Alain tramped down the stairs and entered the kitchen. To his surprise Izzy sat at the table with Lee and Bebe. As he entered the room, Jo was placing a large teapot on the table. He caught Jo's eye and she opened her mouth to speak, but was prevented by the noise of Master Barwick opening the door and joined them.

At the sight of Izzy sitting at the table, he stopped and glared. Shutting the door, Jo moved her body to force him into the room. 'Ah Barnaby, good timing. Please come in and take a seat.'

Pulling out a chair for him, Jo waited patiently while he made up his mind to stay. As Alain took a seat beside Master Barwick, he realised he had understood Jo. Once again, he searched around for Trouble. Unable to find the dog anywhere he raised a questioning eyebrow in Master Barwick's direction. The old man shook his head and shrugged.

After she finished pouring everyone tea, Jo sat beside Izzy and took the other girl's hand. A quick glance around the table showed Master Barwick was not the only one staring daggers at the Time Wrecker. Bebe glared at the girl over the rim of her teacup, and Lee sat back arms folded, his eyes challenging Izzy. She lounged back in her chair, appearing unconcerned, but the frequent eye contact she made with Jo told a different story.

'Alice took my shift at the store because I worked late at the vet's last night,' Jo started. 'After talking with her, I decided rather than rest I should bring you all here so we can work together to resolve things with the other coven. She agreed with me, so long as we do not make any firm plans without running them by her—especially you two.' Jo stared directly at Lee and Bebe.

Jo, how is Trouble doing this? I cannot reach him, Alain sent

It's not him, you dolt. It's me.

Alain's eyebrows almost flew off his head. *Izzy?*

'When I left Trouble early this morning, he was doing much better,' Jo told them, seeming undisturbed by the second conversation going on in her head.

'Excellent. When can he come home?' Alain asked. *Why? Why are you doing this, Izzy?*

'He is not out of the woods yet. They are keeping him sedated until lunchtime today to give his body a chance to heal. Before they wake him, they will do some more tests, but they are hopeful he is over the worst of it.' Jo's words warmed Alain's heart and everyone murmured their gratitude and relief.

Because I can. And ... well... what is going on is too wrong for me to stand by and do nothing. We have to stop it. This is not the right way to fix the ills of the world, Izzy sent.

'Sadly, two more dogs came in last night with similar symptoms. The numbers are on the rise. Susan, the vet, let me try Barnaby's cure on one of them–with the owner 's permission of course. They are both at the same stage of the diseases development, so we should get an idea of whether or not the cure helps.'

I do not trust you, girl. You are a Time Wrecker. Master Barwick cut into the second conversation, and at the same time he responded to Jo. 'I can make up some more if it helps, for the other animal, but I am pleased they let you test it. '

Time Wreckers is the Guardians' name for us. We call ourselves the World Fixers, Izzy told them.

Bah, semantics, Master Barwick dismissed her.

'Let's not get ahead of ourselves,' Jo said. 'It will take twenty-four hours before we know whether or not it helps. Remember, Trouble had an accelerated dose of the bacteria.'

'Yes, one given to him by your friends,' Bebe spat the words out as she pointed at Izzy. 'You almost killed him.'

'Bebe!'

The hurt in Jo's voice did not deter Bebe. 'I know you like her, Jo, but that does not change the fact she is part of Tabitha's coven, and therefore is responsible for what happened to Trouble in the first place.'

Tears welled in Izzy's eyes. *It is not semantics; it is name-calling. The Time Guardians want time to flow exactly as it always has, without change. We want to fix things that are setting the world on a course for destruction. Who is to say whose approach is right or wrong?* Izzy defended herself against Master Barwick. At the same time, she turned and faced Bebe. 'I would never hurt Trouble, and I would never let anyone else either. In fact, I am here because I think my coven is going too far. Making a few dogs sick is one thing, and even that got out of hand. Giving this disease to humans is a whole other proposition—one I can't support.'

Bebe's jaw dropped, and Lee put down his phone.

In all the furore over Trouble there had been no opportunity to tell them about what Izzy had said last night. She resolved that problem by outlining the coven's discussions from the night before.

Throughout, Master Barwick was strangely silent. He stroked his beard and gazed thoughtfully at Izzy. She pretended not to notice, but Alain watched as she glanced at the alchemist through her lashes every now and then, as if watching and waiting for his next attack.

'So, what did they decide after we left?' Lee's question brought Alain's attention back to the matter at hand.

'Tabitha managed to persuade most of them to go ahead with the plan tomorrow night—the plan to release a new version of bacteria that can infect humans.' Izzy's voice was barely a whisper. 'That was why I searched out Jo this morning—to tell her everything in the hopes you can stop them.'

'Why can't you stop it?' Bebe turned on Izzy again.

'I would like to. In fact, I tried, but Tabitha is no longer listening to me. I cannot prevent the spread of this abomination alone—I need your help.' Izzy's gaze did not waiver as she admitted she needed them.

You cannot influence anyone else to act against those you've been helping, can you? Master Barwick asked. *But as we are already actively trying to stop the spread of bacteria, you can nudge us in the right direction?*

Correct. My Council will pull me out of here before I have time to convince anyone to oppose Tabitha. However, they cannot watch every move I make, and they are aware of my relationship with Jo, so they will be expecting me to be in contact with her, and they are a little distracted at the moment ...

So I heard, Master Barwick said dryly.

Izzy ignored the comment. *I told the coven last night I will use my friendship with Jo to spy on what you are doing to ensure you do not get any whiff of their plan, so they won't be too suspicious. Now I can tip the scales in your favour when I am able—without being obvious of course.*

This is a dangerous game you are playing, missy, Master Barwick said, frowning at her.

There is no other way to stop this abomination, she declared.

'Izzy suggested she spy on us for the coven, when in reality she is keeping an eye on them for us,' Jo informed the group.

'How do we know you are not playing us both?' Although it was Lee who spoke, he asked the obvious question.

How do we know we can trust you? Alain added.

'You don't,' Izzy said out loud, answering both questions. 'In fact, I'm not sure that if I were you, I would trust me either. But what choice do you have? Can you do this without me?'

'Perhaps,' Lee said.

'But it would be harder,' Izzy told him. 'All I can say is, we cannot let this abomination be released. I will undertake to tell you where they are planning to spread the bacteria, and I will tell them I convinced you nothing is going on, or that they will be at another location. It is up to you how you stop them.'

'Are we going to wait until they are actually spreading the disease? Isn't that risky?' Bebe asked.

'Yeah, it would be better if we destroyed the bacteria before it got to that stage.' Picking up on Bebe's question, Lee proposed the beginnings of a solution.

Izzy sighed. 'Don't you think I haven't already thought of that? The vial containing the bacteria is locked in Tabitha's safe. I tried to break in, but it's state of the art and impossible to open for all but the most talented safecrackers.'

A slow smile spread across Lee's face. 'Alain and I are very good at blowing things up.'

'Honestly, Lee, I sometimes wonder if you still have the brains you were born with. If you blow up the safe with the bacteria in it, you risk releasing it into the world anyway,' Bebe said, shaking her head.

'Oh, yeah.' Lee laughed wryly. 'Perhaps not my best plan.'

'That's not such a bad idea,' Master Barwick mused. 'A small, local release of the bacteria might be able to be contained and dispersed harmlessly using magic. I am assuming the release is timed for tomorrow night so that your coven can use magic to ... um... accelerate growth perhaps, so it can multiply faster and spread further.'

Izzy nodded.

'So, let me summarise our two options. The first is Lee's: to steal the vial now, which would possibly result in a minimal release of the bacteria. The second is to stop the coven at the site of the dispersion. This course of action also has risks. We might cause the same bacterial spread as option one if they release it and our counter measures are not strong enough. Or, if they disperse it before we get there, the impact may be larger.' Master Barwick's gaze swept around the table as everyone seemed to confirm their agreement.

Everyone except Alain nodded. 'There is a third option. Izzy, do you think the coven would go ahead without their full contingent?'

Izzy seemed to consider his words. 'I am not sure. I think if it were Tabitha. Or perhaps Ruth, a couple of the others sympathise with her and they might develop cold feet and refuse to go through with the plan.'

'So if we stop one of them from getting there we might be able to prevent the spread happening tomorrow, and that would buy us some more time.' Alain picked up her idea and took it to the logical conclusion.

'All these options are short-term,' Bebe said. 'If we destroy the bacteria, what is to stop them making more? And if we stop them tomorrow night, the coven will simply wait until the next full moon to try again. What we need to do is choose the one that gains us the most amount of time to come up with a long-term solution.'

'And don't forget, we still need to talk to Alice and get her agreement,' Jo added.

Master Barwick frowned. *If Sigma was here, he would be able to sense the possible futures and tell us which one would give us the best result.* He looked at Izzy. *Can you do that?*

Izzy shook her head. *Only our most senior agents are granted that ability, and I'm not at that level yet. If this mission had been successful I might have been promoted, but now who knows?* She sounded a little sad as she spoke of what she was giving up to help them.

The others waited for Master Barwick, the only adult in the room, to provide guidance, but he seemed reluctant to make a decision.

Maybe we should wait and see how Trouble is this afternoon before deciding what to do. Alain tried to help out his mentor.

Delaying doing anything in itself is a risk. There are times to wait and think, and times for action. I believe this is a time for action, Master Barwick was decisive. *There are a lot of things we need to take into account though.*

'All right. Bebe and Lee, how about you go to your aunt's store and search for anything on how to stop growth spells? Bebe, please also bring her up-to-date on everything we discussed this morning. And Lee, would you be able to spend some time on your internet thingy researching safe cracking?' Master Barwick took charge of the situation. *That also means they are out of the way when Izzy leaves and we can no longer understand their language.* He smiled.

Good thinking, Alain sent.

'Will do,' Lee said as Bebe nodded.

'Jo, do you think this Ruth person might listen to reason if you spoke to her today?' Master Barwick continued.

Don't you trust me to do it? Izzy asked.

'I am not sure, Barnaby, but it's worth a try.' Jo shrugged.

Jo is a better choice because of her history with Ruth. Alice tells me they are close, Master Barwick responded.

'I can go with her and tell her about what happened to Trouble last night,' Alain offered.

And how would she understand you? Izzy asked.

'And would she believe you. I mean, she doesn't know who you are,' Jo tried to dissuade him, and given Izzy's comment, Alain was reconsidering his offer.

'I should go too,' Izzy said, and the others looked at her in surprise, but it was Alain who spoke.

'How can you keep up your ruse if you are seen with us?'

How will you be able to understand what she is saying, or she you, if I am not nearby? Izzy mind-spoke. Out loud she said, 'If I look like I am wavering in my support of Tabitha, it might help to change her mind. And if she stands firm, I can find some way to let her know I am only with you because I need to stay in good with you guys to find out what you are up to.'

'Man, you are good.' Bebe's admiration at Izzy's plotting skills made Alain laugh.

Ignoring the girls, Lee turned to the alchemist. 'And what will you be doing, Barnaby?'

'I shall be here working on cooking up a new batch of the cure for the dogs, and seeing if I can figure out how they might mutate the bacteria to affect humans. If I can do that, I might be able to come up with a vaccination or a cure.'

'Do you need me to stay and help you?' Alain asked. *If you do, Izzy and I can stay behind. She can help with any books you need to read.*

'No, no, I am fine. You go with Jo. I will work faster alone.'

Master Barwick clasped his shoulder. *I will be working from my notes mostly and ...*

... and he still does not really trust me, so he wants

me far away from his work, and he wants you to keep an eye on me, Izzy finished.

'Right, everyone has a job to do. Let's go,' Master Barwick dismissed them, and he used the hand on Alain's shoulder to help himself up.

And let's do Trouble proud, Alain added to himself.

The strained atmosphere in the car during the journey to Southampton was uncomfortable to say the least. After a whispered conversation during which Alain gleaned Jo had not wanted Izzy to come with them, the car remained silent until Izzy turned on the radio. However, the music she finally settled on did nothing to mask the tension between the two girls.

Jo concentrated on driving. Izzy sat beside her, glancing at her friend every now and then. A couple of times she moved as if to say something then, catching sight of Alain in the back, she stopped herself.

Watching the countryside speed by, Alain continued questioning his decision to come along. Maybe he'd read Master Barwick wrong. Maybe the alchemist had suggested he come not to keep an eye on Izzy, but merely to give him something to do other than fretting about Trouble. If that was the case, he could have stayed behind and helped Master Barwick, even if only to clean up a little, and avoided the argument brewing in front of him.

The scene outside the car changed from country lanes to a main road with houses on either side. The number of cars and houses and people overwhelmed Alain, making him feel very small and insignificant. Southampton was even bigger and busier than the London he'd left a couple of days ago. As they entered the city proper, Jo followed the blue signs directing them to the hospital. Upon entering the grounds, she found a place to park the car and they all piled out.

'You cannot possibly think you are coming in.' Jo turned to Izzy in astonishment.

'I most certainly am.'

'I can handle this. Ruth and Mum have been friends for years, and she and I ... well, we have a history.' Jo stood in front of Izzy, blocking her way forward, hands on hips.

'I am well aware of your history. We discussed it at the meeting in detail after you left. Tabitha believes Ruth is protecting you because of it. But that's not why I am going with you—I am going to give Ruth cover if she needs it. When we ask her to stay away tomorrow, if she thinks another coven member is prepared to try and thwart Tabitha's scheme then she might be more likely to consider it.'

'"We" ask? See how easy it is for you to slip into talking about you and I as a team? What if you let slip you told us about the bacteria skipping to humans?'

'I wouldn't,' Izzy protested.

'It is too risky. You should stay here.'

Unwilling to become involved in their quarrel, Alain moved away and surveyed the car park. In his wildest dreams, he would never have imagined so many cars in the world, and this was only a small number compared to those they had passed on the journey here.

When he closed his eyes, the air filled with the sounds of their movements. Taking a deep breath, he coughed as his lungs filled with unclean air. He imagined if you lived in Southampton, the smell and noise from cars would be a constant backdrop to your life. He was beginning to appreciate why Izzy fought so hard to save the world form this sort of thing.

Jo sighed a loud and exaggerated sigh—she must have realised she fought a losing battle. She swivelled on her heel and walked off towards the closest building. Izzy stalked after her, leaving Alain behind. Had they even remembered he was there?

As they approached the building, Alain read the sign by the door, "Adolescent Behavioural Support Unit", and he realised how Jo knew Ruth—she was the person who'd guided her back on the straight and narrow after her father left. This meeting was going to be way more difficult than he'd first imagined.

Alain trailed after the others through a maze of corridors. If he got lost, he would never be able to find his way back out alone. Finally, they reached a door with the name *Ruth Claremont* on it. Jo stopped and raised a hand to knock, but stood frozen as the door opened before she'd had a chance to complete the action.

'Oh, Jo. Was I expecting you?' A tall woman in a white coat stood in the doorway. Perching her glasses on the top of her head, she glanced past Jo and saw Izzy. Her eyebrows raised questioningly. 'And Izzy is with you too. So, is this a social call, or something more?' Her eyes met Alain's. 'And who are you?'

'I am very uncomfortable at the moment, and not quite

sure why I am here.' Alain shrugged, and caught a playful glint in the other woman's eyes as her lips turned upwards.

'I bet you are. But what can you expect when you spend time with such ... shall we say ... mavericks.'

'Ruth, Alain. Alain, Ruth. Now we have that over, Ruth, do you have time for a chat?' Jo asked.

'I was just on my way to the cafeteria for lunch if you want to join me. My schedule is pretty full this afternoon, so this is my only free time for the rest of day.'

The two girls looked at each other, and then nodded as if they shared a single thought. Minutes later, Alain found himself once again trailing behind the others with no idea where they were going or how to find his way out if he got lost.

The cafeteria was a large room full of tables. There appeared to be a rush for lunch, leaving only a few vacant places. On one side ran a self-service counter facing a wall of picture windows that framed the grey day outside.

Jo ordered teas for them, and they followed Ruth to a table by the window. Once seated, Ruth began eating her pie as if they weren't there. Alain watched as the two girls stared at each other, Izzy nodding towards Ruth, encouraging Jo to take the lead.

'Um, it's about Tabitha, and her scheme.' Jo opened the conversation.

Ruth smiled, tucking a strand of greying brown hair that had escaped its bun back behind her ear. 'You do surprise me,' she said before carrying on eating.

Alain grinned—he liked the woman sitting in front of him. She was not only confident and self-assured, but she was enjoying the awkward situation they found themselves in. That very fact relaxed him, and for a moment he forgot his worries about Trouble and the bacteria while he enjoyed the show.

'Well, I saw at the meeting you were not happy with her escalating things, and I wondered if you would consider returning to our coven.' The last words rushed out of Jo's mouth as if they had a momentum of their own.

Alain smiled at the look of shock on Izzy's face. This was not what they had agreed. Had she done it to show Izzy was not really privy to this?

Ruth laughed. 'Is this coming from you, or Alice?'

'I didn't tell Alice I was coming.' Jo raised her eyebrows defiantly as she answered.

'Mm, interesting,' Ruth said, pausing with her fork halfway to her mouth. 'So, the coven has not changed its stance; they will not take any action to preserve the forest beyond their growth and energy spells?

When Jo did not answer, Ruth ate another mouthful of food, then turned her attention to Izzy. 'And what is your role in this? You did not speak out against Tabitha's plan last night, but you clearly were not comfortable either. Have you left our coven?'

'I am considering it.' Izzy's voice sounded uncertain even to Alain, leaving her motivation open to interpretation. 'Okay, I don't want to. But I have thought things over and I'm not really happy taking part in what is essentially the murder of animals,' she added hastily, clarifying her position.

Sitting back in her chair, Ruth regarded her three guests through hooded lids before leaning forward and resuming her meal. As if unnerved by the silence, Izzy spoke to fill it, and Alain saw how Ruth might work as a therapist.

'That wasn't our intention when we started this. We thought a few more dogs might become ill, forcing people to think more about protecting the forests. But you've seen how the virus works, what it is doing to dogs, what it could potentially do to—'

'Come on, Ruth. I can't believe you think hurting people's pets is the right way to go about changing things.' Jo spoke before Izzy could let on she had told them about the new bacteria that would kill humans. 'It breaks my heart when they come in to the surgery with this illness. If you saw them too, I know you'd change your mind. Perhaps if I pick you up and take you to the vets after work tomorrow.'

Nice, Alain thought to himself. You hid the fact that Izzy told us the whole plan, and you have given her an excuse not to go tomorrow.

Although Jo offered her an out, Ruth was not taking the bait. 'I am sorry, Jo. I am busy tomorrow night. Perhaps we might do it on Sunday.'

'I guess so, if the dogs are still alive then.'

'Jo!' Ruth's tone held a definite warning note. 'You are well aware of my feelings on emotional blackmail. I said I will catch up with you when I have some free time.'

Alain sensed Jo bursting at the seams, wanting to talk Ruth out of supporting Tabitha's scheme. Unfortunately, if she pushed any harder Ruth might guess they knew the truth. Alain held his breath, willing Jo to let it go. Finally, her shoulders slumped in defeat.

'Well, if you are certain you will not let me convince

you, I guess we should leave you to finish your lunch in peace.' Jo stood and pushed her chair back, scraping the legs along the floor.

The girls' disappointment seemed to be the only thing that got a reaction from Ruth, but Jo turned away before she could see the conflicting emotions cross her mentor's face. As Alain stood to follow Jo, Ruth gabbed Izzy's arm. Izzy sat back down and he moved until he was out of Ruth's line of sight, but close enough to overhear their conversation.

'After our meeting last night, Tabitha's friend Gavin visited me. He informed me I should be careful because accidents can happen to anyone at any time, and if I wanted to stay safe I should stay close to our coven. I can't tell if you are playing along while you spy on Alice's group, or if you are wavering from Tabitha's plan. Either way, I would be very careful if I were you. I don't think this guy fools around.'

Izzy whispered, 'Do not fear. I am only keeping in with Jo to find out what her coven is doing. I will be there tomorrow as planned.'

Alain headed for the door before Izzy was out of her chair, but she rushed to catch him up.

'I guess you heard that?' Izzy said

Alain nodded.

'She is really scared. There is no way we are going to be able to stop her or any of the others from going tomorrow night.'

'I know. We need to think of something else.'

By the time they reached the car, Jo was already in her seat and buckled up ready to go. Tears rolled down her cheeks and she gripped the steering wheel so tightly her knuckles had turned white.

'I cannot believe it,' she said. 'I just cannot believe Ruth is involved in hurting animals and is considering doing something that will hurt a lot of people.'

Izzy placed a hand on her arm. 'To be fair, Ruth argued against hurting animals, as did Gladys. They suggested we cast spells to make people uneasy when they visited areas of the forest being considered for development. I thought it was rather a good idea, but Tabitha wanted something more extreme. The others went along with her, so I agreed as well. Now Gavin is threatening Ruth, and she feels she has no choice but to go through with this.'

'But she cast the first spell without him bullying her into it.'

'Yes, she helped cast the spell. Beth always finds an excuse not to be available, and I pretended to be sick because I could not be involved, and Ruth had to fill in to make up the five. Then when we saw what was happening to the dogs, and how more than normal were dying, even Tabitha wanted to stop. But Gavin stepped in and convinced her to carry on.'

Rather than calming Jo's fears, this news made her cry all the harder. 'Ruth will never forgive herself if she casts the new spell. We have to find some way to keep her from participating.'

Taking a deep breath and wiping the tears from her eyes, Jo started the car. 'Let's head home. We have some more planning to do, and I want to ring Susan and find out how Trouble is.'

CHAPTER TWELVE
SOLDIERING ON

Although no one spoke, the journey back to Burley was a little less tense than the one to Southampton had been. As the car pulled up outside Alice's house, Alain leapt out. He wanted to get away from the others and clear his head. Heavy with fatigue, his shoulders slumped as he let himself in through the back door.

Lee and Bebe sat at the kitchen table with a distraught Master Barwick. Wearily smiling his hellos, he noticed Bebe's hands trembling, and he froze as he attempted to work out what was going on.

Alice paced back and forth in front of the bench while Lee sat beside his sister, arm wrapped along the back of her chair. Master Barwick glanced up as he entered, his hands clenched and his brows furrowed.

Thank goodness you're back. Now I might be able to

work out what is going on. Please tell me Izzy is with you.

Jo and Izzy bundled Alain through the door and went to stand in front of the Aga to warm up.

Alice stopped walking and stood with her hands on her hips, glaring at Master Barwick. 'Are you silent because you think I'm over-reacting? I might be, but I really want to hear what you think.'

'On the contrary, my dear, you may well have every right to be angry. How about you sit down and recount your story for the others, and we can all decide what to do together.'

Alain admired Master Barwick's handling of the situation. No one would ever have known he had not understood a word Alice said up until their entrance.

Jo pulled out a chair for Alice to sit on and placed a hand on her shoulder. 'Tell us what happened,' she encouraged.

'We were in the shop—the twins in the book room doing some research and me by the counter—when I heard the screech of tyres. Thinking it was just some young kids letting off steam, I looked out the window to find out who'd done it in time in time to catch the back door of a car open. A man half reached out and threw something, and next thing my small plate-glass window was in pieces. As I rushed over to inspect the damage, the car door closed and the culprits took off.'

Alice clasped the mug of tea in her hands, the tremors causing her to spill a little on the table.

Lee picked up the story. 'Someone threw a brick. It hit a stand on the way through, which fell on Bebe, cutting her face.'

On cue, Bebe pulled her hair back off her face, revealing a dressing. 'Only a small cut,' she said. 'No concussion, and the doctor told me to go home and drink heaps of sweet tea.' She pointed to the cup in front of her. 'And I always follow doctors' orders.' She smiled wanly at them all.

'It could have been much worse.' Lee's voice belied his barely controlled anger.

'Yes, we should be thankful it wasn't.' Alice said, patting him on the arm as if to calm him down. 'What was more disturbing, though, was the note tied to the brick.' Alice indicated the crumpled piece of paper in the middle of the table.

Jo leaned over to read it. 'Keep your nose out of other people's business. You have been warned.' Moving back to the heat of the Aga, she said, 'It's like something out of a bad seventies cop show. Did you recognise the car, or the person who threw the brick?'

Alice looked at Izzy as she answered, 'No, I didn't. But I can hazard a guess at who the message is from.'

Izzy shifted in her chair, but her chin lifted as she met Alice 's gaze. 'After what I heard today, I suspect you may be right.'

'You are part of the coven, so you are responsible for their actions,' Alice shot back.

'Hold on you two,' Jo interrupted what had the potential to turn into a major argument. 'Izzy's been helping us this morning, and she is as concerned about the way things are going as we are. I, for one, do not believe she supports any of the threatening activity going on.'

'You mean there has been more?' Lee asked, and Izzy recounted her conversation with Ruth.

Sighing as if the weight of the world was on his shoulders, Master Barwick leaned his arms on the table. 'If the one person who stood up to Tabitha is too scared to oppose her, then we have no hope of changing anyone else's minds.'

'I just want to clarify, it was Gavin who threatened Ruth,' Izzy said.

'But it is Tabitha who has the power to put a stop to this,' Alice said.

Alain intervened before things got heated again. 'It doesn't matter who is leading the coven. We need to change our tactic, as it is unlikely we will be able to prevent members from going along with the plan if they are too frightened to protest.'

'Hold on,' Jo said. 'We might not be able to talk Ruth into voluntarily boycotting tomorrow night's activities, but there are other methods of keeping her away. I would like to try them if only because I get the sense she does not want to be involved in this any more than Izzy does— but she is too scared to say no.'

Lee sat forward in his chair. 'You mean something like kidnapping her? How cool.'

Master Barwick held up his hand. 'Now Lee, I don't think we need to go quite that far. Not only is it illegal, but it might also be very dangerous.'

'More dangerous than facing a terrible epidemic if they succeed tomorrow?' Lee was ready to argue his point further, but Alice put a quick stop to the potential solution.

'Barnaby is right,' she said. 'Your parents would never forgive me if I allowed you to do anything that might jeopardise your future career.'

'But ...' Bebe's face wore the same expression as Barabal's did when she was scheming. '... if we managed to figure which tourist attraction the coven are targeting, we might be able to work out the route Ruth will take. Then we could block the road, force her to stop, and delay her long enough so she misses everything all together.'

'Why a tourist attraction?' Alice asked.

Jo's face lit up. 'Because they will attract the greatest number of people this time of year.'

'Of course.' Alice nodded. 'Most of the roads around the forest are so small, if someone broke down ... say with a flat tyre ... they could block the way, and she would not be able to drive past. Also, Ruth is basically a good person. She would not leave anyone stranded on the side of the road.'

'It would have to be ...'

Before Izzy finished her thought, Alice's phone rang. She took a quick look at the screen and picked it up. 'Sorry, I need to take this. It's Donald and he never rings at this time of day unless it's important. I won't be long.'

Once she left the room, Izzy continued, 'As I was saying, Ruth will recognise you, Alice, Alain and I, so it has to be Bebe or Lee.'

'Leave it to us,' Lee said. 'We would have to hire a car though, because Ruth must have seen Alice's and Jo's mum's cars before. We would also need a good idea of which way she is travelling to make this work.'

'I can arrange car hire,' Alice said, returning to the room and putting her phone back on the table.

'Is everything ok with Uncle Donald?' Bebe asked.

'What? ... Yes.' Alice was running the charm on her

necklace back and forwards along the chain. I have a friend in Southampton who owes me a favour or two and will do me a good deal on a car.'

Bebe frowned at her aunt, and looked as though she was about to say something when Izzy spoke. 'And knowing which way she will go should be easy to work out. There's a meeting this evening to finalise plans, so I should be able to give you the location,' Izzy said.

'I hope you all understand, removing one of the coven may not be enough to stop the ceremony from going ahead,' Master Barwick said once they finished planning Ruth's diversion.

They nodded, and Bebe said, 'We're not going to stop looking into other options, but this may be the best shot we have.'

'So long as you know,' Master Barwick said before moving on. 'Lee, did you manage to find out any safe-cracking methods that might help us break into Tabitha's tonight?'

'No. I did a web search, but everything mechanical required some technology that is not available in local stores—in fact, we would need to send overseas for most of it.'

'What about the old-fashioned ways?' Jo asked.

'Yep, I did some research on that as well. I watched a few online videos and it would take weeks, even months to develop the techniques to a level to be able to open even the simplest safes, and we simply don't have that much time.'

'Sound like your day was a complete bust,' Jo said.

'Not exactly. We did find a protection spell in one of Alice's books that might work for us. Alice checked her stock and she found everything we would need to cast it.' Bebe nudged Lee, who leaned down and pulled his backpack out from under the table. He rummaged inside before producing a book from its depths.

'It is an ancient rite that prevents anyone from casting a spell with malicious intent in an area,' Alice told them all. 'Do you think it might help, Barnaby?'

Lee pushed the book on the table over to Master Barwick, who opened it at the marked passage and read.

'Yes ... oh, this is good. If we were able to cast this in the same area the coven plans to work their magic it should be enough to stop them from being effective.' Master Barwick tugged at tufts of hair as he read some more. 'We need enough for five people. Did you take that into account?'

Lee pointed to a box on the bench. 'Already sorted.'

'I thought as Tabitha's coven were casting in a pentagram formation, to effectively counter then we would need to do the same. I believe we are prepared,' Alice said.

Alain, are you there? I cannot reach Barwick.

Trouble?

Yes, it is me. A weak groggy voice answered, but it had never sounded better to Alain.

Master Barwick is a little busy at the moment. I will explain later. How are you?

Better, still a little tired, but I can no longer feel the bacteria eating away at me.

Alain smiled; things were looking up. *Rest a while. Things are under control here for the moment.*

Returning his attention to the conversation, he found himself in the midst of a debate over who should make up their pentagram. Alain, Master Barwick, Alice and Jo were a given. Alice seemed to favour asking Jo's mother, but Jo wanted to leave her out of it.

Can Trouble cast a spell? Alain asked Master Barwick.

Yes, if he were well enough.

'How about we wait until tomorrow to decide who will be the fifth,' Alain suggested.

Jo eyed him suspiciously. 'Why?'

'I just thought of someone else, but I need to check if they can be available,' Alain responded.

'Wait a moment—even if you find someone else, we might still need your mum as a backup, Jo. Donald called to tell me there is a delay with getting some equipment for his project and, as classes are finished for the year, he is coming home until after Christmas. He is waitlisted for a flight and might be here as early as tomorrow.' Alice dropped the news in ever so casually into the conversation.

'Would your husband forbid you from helping us?'

The others around the table tensed at Master Barwick's question, their eyes fixing on anything except Alice. Having been out and about a bit more than his master, Alain realised that women were no longer subjugated by their husbands, and could do as they pleased.

Fortunately, Alice took the question in good humour, ignoring everyone else's discomfort. 'Goodness no. It is just, well, getting him up to speed on this hours after he has arrived home might be a bit much. Jo, perhaps you might have a word with your mother—just in case. '

Jo was still staring at Alain, then it was as though a light clicked on.

'Oh, oh, of course you have someone else to help, and

yes, Alice, I will talk to Mum tonight. Can she call you if she needs to? Because this all sounds a little kooky, and I'm not sure she will believe me.'

'Of course. I might give her a call later anyway,' Alice said.

'Okay. If we are finished then I'd best go and ring the vet to check on Trouble. Izzy, shouldn't you be getting back to work? You don't want Gladys to become suspicious—otherwise your coven may decide to expel you, and you'll lose your chance of finding out where they are going to be tomorrow night.'

'You are right.' The other girl followed Jo into the hallway. *And I must ensure my council does not suspect I am helping you and pull me out—or worse still, send someone else to finish the job.*

'And I need to return to the shop to see how the window repairs are going, and organise a car for tomorrow,' Alice said, rising and grabbing her coat from the back of the chair in a single motion.

'Now that we have a plan, Alain and I need to prepare the casting.' Master Barwick picked up the book and stared at Alain, waiting for him to move.

'Hold on, I've something that might help you in our room. Alain, can you give me a hand?' Lee said, standing to leave. Alain followed him out but stopped in the doorway and looked back over his shoulder—Bebe had not moved.

'What are you going to do?' he asked her.

'Oh, sorry. I was miles away. I have some things I need to look into—on another matter.' She winked at him and he grinned back, then turned to go after Lee.

As he walked up the stairs, he could not help but

overhear Jo and Izzy in the lounge.

'Please Jo, there is still time to back out. I am scared of Gavin, and I couldn't bear it if he hurt you.'

'But you are still going to go to this meeting and place yourself in danger?' Jo's voice was angry.

'I am, but you know I have other commit—'

'No buts. I am prepared to fight for what I believe in, the same as you are. If you care for me as you say you do you should try to understand that and support me.' Jo stormed to the door, flung it open and ran out.

'I do support you,' Alain heard Izzy mutter. 'I am just not sure I could survive losing you again.'

Alain tried to figure out what Izzy had meant but, not knowing the pair's full past, he decided to ask Trouble about it later, and continued up the stairs.

'Quickly. There isn't much time before Izzy goes.' Lee handed him his laptop in the hallway. 'If I have worked things out right, Izzy has been allowing you to understand us when she is here. That means you cannot study the book without a translator. I set this programme up to change modern English into old English. It may not be perfect, but it should help you keep working.'

The door slammed below.

'Thank you,' Alain said, but the confused look on Lee's face told him Izzy was no longer working her magic.

Izzy pulled into Tabitha's drive. The number of other cars already parked suggested she was almost the last to arrive—only Beth's vehicle was missing. She sat for a few minutes to gather her thoughts. What was she doing? She was throwing away everything she had worked for. No, she could not doubt herself now—there was a line between right and wrong, and the coven were about to cross it.

The door creaked as she opened it, and she slipped out of the car. She reluctantly made her way inside, not quite knowing what to expect.

She knew immediately that Ruth had told them of her visit today.

'I was not sure you were going to join us this afternoon.' Tabitha's voice was syrupy sweet. But Izzy knew from experience this was Tabitha at her most dangerous, and she prepared herself for the strike.

'I am not sure we should allow her to remain.' Gavin sat in an armchair, watching proceedings, no longer hiding in the shadows.

'You allowed a man into our coven,' Izzy spluttered, diverting attention to buy herself time. Although, to be fair, she was a little surprised at Tabitha so openly acknowledging Gavin's role in the coven's recent activities.

'I invited him to attend. With his international experience, he brings a different perspective,' Tabitha said, her hard face daring anyone to object.

'What? Even if he was not a man, we haven't inducted him into our group.' Izzy attempted to suppress her anger and fear by arguing points of order.

'He has as much of a stake in this as we do—he stays. What I am not so sure about is whether we allow you to.' Tabitha's voice was like steel. 'Ruth said you attempted to convince her not to turn up to tomorrow's casting.'

Izzy glanced behind Tabitha to find Ruth at least had the good grace to appear ashamed at having ratted her out.

'I did, and I would have reported that to you when I updated you of Alice's coven's activity, if you had given me the chance. May I remind you, you all agreed to me using my connection to Jo to spy on her group to make sure they don't find out what we are doing. '

A couple of the women nodded in agreement, and this gave Izzy the courage to go on. 'If I had not gone along with Jo today she would not have believed I was truly with her. However, if you no longer trust me, I will leave.' Izzy's stomach fluttered as she wondered if she had overplayed her indignation, and if they might allow her to actually walk out.

'Come on, Tabitha, she is part of our group, and we did support her offer to spy on the others.' Mona, one of the quieter members of the group, spoke out in support.

Tabitha's index finger tapped her lips as she stared directly at Izzy. 'All right, you can stay. But you best have some good information for us to make this all worthwhile.'

As she took her seat, Izzy attempted to hide her relief, but noticed Tabitha look towards Gavin in the corner as if to confirm she had made the right decision, telling her once and for all who was really in charge now.

'As you heard from Ruth, Jo and her friend Alain and I went and visited her today. It was Jo's idea. After last night, she wanted to save Ruth from herself.'

From the corner of her eye she caught Ruth squirming in her seat, and she was not the only one. To her amazement, Tabitha blushed, then seemed to cover it by taking a long drink from her coffee cup.

'Jo also asked me what else we were into, and what the vote to escalate our campaign was about. I said it was for the same—spreading the bacteria in more places— but it didn't matter as the vote failed. She didn't believe me. Even though I had her convinced I wanted to join their coven, she was sceptical about me giving up our secrets that easily.' Izzy sat back in her seat, attempting to appear more relaxed than she felt—would they buy her explanation?

'That sounds like Jo,' Ruth said. 'I am sure she wanted to believe you, but she would not like you so much if she didn't think you had integrity.'

'She is so worried about your involvement in this, Ruth.' Izzy turned slightly to better read the other woman's face. 'She could not believe you would be happy about hurting animals, no matter how much you wanted to save the forest. She was sure she could talk you out of supporting the coven, and I went along to talk with you to prove myself to her.'

Knowing how much the morning's meeting had upset Jo, Izzy took a certain amount of pleasure from Ruth's discomfort at her words. As she looked around at her fellow coven members, few of them would meet her eye. Only Rosalind appeared defiant. It caused her to wonder how many more of them Gavin had threatened, and how far this man would go to enact the final step in his plan.

'So they guessed about our involvement in the dog disease, and Jo confirmed it, but have no actual proof?' Tabitha asked.

Izzy nodded.

'Do they know anything about tomorrow night?' Gavin said from the sidelines.

Izzy hesitated before answering, giving herself away. Gavin sat forward, bringing his face into the light.

'Come on, girl, spit it out,' he commanded, and all pretence of Tabitha running the meeting evaporated.

'Well, it is a full moon, so they suspect we will be doing something, especially after the Jo being here last night.' Izzy had a brainwave. 'Then when Jo asked Ruth to visit the dogs tomorrow with her and Ruth said she had something on, it made Jo even more suspicious. I assured her we had no plans but, once again, I don't think she believed me.'

Gavin's face drew into a snarl. 'We need to make sure they do not interfere.'

Tabitha stepped in between Izzy and Gavin. 'Come now, we need not do anything hasty that might draw the wrong type of attention to us. We were lucky Alice did not involve the police today after that ... um... hasty move of yours, Rosalind.'

Gavin stood and moved beside Alice. 'I agree. Stupid things like that draw unwanted attention to the area just when we need to be most careful.'

Rosalind's lips drew themselves into a snarl. 'I can't believe we are still afraid of that woman and her group. She needs to learn to keep her nose out of other people's business.'

'Is this really to do with the work of our coven, or is this payback for Alice telling her son you were not as devoted to him as you made out—that you were also seeing that drummer in Southampton?' Gladys, who did not often speak at meetings, locked eyes with the younger woman as though daring her to continue.

'It doesn't matter why she did it,' Tabitha said, bringing everyone's attention back to her. 'What matters is that we cannot tolerate anyone else here going off and doing their own thing.'

There were mumbles of agreement, and Rosalind huffed, 'Whatever.'

'Okay, from Izzy's report we can assume Alice and her coven are steps behind us. She is still trying to find out what we are planning to do, and we can take measures to ensure she never does.' Tabitha's shoulders relaxed a little as she spoke.

'Who is the boy? The one who went with you to Ruth's office.' Gavin was not yet ready to give up.

'He's a new boy in town. He and his uncle rented a room at Alice's—Jo's taken him under her wing. I think he has a bit of a crush on her.' Izzy improvised, and she must have been convincing as the others settled back down. Even Tabitha's stance was more relaxed. However, Ruth eyed her sceptically, and Gavin still glowered at her as he returned to his seat.

'Now that's all sorted, let's move to the plans for tomorrow.' Tabitha paused a moment, but no one had anything to add, so she continued. 'We will meet at The Sir Walter Tyrell pub near Lyndhurst at nine thirty—do not, under any circumstance, be late. With Beth in London helping her sister with a new baby we need all hands on deck. Also, our spell must be cast as the moon reaches its zenith to ensure we maximise its effectiveness.'

'Are we going to do the spell in the car park? With

everyone watching? I thought we would stay anonymous.' Mona, often called Mona the Mouse behind her back because people tended to forget she was there, seemed confused—then, she often was.

'No, Mona, we are meeting at the pub. We'll travel to the site Gavin and I have chosen together. This is just a precaution so no one can let slip where we will do the casting.' Tabitha stared pointedly at Izzy.

In response, Izzy tried to appear nonchalant, containing her disappointment. Not knowing the location in advance would make things harder for the others.

'I also want everyone there. We only need five for the casting, but with Izzy being sick the last two times we cannot be too careful.' Turning to Izzy again, Tabitha said, 'I hope you don't feel anything coming on this time.'

'No, I am fine. I'll be there.' In an attempt to appear nonchalant Izzy leaned back in the chair, but unfortunately heat in her cheeks probably gave her discomfort away.

Having scored her point, Tabitha smiled and expanded her gaze to include the entire group. 'Okay, on the table is a list of what you are to bring—take one as you leave. Please make sure you are prepared and that you memorise the spell. Any other questions?'

When no one spoke, she declared the meeting closed, and the coven could not leave the house quickly enough. It was not a good sign that the witches did not linger for their usual after-meeting chit-chat.

As she fumbled in her bag for the keys to her car, Izzy felt a presence behind her. After opening the door, she turned and found Gavin looming, a shadowy figure standing just out of reach of the light spilling from the car. Standing taller, she tried not to let the knot of fear in her stomach show.

'I hope for your sake you turn up tomorrow ... alone.'

'Of course,' she said, slipping behind the wheel. She resisted the urge to lock the doors, not wanting to show the man how much he rattled her. Her hands shook so much it took two attempts to put the key in the ignition, and the tyres screeched as she took off. She swore she caught a glimpse of him laughing in her rear-vision mirror as she exited the driveway.

Studying the spell they needed to do tomorrow night was slow-going with having to type each phrase into the programme, wait for it to translate, then put it into a document to be read later.

As he worked, a thought occurred to him. 'Master Barwick, magic is stronger in our time than in this one. Would it create a stronger spell if we spoke it in our language?'

'When Trouble translates for us, we are speaking as normal in our language—others just hear us differently. You do realise that, don't you?'

Alain considered his master's words a moment before answering, 'Huh? ... I never really thought about it before. Now you have said it, it is so obvious.'

'The lack of magic in this time is to do with the decrease in people's connection with nature. In fact, population growth and overdevelopment means very little land remains in its natural state. Each time a town expands, or a farmer clears a field for planting, humanity distances itself a little more from the earth and some magic is lost. That is why we require five magicians in a pentagram formation to cast a spell that in our time, you or I would be able to do alone.'

'Oh.' Alain went back to his study, all the while thinking he could not wait to go home where things were in a much better balance.

Then he shook his head. Back home, people died of many things able to be cured now. Fewer people starved in the winter here and most people had access to education, meaning they had a better standard of living. And the food was delicious. It was one thing he was going to miss when he returned to his own time.

Oh no, was he really prepared to sell out the earth and the magic it created for creature comforts? Or would he choose his home with all its failings but an abundance of magic? Ah, so maybe that was why the Time Guardians preserved history—because no one person had the right to decide which direction humanity moved in, and that was what they were fighting for.

The Time Wreckers had no right to give Gavin and Tabitha the ability to wipe out a large number of people simply because they believed the world was heading in the wrong direction and needed to be saved.

Staring at the wall, he stilled his mind. These problems were too big for him to deal with. Besides, he still had to face his own ones. When he returned home, would he stay in London and study with Master Barwick or go back to the New Forest and fight for it to be returned to the people?

ALCHEMIST

When they'd left London, the decision was difficult as the urge to return the land to the people William the Conqueror stole it from was strong. Now he had seen how the forest had flourished because of its royal protection, his decision was even more difficult.

Shaking his head, he laughed at himself. He need not decide now. Firstly, Trouble was in no fit state to take them back. And secondly, Trouble had achieved his goal by bringing Alain here—he was now thinking through the consequences of his actions rather than reacting to situations. That dog certainly was smarter than he looked.

Returning to his work, he typed in the next line of the spell instructions and began copying out the translation. Both copies looked the same—he had obviously been working for too long. He shook his head, then blinked a few times. No, it still looked the same. That could only mean one thing.

Dropping the computer on the sofa, he flung the door open and dashed downstairs and into the kitchen. Jo had her back to him and was placing something in front of the fire.

'Trouble?' Alain rushed forward and knelt beside the dog bed. Trouble raised his head, then his eyebrows as he looked at Alain.

'Susan said he made a miraculous recovery—he's almost back to normal. He is still very weak, and a bit dopey from the anaesthetic, but he is clear of bacteria and on the mend.' Jo gently scratched Trouble under an ear.

'Thank goodness. Does he need anything? Water? Food?' Alain stood, ready to do the dog's bidding.

I am just here, you know.

'Trouble, I warned you.' Jo frowned at the dog, then pulled Alain away for an explanation.

'On the way here, I struck a deal with Trouble. He can translate for you when Izzy is not here so long as he stops when you go to bed so he gets some rest. No mind-speak unless it is urgent, because it is even more tiring than translating. We can reassess the situation tomorrow when the anaesthetic is out of his system and he has rested. And yes, he would like water and food. I think Alice mentioned some leftover chicken breasts in the fridge, which should be perfect.'

'Thank you, Jo, and thank Susan the vet for us. I am kind of fond of this mutt.'

Mutt?

'Trouble!' Alain and Jo admonished together as Bebe appeared through the door from the hallway.

'Trouble, you are back.' She dropped down beside the dog and scratched him under his ears. Leaning his head into her hand, Trouble looked up at Alain, and Alain could have sworn Trouble was saying, "See? Someone truly appreciates me."

Bebe stood, walked over to the fridge and opened the door. 'Let me get out the meat Alice left for him. Ah, and here is the lasagne she asked to be heated for dinner.'

As Bebe pottered around the kitchen looking after Trouble and preparing a salad, Jo put the kettle on and busied herself making a pot of tea. With nothing else to do, Alain made himself comfortable beside Trouble and ran his hands though the dog's fur, not sure whether he was comforting the dog or himself.

Closing his eyes, he was enjoying a few minutes of

calm when the sound of thundering footsteps came from upstairs, and he opened his eyes to a kick as Lee stumbled over his outstretched legs. Quickly recovering, and saving his tablet from the hitting floor, the boy exclaimed, 'Dude, do you have to sit right in the doorway?'

'What's the rush?' Bebe asked as she joined Jo at the table.

'Someone's attempted to assassinate David Cameron.'

'What?' Alain said, just as Bebe said, 'Who?'

'Bee, for someone who is very smart, sometimes I wonder where your head is at. David Cameron is the Prime Minister of Britain.'

'Oh.'

'Don't worry, Bebe. I didn't know who he was either. Lee, why would someone try to kill him?' Alain said from his seat on the floor.

'Brexit,' the others spoke in unison, which was kind of scary.

'And Brexit is ...?'

'David Cameron and his government called for a referendum on whether or not the United Kingdom should leave the European Union. It is all anyone is talking about. Both sides feel very strongly about leaving or staying, so the country is getting to vote on it,' Jo explained.

'Why would someone try to kill the Prime Minster though?' Bebe asked. 'His only sin is avoiding dealing with the issue by calling for a referendum.'

Panic and disruption at a critical time in the country's development. This must be Time Wreckers, as an attempt on the Prime Minister's life runs contrary to history. Trouble's head dropped back to his paws as if speaking the two sentences had tired him out.

'Disruption,' Alain said.

'Yes,' Bebe acknowledged. 'His death now would not only cause a lot of unrest, it would also bring other elected representatives to the forefront of the debate, whether they wanted it or not.'

'Dinner is ready,' Jo said as a buzzer sounded moments before the front door opened. 'Ah, that must be Alice. Alain, can you please go and call Barnaby so we can eat? Tomorrow's a big day, so an early night would benefit us all after last night's drama.'

CHAPTER THIRTEEN
PREPARATIONS

Sitting on the drooping bed with her arms leaning on her thighs, Izzy clenched her hands into fists to stop them from shaking. Taking some deep breaths, she attempted to calm her scrambled thoughts.

Standing, she paced around the small bedsit she rented above Gladys' shop. Thanks to the bed, chairs and side table in the room, the space available for her pacing was almost non-existent. A wry smile crossed her face. Thank goodness the bathroom in the shop and the small kitchenette downstairs meant she didn't have to squish anything else into her living space.

When she'd arrived in town and offered to do a few shifts in the shop in return for a place to live, she'd assumed the upstairs quarters were an actual flat. When she saw the room she almost backed out, but then she would have had to find another way to meet Tabitha and be invited to join the coven.

As she circumnavigated her sleeping quarters, her mind searched for solutions to her current problem. She didn't believe the Council would support the extreme measures Gavin and Tabitha had put in motion, but it was difficult to be certain about that in the current leadership vacuum.

During their last contact, her mentor had let slip the number of operations going on in this particular time had stretched their resources to the limit. Even so, it was unusual for someone new to the team to be left to their own devices for so long.

Then again, lack of contact was a good thing. No doubt the Council would stop her working with Jo and the others, not only because of the prohibition on working with Time Guardians, but also because of her's and Jo's past.

Before she left for this mission, her mentor had expressly forbidden her from making contact directly with Jo, especially after the debacle Isolde caused at King Henry's coronation. But she had not been able to stay away. There would be a price to pay for spending time with Jo, let alone assisting the group in their plot to stop the spread of the bacteria Tabitha and Gavin created. Sighing, Izzy lay down on the narrow bed, hands clasped behind her head.

Should she attempt to contact the Council again and risk being pulled out of this time, or should she carry on with her own plans? As the tension of the day got the better of her, she drifted off to sleep.

She slept restlessly that night and woke early. She made her way downstairs, and got herself a cup of coffee and dressed while it cooled. With nothing left to do, she sat at the table and stared at her phone. In her heart of hearts, she knew the decision was already made—she would use any means necessary to stop Tabitha and Gavin.

Picking up the phone, she texted Jo.

Alain stumbled downstairs in the half-dark to the front door. As he started to open it, Jo pushed her way in.

'Why aren't you dressed? We need to get a move on. There's so much to be sorted before this evening.'

Shoving past him, Jo headed for the kitchen. The sounds of the kettle being put on filled the house as he shuffled after her.

'What time is it?' Alain pulled out a chair as he spoke.

'Six thirty already.' Jo took cups out of the cupboard and banged them on the table.

'Jo, the coven are not gathering until tonight.' Alain ran a hand through his hair, making it stand upon end.

'Izzy just texted me. She told me where they are meeting but not the actual place of the ceremony, so we will need to get together and try and figure as best we can where they are going.'

'Still, it is very early.' Alain yawned and stretched.

Jo sunk into a chair, almost as if the air had been punched out of her. 'Once I got the text, I couldn't sleep. I am full of energy and need to be doing something—anything.'

'Couldn't you do that something at your place?' Alain asked, barely able to keep his eyes open.

Trouble stretched himself out and wandered over to

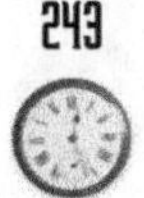

Jo. He nudged her hand with his head and sat, looking expectantly at her.

'My mum is on nights. She'll be home around seven and my moving around would keep her awake.'

'And perhaps you did not want her asking questions because you would tell her everything and then she would offer to help tonight? And you don't want her involved?' Alain suggested.

'She would have to change shifts and … well I'd just feel better if she wasn't involved in any way with Gavin.'

Jo's smile was wan as Trouble reached out a paw and dragged at Jo's hand.

'I think Trouble wants your attention.' Alain smiled.

After absent-mindedly looking down, Jo's face brightened when she saw the dog staring back at her, tail wagging in great sweeps across the floor.

'Wow, you look great this morning. The anaesthetic is mostly out of your system and you look—well, you look almost normal.' She smiled a sheepish smile. 'Of course, you can tell me yourself. How are you? Do you feel better?'

I am much better, and ravenous. Thank you for asking.

She stood and walked to the fridge, and pulled out some food for the dog. As she worked, she told him, 'Given our job tonight, I think it best you stick to resting today. Later on we may need your help, so we do not want to tire you out before then.'

As Jo placed the bowl of food in front of him, Trouble's tail wagged so much it turned full circles and he almost hit himself in the face with it.

The sound of something hitting the floor drifted down from upstairs.

244

ALCHEMIST

'We must have woken the others.' Alain rose to make him and Jo some toast as he spoke.

As he placed their plates on the table, Bebe appeared, followed closely by Alice and Lee. Turning to her nephew, Alice said, 'Can you please go and call Barnaby? We need to plan out our day, and he should be here to help us.'

Muttering curses under his breath, Lee left the warmth to fetch the alchemist. When the two of them arrived, the kitchen was a bustle of activity, and it was some time before anyone spoke.

'Jo, I know you are an early riser, but this is extremely early even for you. What's up?' Alice looked over the rim of her teacup at her assistant.

'Izzy texted me this morning. They are meeting at The Sir Walter Tyrell pub at nine thirty tonight, and they will go on to the actual site from there. We need to check out all the tourist spots within a thirty-minute-or-so drive from the pub to work out where they might be going.'

'Only thirty minutes?' Alice asked.

'Yep. Jo says they need to be in pace ready to cast when the moon reaches its zenith.'

'All the places?' Bebe grimaced. 'There could be hundreds. How are we going to cover all of them?'

'We can narrow it down, I think. We are looking for areas of high tourist activity even in winter, that are still within the forest, and are sheltered from the road,' Lee said.

'We should concentrate on sites with magical significance, so that cuts out a few of the more popular attractions,' Alice said.

While the others discussed how to frame their search, Alain was chuckling to himself.

Jo glared at him. 'I don't see what is so funny.'

'They named a pub after Tyrell, the man who killed King William Rufus. You must find that funny,' Alain said.

'They only think he killed William,' Jo said.

'No, he definitely shot the arrow that killed the king,' Alain told her.

'How do you know ... oh.' Jo's eyes grew wide.

'Yes, how do you know?' Bebe asked.

Deftly changing the subject, Alice explained, 'The Sir Walter Tyrell is quite appropriately named since it is not far from the Rufus Stone.'

'The Rufus Stone?' Alain searched his memory for a stone named after Willian Rufus.

'Yes. Centuries ago, the people erected a stone marker on the spot where William Rufus died,' Alice said.

'How close is the stone to the tavern?' Master Barwick asked, stroking his beard.

'Less than five minutes' drive,' Alice answered.

'Then we need not waste our day looking for the site of tonight's rite. What place in the New Forest will have stronger magic than the spot where an anointed King of England spilled his blood?' Master Barwick delivered his verdict, then carried on eating as if the subject were closed.

'Are you sure? It is almost too obvious a place when Gavin and Tabitha are being so secretive.' Jo twiddled a knife in her hand as she spoke.

They are going to hold the rite at William Rufus' place of death. You and Alain need to convince them of this, Trouble spoke to Barwick.

Why don't you? Alain asked. *Bebe is the only one we haven't told that you are a Time Guardian and can speak.*

Would it not be easier for everyone if we just came clean and told her the truth?

She is not yet ready. It would do her soul more damage than good if she knew. Trouble slumped back down on his bed, head on his paws, his soulful eyes regarding Alain.

'Alice, you know the New Forest. What do you think?' Alain asked.

'There are places in the forest that are great for magical spell casting, depending on the spell. Given that this one is going to spread an evil disease, I believe a place of death would provide the perfect energy. Barnaby is correct; they will likely go to the Rufus Stone site.' She held up her hand to prevent Jo from objecting. 'We could debate this for hours and discuss options like following one of the coven for confirmation, but we need to make a decision quickly so we can prepare. If you have a better idea, now is the time to speak.'

Jo opened her mouth as if to object, then closed it. 'It would be just like Tabitha to tell everyone they would be travelling to another site, then go just a little way down the road. Perhaps you are right.'

'So where will we set up to waylay Ruth?' Lee asked.

'If we look at a map we might get a better idea about that.' Alice stood and opened the bureau draw behind her. Rummaging around, she eventually found a tourist map for the New Forest. Opening it up, she placed it where they all could see. As she spoke, she traced the roads she talked about. 'Here is the stone, and here is the pub.' Alice pointed them out, and Lee reached behind her. After pulling a pen from the drawer, he circled the two points on the map.

'Everyone coming from Burley will take the A31 and turn up this lane to get to the meeting place. In fact, to go to The Sir Walter Tyrell they will pass the Rufus Stone car park.' Alice traced the route on the map with her finger.

'Ruth's youth support group is today,' Jo said. 'That means she'll be coming from Southampton.'

'How do you know that?' Lee capped the pen and placed it down on the table.

'Because she used to attend, nosey.' Bebe punched her brother on the arm.

'She often used to give me a lift home, so I think it is likely she will take the same route she used when dropping me off—the A336 through Netley Marsh, onto to the B3079 and B3078. The road goes on to Frogham, where Ruth lives, so it is the way she is most familiar with.'

'And that helps us how?' Alain's attempts to follow the road numbers on the map confused him, and he really couldn't understand how knowing her route would help them.

Lee smiled. 'Because, due to the lateness of the hour, Ruth will no doubt want to drive a familiar route. She will approach the pub from the other end of the lane off the B3079.' He pointed to the place on the map for emphasis. 'That means Bebe and I can set up our ruse around nine fifteen.'

'Ah, I see. If we wait in the car park by the Rufus Stone, and you and Bebe are at the other end of the road, and we are wrong about the stone being where they are heading, we will be perfectly positioned to find out which way they go from the tavern.' Alain grinned, feeling pleased with himself.

'Yes,' Lee said. 'Although we are almost certain they will be going to Rufus Stone, just in case they aren't, we need to be able to follow them and find out where they end up.'

'This all sounds fine, but what if someone else stops to help us?' Bebe managed to tease out the holes in a plan just as Barabal did, and Alain smiled.

'Good point,' Lee said. 'And it doesn't take long to change a flat tyre anyway.'

'Maybe if you hide the jack somewhere, that might buy you some time,' Jo said.

Bebe nodded. 'Good idea, Jo.'

To Alain's ears it was as though they spoke a foreign language, so he kept silent.

'We will need to make sure our car is well hidden,' Alice said. 'Tabitha and Gavin are already suspicious. We don't want to make them more so by telegraphing our presence, especially as Tabitha knows my car.'

'That reminds me. Gavin and Tabitha are wary of Izzy at the moment, so she is going to keep away from us today,' Jo told them.

'Then that makes it all the more important that we go about our day as if we suspect nothing untoward is happening,' Master Barwick said. 'We don't know who might be watching us, and after yesterday ...'

'You're right, Barnaby, and I am already late for work—must dash.' Alice rose as she spoke.

'Ah, just one more thing, Alice,' Master Barwick said. 'Your husband—have you a time for his arrival today? Does Jo's mother need to be alerted to be on standby?'

'No, no, I shall be fine. There was a flight due in this

evening, which would have had him home about eight, but it was full and he couldn't get a seat. He won't be here until tomorrow morning now.'

'Excellent.' Master Barwick smiled. 'It looks like we are all set then.'

'I will leave you kids the keys on the dresser by the door so you two can drive to the station in Brockenhurst when you go to pick up the rental car,' Alice said. 'The rental place is about five minutes' walk from Southampton Central. Directions are on the dresser. Jo, don't forget your extra shift today to do the internet orders. And you can take me to the station at closing so I can pick up my car.'

'A whole day with nothing to do.' Lee sighed. 'How can we make it look like we are doing something?'

'I have an idea,' Bebe offered almost tentatively. 'We have to pick the car up in Southampton, and I am supposed to be looking for something to do next year ...' Rather than meeting Lee's eyes, Bebe followed her finger tracing the grain on the table.

'Come on, Bee. If you've something on your mind, just spit it out.'

'After we pick up the car, we could head to the main campus of the university and get some information on courses,' Bebe said.

Lee turned to his sister. 'On any one course in particular?'

'Maybe.' Bebe may have been coy with Lee, but she winked at Alain as she stood. 'I'll just go and get my things.'

Lee rose to follow Bebe out. 'Alain, are you coming with us?'

'No, I have something I have to do.'

Once the others had gone, Alain turned to Master

Barwick. 'I have an idea for a Plan B for Ruth. Do you fancy helping me make a sleeping draught?'

Alain waited for the others to leave before rummaging in the kitchen for the things he needed to make his draught. In the fridge, he found some lettuce leaves, and the store cupboard yielded some vinegar, but Alice's pantry would not give up any of the other ingredients he needed.

'What a noise. I am sure they can hear you all the way in Southampton,' Bebe said.

Alain jumped at the sound of her voice and hit his head on the shelf. 'Ouch'

'What on earth are you looking for?'

'Opium, or poppies.'

The girl's eyes widened in surprise, and she took a step back. 'I didn't realise drugs were your thing.'

Alain frowned. 'What? ... No. You think I want opium for me? To get high?' He laughed. 'No, it's for a sleeping tonic.'

Still keeping her distance from him, Bebe moved to the opposite side of the table. 'A sleeping tonic? For whom?'

'Ruth. It's my Plan B.'

'Still, you can't use opium or poppies in it. They're illegal.'

Dwale was so readily available in his own time he had not even considered he might not be able to find all the ingredients. Suddenly, Master Barwick's job of trudging the lanes to find hemlock and henbane did not seem so bad.

'What exactly do you need opium for?' Bebe's tone was still wary.

'The opium makes the person sleepy, detached.'

'Oh. Well, there's codeine in Alice's medicine cabinet. That is a manmade substitute, and it is perfectly legal.'

'Mmm, it might work. Let's take a look.'

Bebe returned a few moments later, a white packet in her hand. Having read the ingredients on the back of the box, Alain decided they might still be able to make the brew. If he used the standard adult dose of the codeine-based drug, it should be enough. Maybe he would put an extra tablet in for good measure.

When Master Barwick returned, they would dry the henbane and hemlock in the oven. Once it was done they would grind it down. All he needed now was the agent to help the body absorb the tonic. As if reading his mind, Bebe said, 'Do you need anything else?'

'Just one more thing—sow's bile.'

'You're kidding, right?' Bebe's laughter was nervous, as if she were afraid he might not be.

'Um ... no. Actually, bile from a gall bladder helps the draught act more quickly. Obviously being from a female animal will make it stronger.'

'Yuck, this is going to be foul. You might need something to disguise the taste. How about star anise? I think I saw some in the cupboard.'

'Are you kidding? That would counteract the bile—that is, if I can find some.'

'What about spearmint?'

Alain considered this for a moment. 'Yes, that might improve the flavour and it would not affect how the tonic works.'

'Good, because I put some packets of dried leaves

away in Alice's shop the other day. Actually, now that I think of it, I also saw some dried ox gall bladder. Could you use that for the bile thing?'

'It might do at a pinch. These ingredients are all a little different to the ones I normally use, so I'm not sure how well they will mix together.'

You should check with Master Barwick when he returns, but if all the ingredients are as you described, then it will work in a fashion. Perhaps I would err on the side of caution with the codeine though—maybe don't use that extra tablet you were planning on.

He had forgotten the dog sleeping in front of the Aga, and started at the sound of his voice.

Thanks.

'Alain, are you listening to me?'

'Huh?'

'I said Lee and I are off in a minute if you want a lift?' Bebe asked.

'Ah, no, I should be fine walking.'

Bundled in his warm jacket, Alain trudged up the road towards the Main Street and Alice's shop for the final ingredient for his tonic. As the icy wind slipped through his jacket, he wished he had taken Bebe up on the offer. Checking for traffic, he crossed the road and entered Alice's store. She was standing behind the counter reading a book when he entered.

'Hi Alain. What can I do for you?'

'Do you stock dried spearmint and perhaps some dried sow or ox gall bladder?'

'Ah, you are making a tonic then,' she said as she emerged from behind the counter and headed towards the back room, then returned with two packets for him.

'Here you are. The gall bladder is powdered, so I would use about half of the normal amount. It does dissolve better this way though.'

Alice popped them in a bag and was handing them over when the door opened, and a cool rush of air entered the shop.

'Good morning, Alice.'

As the customer spoke, Alice dropped the bag on the counter. 'Tabitha.'

'Ah, hello boy. Did you ever find your missing dog?'

Surprised Tabitha recognised him, Alain went on the defensive. He was unsure what she had managed to piece together about his involvement in recent events—like, for instance, did she know it was his dog her friend had almost killed?

He masked his anger as he replied. 'Thank you, yes I did.'

'Not too busy today I see, Alice.'

'Not in the shop, but we are coming up to Christmas and internet sales are crazy. Jo is coming in later to help me with those so I can get them to the post office for last pickup.' Alice's tart tone did not invite further conversation, but Tabitha ignored it.

'Nice to find our local businesses doing well even though foot traffic is generally quiet this time of year.' Tabitha picked up a deck of tarot cards from the counter display and turned them over in her hand. 'I suspect after that you will be able to close early.'

Alice frowned at Tabitha as the woman replaced the cards. 'What a nice thought, but some new stock arrived yesterday and it won't process itself. Just because there are no customers does not mean I have no work to do.'

Tabitha opened her mouth to continue the conversation as the door opened again, and Jo entered bearing two takeaway cups of coffee. On seeing who was in the shop, she stopped. Her eyes widened like a deer caught in the headlights. She looked from Alice to Tabitha.

'Come in, girl. You're letting out all the warm air.'

Alice's fingers tensed into a fist as the other woman ordered about her staff in her shop, but she bit her tongue. 'Can I do something for you, Tabitha? Only I must be getting on with those orders.'

'Well, yes, you can. I'm looking for some purified rock salt. I need rather a lot—around ten packets.'

Alain held his breath, hoping Alice would not refuse to sell her the salt. That would only make Tabitha suspicious, and if Alice didn't sell her the ingredients she had plenty of time to drive to Southampton and buy her supplies before this evening.

'Of course. Let me check my stock. Do you need it for anything in particular?' Alice said as she moved from behind the counter.

Tabitha's laugh grated as she assured Alice she was working on a new spell. 'It's not quite perfect yet, so I want enough on hand to cover any mistakes.' She followed Alice into the back room.

Jo poked her tongue out at Tabitha's back as she walked past, and said under her breath, 'How can Alice be so pleasant to her?' She placed the coffees on the counter. 'Sorry, Alain. I didn't know you were going to be here so I didn't get you One.'

'That's okay. I should be getting back soon anyway.'

'You have plans for today?' Tabitha said, coming around the corner laden with bags of rock salt. 'Anything interesting? Perhaps taking in some of our local sites?' Tabitha's eyebrows raised in query.

'Um, no … not really. It's just …'

'… his uncle will wonder where he is,' Alice finished for him. 'Barnaby is not well today, and Alain just popped in for some ingredients for a tisane.'

'Oh, I am sorry to hear that,' Tabitha said. 'That reminds me, Alice. Have you heard anything about Jenna's Pepe?'

'He died,' Jo said bluntly.

Tabitha's face blanched, and her voice lost some of its false friendliness when she spoke 'Oh, I am sorry to hear that. I thought he was on the road to recovery.'

'He was, then he took a turn for the worse. The poor old boy just had no fight left in him and …' Jo glared at Tabitha.

The other woman pulled herself upright and her face became impassive as she looked down her nose at Alice. 'I will pay for the salt on Visa,' she said as she turned away from Jo and put the bags she carried on the counter.

' … and it's your fault,' Jo finished.

Alain held his breath, waiting for Tabitha to explode. However, she ignored Jo's words, finished paying for her goods, then packed her bag with controlled, deliberate movements. As she reached the door she turned slowly and said, 'You should be very careful flinging around accusations like that Josephine Brown. You could land yourself in very deep trouble—trouble there is no way out of.'

Before anyone could react, she was gone.

CHAPTER FOURTEEN
OPERATION DIVERSION

Lee bent over the tyre and attached the deflator tool he'd purchased from the hardware store in Southampton. The salesman had said the process was quick, but it seemed to him it was taking forever. A noise in the bushes beside the road caused Bebe to turn, redirecting the light from her phone.

'Bebe!'

'What?'

'Pay attention. This is England, not Australia—there's nothing in the bushes that will hurt us. I need the light over this way so I can see what I am doing.'

'Lee, it doesn't need to be completely flat—just flat enough to be unsafe to drive on. You do realise that, don't you?'

'Uh? No, I didn't think of that.' He looked down at the

tyre. Was it deflated enough to be a hazard? 'What do you think?'

Bebe kicked the tyre and her trainer toe sunk into the rubber. 'Yeah, that's enough.'

Lee took the tool off and stood, stretching his back as he did. 'All right, where's the bag?'

Bebe handed it to him and he placed the deflator tool inside. After walking around the back, he opened the boot and removed the jack. The cheap gym bag sagged as he carefully placed it in. Zipping the bag up, he walked to the edge of the road and shoved it behind a tree, covering it in debris from the forest floor so it could not be easily seen.

'How are we going to remember where it is?' Bebe asked.

Lee looked around, found a branch and leaned it against the trunk. Wedging it securely, he turned around, dusting the dirt off his hands.

'Good. Can we get set up now? It is gone quarter past.' Bebe tapped her foot.

'Gosh, you are impatient.'

'Time is ticking and we need to be ready for when Ruth arrives.' Bebe was in bossy mode. Being scared did that to her. Choosing not to respond, Lee eased himself behind the wheel and waited while she walked around the car to the passenger seat. Once they clicked on their seat belts, Lee started the engine and eased the car forwards a little before quickly accelerating and turning the wheel to make it appear he had lost control and ended up half in the shallow ditch and partway across the road, taking care to ensure there was not enough room for another car to drive around them.

'Right, showtime,' Bebe announced.

Opening the door, she took some cases out of the back seat and flung them on the ground behind the car, creating more of an obstruction. In the meantime, Lee opened the boot and proceeded to take out the spare tyre. He had just wrestled it to the ground when car lights swung along the road.

'Here we go—showtime,' he said, mimicking Bebe as he mimed looking for the car jack.

As the lights hit them, Bebe leaned against the rental car and averted her face. Lee shaded his own eyes from the glare and tensed as the person pulled over, hopefully to help.

'Dammit,' Lee said under his breath. 'The driver is a male.'

'Need a hand?' The man asked as he got out of his car. His tone was clipped, and his accent sounded like the ones they heard on BBC news bulletins.

'Um ...' Lee couldn't think what to say. Fortunately, Bebe took over.

'We just picked up this rental today, and I can't believe it—it's got a flat tyre. And what's worse, we can't find the jack to change it. Do you keep it somewhere different over here?'

'I don't believe so. Here, let me look.' The man walked purposefully towards them.

Lee tensed, wary of letting a strange man help them out. But out of the glare of the headlights, the man appeared less threatening. He was medium height and with a slight build. The silver hair cut close to his head placed him perhaps in his fifties. His twinkling blue eyes were friendly enough so Lee relaxed.

'These rental companies charge the earth and they don't care for their vehicles,' the man said as he leaned over to search the boot.

As he rummaged around, another set of car lights turned down the road, lighting his view.

'Yep, you definitely are short one jack. I'll just get mine, and we'll have you on your way in a jiffy.'

The second car stopped and a tall woman with wild curly hair half-stepped out. Lee relaxed a little, she was exactly as Jo described her.

'What's the hold up?' Ruth's impatience gave her voice a sharpness in the evening air.

'Rental car company stiffed these poor kids. Gave them a car with no jack and a flat tyre,' the man answered on their behalf.

'Will it take long to change it, do you think? I am running late for a meeting.'

Lee glanced at his watch. It was nine twenty-five. They only needed to delay Ruth for another fifteen or twenty minutes for their plan to work, but he estimated the job would take way less than that.

'Sorry, I lost control on the narrow road. I don't know whether I punctured it when I spun, or whether I lost control because the tyre was flat.' Lee's apology was not only genuinely polite, but also a way of playing for time. While they talked, tyre-changing activities stopped.

'And I guess you are not used to these narrow lanes.' Ruth's voice was a little more sympathetic. 'Do I detect an Australian accent?'

'Yes, ma'am,' Lee said. 'And you are right. Our roads

at home are nothing like this. If we were there you'd be able to whizz past us no problem.'

The man returned with his jack. 'Is there a wheel brace in the boot? I didn't think to grab mine.'

Lee took his time in the boot, rummaging around, and stood with the tool in his hand. 'At least they left us with something,' he declared.

Lee and their rescuer placed the jack under the car and began the process of changing the tire. Out of the corner of his eye, he watched Bebe move around the front of their vehicle. In the meantime, Ruth returned to her car and turned on the headlights. Initially, Lee thought she was doing it to help them; instead, she walked around the rental car, using the light to work out if there was any way she could get past.

She drove a four-door hatchback, and from where he crouched, he guessed she could just about squeeze by them if she wasn't too worried about scratches to her paintwork from the bushes on the other side of the lane.

His car was now off the ground, and Lee attached the wheel brace, making a show of attempting to loosen the first nut. At the same time, he looked over to Ruth's car. It was well tended to, and he hoped she would not want to risk damaging it.

'Would you like me to give it a go?'

Lee had almost forgotten about the man who was helping him. He leaned over, clearly thinking he could do a better job of removing the wheel.

'No, it is all right. Dad insisted we learn how to do these things ourselves. It is just the initial loosening that is taking time.' He gave a good heave and the first bolt popped loose. 'See? This one's done.'

Three more to go, he thought to himself. He checked his watch; it had only counted down ten minutes. This would be close, and they were relying on Tabitha getting frustrated with Ruth's delay and leave without her if she were late. What if she didn't?

While he worked on the second nut, he listened as Bebe and Ruth discussed the possibility of getting her car by them. He could see Bebe fingering the vial Alain gave her in her pocket as she tried to discourage the woman from attempting the manoeuvre.

'We won't be long. I am sure whoever you are meeting with will understand why you are late,' Bebe said, using her most reassuring tone.

'That's just it—I'm sure they won't understand in the least.' Ruth's voice sounded fearful and her pacing was becoming more agitated. 'I think I will walk.' She turned on her heel and headed back to her car.

'Are you sure that's wise?' Bebe followed her. 'I mean, it is pretty dark. Other cars on the lane may not see you. Do you have a torch or something?'

Ruth got into the driver's seat, backed her car over to the side of the road and turned off the lights. Opening the rear door, she removed a leather backpack and slung it over her shoulder before locking her car.

'I can use the one on my phone.' Taking her phone out of her pocket, she turned the light on. 'Why tonight of all nights?' She switched it off. 'Less than twenty percent left on my battery. It can only be ten or fifteen minutes' walk up the road and the traffic down here is pretty light mid-week. I should be fine.'

'Wait a moment,' Bebe said. 'Lee, I am going to use my phone to help this lady to her meeting. It is the least I can do after we held her up. Can you pick me up after you've changed the tyre?'

'Fine,' Lee said, loosening the third nut. 'We should only be another ten minutes though. Wouldn't it be quicker, and safer, to wait?'

Ruth's phone pinged and her eyes went to the screen. 'No, I don't think that is the safer option at all,' she said as she typed something and started walking.

Bebe grabbed a bottle of water out of the car, drunk some until about a quarter remained, added the contents of Alain's vial of sleeping drought, and jogged off after Ruth.

Knowing it was now up to Bebe, Lee sped up changing the tyre so he could catch her sooner rather than later.

In moments, Bebe caught Ruth up and turned on her phone light so they could see where they were going.

'I am Bebe, by the way. Sorry we put you out. We always thought England was so built up we could never get into any trouble, but here we are, caught out on our first day of touring round.'

'I am Ruth. And I am sorry, but I think you should go back to your brother. It's not far to the pub, and I really don't need the light or the company.'

'But I feel so bad that we put you out. Please let me try and help you.'

'It is one of those things—you need not feel guilty. And I'm sorry, but I can't chit-chat—I have to get to this meeting.' Ruth's tone was dismissive as she stalked ahead.

'I don't want to be nosy, but are you sure you really want to get to where you're going? I mean, I don't know you or anything, but you sound scared.'

Ruth stopped mid-stride and turned to look at Bebe, a frown furrowing her brow. 'Who are you and who told you about us?'

I guess we will find out if all those times I twisted the truth to my own benefit will come in handy now. Bebe smiled her most open smile and calmed the butterflies in her stomach before she spoke. 'As I said, I am Bebe, and I am spending some time in England with my brother before our parents join us here for Christmas. He is off to university in the new year, and I guess this will be the last holiday we spend together for a while.'

Ruth relaxed, seeming to take Bebe at face value. She asked, 'And you? What are you doing next year?'

'I am hoping to start university in Southampton. I took a tour today. My application is completed and ready to post in; I just need to talk it through with my mum and dad when they arrive here. Well, that and I need to find some work for the next six months, and some work experience for my course to ensure I can get entry.'

'Oh, and what course are you looking at doing?'

'A degree in psychology, with a major in youth issues,' Bebe said

'How strange. I work in that field. Maybe our meeting tonight is not such a coincidence. Perhaps the fates brought us together.' Ruth reached into her bag and pulled out a card. 'When you are settled somewhere, give me a call. I may be able to arrange work experience for you.'

Bebe took the offered business card, certain it was a waste of time because once Ruth found out about their delaying tactics she would want nothing to do with Bebe. Then again, perhaps they had delayed Ruth for long enough for the coven to have left without her, and she would be so relieved at having missed the casting she would forgive them.

As the thought entered her head, Ruth's phone rang. She turned away to answer it, but Bebe strained to overhear her side of the conversation.

'As I said, there was a car blocking the road ... I am walking up the lane now ... All right, I will run if that is what you need me to do. I mean, for goodness sake, I am only fifteen minutes—twenty minutes late.'

Ruth removed the phone from her ear, punched at the screen with her index finger, then shoved the phone into the pocket of her bag. Turning back to Bebe, she said, 'Sorry. Look, I have to rush. You should head back to your brother. The people I am meeting may not take kindly to your presence.'

Bebe caught the fear in Ruth's voice and felt sorry for the woman. 'If it is dangerous, please don't go.'

'Thank you for your concern.'

Bebe made a snap decision. Stopping Ruth was more important than her future. Her gut told her the woman did not want to be involved in tonight's activities, and she wanted to keep her out of them if she could. Holding out her water bottle to Ruth, she said, 'Here—you may need this more than me. It is water with a little tonic a friend makes for me. It calms my nerves and gives me focus.'

'Thank you, but I am fine.'

Bebe would not give in that easily; the others were

relying on her. Playing on Ruth's need to keep her safe, she said, 'Please. I will feel better returning to my brother if you drink it. It is only herbs and the like. Look, I'll take a sip to show you it's okay.' She opened the bottle and took a small mouthful before handing it to Ruth.

'If I drink this, you will go back to your bother?' She frowned and looked skeptically at the bottle.

Bebe nodded. Ruth took the bottle from her hand and downed the liquid, her face screwing up at the bitter aftertaste. 'Uh, what was in that? No, don't tell me. I don't want to know. Now go back to your brother. And don't forget to give me a call when you're settled.'

Bebe promised and walked back towards Lee. As she did, the sound of a car engine coming from the other direction filled the night. Looking over her shoulder, she saw red taillights speeding down the road. The car stopped by Ruth and a door opened.

'Get in.'

Ruth clambered into the back and Bebe sighed as the car sped off—there was nothing more she could do.

With time to kill before the meeting, Izzy headed to the pub. She had ordered a bar meal and a pint and taken herself off to a seat by the fire. A few locals had come and gone, and she'd spent a pleasant evening until it was time to leave. With great reluctance, she'd pulled herself out of the chair, paid her bill and walked the couple of blocks to her car.

As she drove past the turn-off to the Rufus Stone,

Izzy glanced into the car park but was unable to see much of the area. Although she knew the others would keep a low profile, she felt nervous not knowing for certain if they were there.

Her eyes drifted to the clock on the dashboard. It glowed 9:35 in the darkness. Her tardiness demonstrated her doubts about attending tonight's meeting, and she still had no idea how she was going to get out of taking part in the casting. She let out a long sigh when, moments later, she pulled into the car park of The Sir Walter Tyrell.

Tabitha accosted her before her door was even closed. The woman grabbed her arm and almost dragged her away from the vehicle. Izzy stumbled, and Tabitha's grip tightened.

'You're late. Can none of you keep proper time?' Tabitha said as Izzy wrenched her arm back and returned to the car to gather the rest of her things.

Another vehicle pulled up beside them. Through her car's passenger window, she caught Beth emerging, and the woman sent her a wry smile before locking her vehicle. It seemed Izzy was not the only one who didn't want to be here. Surreptitiously, she searched for Ruth's car, and heaved a sigh of relief when it wasn't there.

'Come on, the two of you. We're over here.' An exasperated Tabitha herded them towards a seven-seater van. It wasn't her normal car; she must have rented it for the night.

Gladys, Mona and Rosalind waited inside. Izzy glanced around, searching for Gavin. Through the windows of the rental she found a similar-sized vehicle parked next door. The American sat behind the wheel. Six burly men who looked as though they would not take any nonsense filled the rest of the seats.

'Ah, you spotted out security detail.' Tabitha almost purred. 'Gavin thought it would be a good idea for them to come—just in case.'

'Just in case of what?' Izzy's stomach tensed with nerves, and she thought she might throw up.

'Interruptions.'

Goddess, Izzy thought. We did not plan for this. I need to tell the others.

Reaching into her bag, her fingers searched for her mobile phone. As she pulled it out, Tabitha held out her hand.

'Thank you—you just reminded me. I am taking care of all phones until after the casting. We don't want anyone interrupting us at a critical time.'

Izzy handed over her device, and Tabitha popped it into her bag before turning to the others and asking for theirs. Izzy slumped in her seat.

'Agnes, where is Ruth?' Izzy whispered.

'Someone broke down on the road and she can't get past. Tabitha is beside herself.'

They waited, and Izzy glanced at her watch. Almost ten and Ruth was still absent. Maybe this would not go ahead tonight after all.

A car door slammed, and moments later Izzy started as someone thumped the side of the vehicle. Tabitha got out and followed Gavin a few steps away, no doubt so they wouldn't be overheard. Gavin's head dropped down to Tabitha's as they spoke.

The conversation started out cordially, but Tabitha's lips began to tighten as Gavin interspersed his words with sharp gestures. An agitated Tabitha pulled a phone out of her pocket and stabbed her fingers at the screen.

She spoke briskly to whomever she called, and returned the phone to her pocket. Under the car park light's, Tabitha's face turned angry. She exchanged a few words with Gavin and he growled something in return before stalking away. Walking back to the car, Tabitha opened the driver's side door and jumped in.

'Make sure you are belted up,' she ordered. As she turned the key in the ignition her hands were shaking, whether in anger or fear Izzy had no way of knowing. The car started and lurched away at speed towards the car park exit.

As they turned towards the Rufus Stone, Izzy released the breath she had been holding. Obviously Lee and Bebe had managed to waylay Ruth; they would be one person less.

Her victory was short-lived.

Tabitha was not a great driver at the best of times, and driving backwards down an unlit country lane in the dead of night could in no way be described as the best of times.

'Tabitha, what are you doing? You'll get us all killed,' Mona squeaked.

'Ruth is behind us, our destination is in front, and I can't turn this blasted car around on this narrow lane. Now shut up and let me concentrate.'

Along with her companions, Izzy grabbed whatever she was able to and held on for dear life. It was a good thing they did because moments later, Tabitha brought the car to an abrupt stop, almost giving everyone whiplash.

'Open the door.' This was no polite request; it was a command.

Izzy leaned over the seat and slid the door open, letting a rush of cold air into the warm interior as she did. A startled Ruth peered inside the vehicle, giving each of them a onceover as if trying to work out who they were.

'Get in,' Tabitha spat at the woman. 'Don't make us any later than we are.'

'Don't worry. We all arrived a little tardy tonight,' Izzy whispered as she helped the rather dazed woman into the car.

As they drove off, Ruth's eyes glazed over and she lay down on the seat. Within moments she was quietly snoring.

CHAPTER FIFTEEN
THE SPELL IS CAST

Alain and the others ducked down low as headlights swept the car park at the Rufus Stone. Popping his head above the seat in front, he watched as the vehicle pulled up under one of the security lights. The driver got out and checked the surrounding area.

'Looks as though we guessed correctly; they are going to use the Rufus Stone's power to augment their spell,' Master Barwick said.

'Phew. I wasn't looking forward to following them all over the New Forest,' Alice said.

'It is as we thought. Gavin is here directing things,' Alain informed the others. 'No, wait a minute.'

He peered through the windscreen into the darkness. The other passengers appeared more heavyset than a group of women would be. Alain sucked in a breath as the doors opened, and a group of large, burly men spilled out.

'Oh no. We didn't plan for that,' he said.

Trouble placed his paws on the front seat beside him to get a better look at the group taking position around the perimeter of the park.

Looks like he has brought some hired muscle along, the dog said.

As the men spread out with almost military precision, Alan silently congratulated Alice on having the forethought to hide the car in the trees. After parking, they had placed a couple of loose branches over the windshield just to be sure the car couldn't be seen from the car park.

'What do we do now?' Alice asked. 'We cannot take them on as well as the coven, but nor can we let the ceremony go ahead.'

'The coven is not here yet,' Master Barwick said. 'Perhaps we should just wait and see what happens before we decide our next move.'

As he spoke, another car pulled into the almost deserted car park, coming to a stop beside the first vehicle. Moments later, the coven bundled out and huddled in a nervous group, glancing wearily at their protectors.

'I spoke too soon,' Master Barwick said.

'Oh no,' Alice wailed. 'Ruth is with them. Their full coven is here.'

'Wait a moment. She is leaning heavily on Izzy and is none too steady on her feet. Perhaps she ingested some of my dwale,' Alain said. 'It will be a while before she is able to help them. That gives us a little time to plan.'

Tabitha handed out baskets to the other witches. Ruth dropped hers, and in her attempt to pick it up almost fell face first on the ground. Her lips pursed and her brow drawn into a frown, Tabitha grabbed and wrapped Ruth's hand's around the handle before letting go.

'We use similar baskets to carry our mobile altars,' Alice said. 'It looks as though the others will cast the spell while she supervises.'

'But Izzy can't,' Alain said. 'She is not allowed to act directly.'

'She will find a way around it.' Master Barwick's confidence in Izzy being able to do what she needed to calmed Alain.

As the coven organised themselves, the hired muscle continued moving around checking their surroundings. One stopped almost in front of the car, his back to them. Alain was sure he saw a bulge in the men's jackets as he passed in front of them.

'I am not sure we can do this,' he said to the others. 'I think they may be carrying weapons of some sort—this has all gotten so much more dangerous.'

'I believe at least one of them is carrying a gun—a handheld weapon that fires projectiles.' Alice added and looked at Alain and Master Barwick. 'Perhaps we should call in the police,' Alice said. 'We can't tell them the truth about what is going on, but if we report strange men in the area almost certainly carrying weapons, I'm sure they'll come.'

That is a very good option, Trouble said.

'And that will meet our objective here?' Master Barwick said.

No, I did not say that. In fact, we are at one of those points in time where the future is murky. I cannot make out the outcome of any particular course of action.

'I think we should stick with our original plan. If it fails we can always call the police as a last resort.' Until that moment, Jo had been silent. 'Our best bet is still to get to the stone before them and protect the area, right?'

'You are correct. And they are almost ready to go, so we'd best move.' Alain made a grab for the door handle.

'Wait,' Alice said before he could open it. 'When we open the doors, the central light will come on. We aren't camouflaged enough to hide that.'

Reaching up above them, she fiddled with something. Moments later, she held up a bulb. 'Now we should be okay. Open the doors away from the car park. Do not bother with shutting them; just push them to.'

'You are quite good at this.' Jo voiced her admiration.

'The product of a misspent youth.' Alice chuckled.

Everyone remain alert, Trouble warned them. *Bebe and Lee haven't made it here yet, and I don't see them being able to sneak through that ring of guards. That means we have no lookouts.*

'All right? Let's do this.' Jo reached for her door handle and opened it as quietly as she could. Still, the small snick it made echoed through the night and they held a collective breath as the closest guard peered around, as if searching for the source of the sound. A few seconds later, his stance relaxed, and so did they.

Jo slipped through the opening, followed by Trouble. Alain reached into the seat well and passed out five bags before sliding over the back seat and joining her outside. Master Barwick and Alice appeared to be whispering. Alice reached down, and Master Barwick disappeared from sight. Next thing, Alain saw his master's butt raised in the air as he crawled up the passenger seat and over to the back of the car.

After the alchemist's awkward exit, Alice reached over and restored his seat before disappearing from view herself. Her departure from the car was even more awkward than his master's, and Alain wondered if it was less noisy than opening a second door. However, frequent checks of the guards told him the babbling voices of the women in the car park more than drowned out any noises they made.

Just as he thought they had managed their escape from the car undetected, Alice lost her footing, pushing the door open and rolling onto the ground.

The guard's head swivelled, and he reached under his jacket. They all froze, unsure whether to run or hide. Before they could decide, lights illuminated the car park, and the guard looked towards the entrance.

The car stopped at the beginning of the driveway, then obviously thought better of continuing, and backed away.

Another guard ambled over and sniggered, 'Bet they thought this was a good place to make out or smoke up. We ruined their plans by being here.' They both laughed as the original guard moved back towards the cars.

They waited until the new guard had taken a wide-legged stance, back towards them, before moving as quietly as they were able through the woods. Even so, the debris of the forest floor crunched beneath their feet and Alain's heart leapt into his mouth at the noise.

Don't worry. I cast a spell to mute the sound, Trouble sent.

And you couldn't have used that before now? Alain

asked in frustration, his ankle twinging as he nearly missed a step.

I cannot influence man-made objects—only nature. Trouble sent, his tone suggesting Alain should have known this fact.

'All right, ladies, let's get moving.' Tabitha's voice rang out in the night.

Oh no, their route is shorter than ours—they will beat us to the spell site, Trouble sent.

'What shall we …?' The sound of another car pulling into the car park muffled Jo's words.

A door opened and a new voice said, 'Why hello, Tabitha. I didn't expect to find you here.'

'Donald?' Alice gripped Master Barwick's arm, halting his progress. 'What is he doing here?'

I don't know, but he has provided a diversion. Come on, let's go, Trouble sent.

'But …'

Jo took Alice's arm. 'At the moment, they haven't discovered our presence. We'll only make it worse if we go to his rescue. Let's hurry and do this, then we can make sure Donald is okay.'

Jo led Alice forward, and the older women moved with them, but kept glancing back over her shoulder long after they couldn't hear the conversation in the car park. She relaxed a little when she heard the sound of a car engine, and Alain hoped that it signalled Donald's departure.

In less than ten minutes of creeping through the forest they found the Rufus Stone. Alain surveyed the clearing as Jo assessed the best places for them to position themselves to form the pentagram needed to increase the spell's intensity. They had to be able to see each other so they could cast the spell in concert, but remain hidden from the coven.

'Do not forget, the spell must be said in Latin for depth, followed by English to tether it to the here and now,' Alain said as he handed out the pre-made altars along with copies of the words to speak. 'Jo, don't forget to flash us with your phone light when we are to begin.'

'Yes,' the girl said. 'All right, Trouble, you stay here by the roadway and save your energy for the spell. Alain will be directly across from you in those bushes over there. Master Barwick, as the strongest of us, I will put you at the point of the pentagram by that tree. Alice, you and I will be the two lower points, behind those two bushes.'

Having been assigned their positions, they dispersed to set up their altars. Placing the candle in the middle, Alain waited for Jo to give the first signal before lighting it, moving his body into position between the clearing and the flame. Moments later he caught sight of the second flash—time to recite the spell in Latin.

Igne ignis effulgens
Ego autem in eaque lucerna lumen est
Sequelae flammae gramina pastus,
incultisque rubens pendebit

Alain lit a bunch of dried hawthorn in the candle's flame, and recited the last line of the spell.

Stringesque tunicam ex terra ignis praesidio

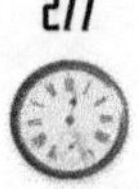

As he readied himself for the signal to begin the English version, the sound of gravel crunching disturbed the night. He could just make out figures entering the park surrounding the sacred stone. Torchlight scanned the area, before falling on the lone dog standing by the edge of the road.

'Are we to be forever plagued by dogs?' He heard Gavin exclaim as he handed the torch to Tabitha.

Strangely, Trouble moved forward to meet him, drawing the coven's attention to him and away from his altar. The eco-terrorist reached down to grab hold of his collar with one hand while he reached for his belt with the other. Alain tensed, preparing to go and help his friend should Gavin do him any further harm.

No, we must finish the spell in English, otherwise it will not be tied to the present, the dog sent.

There are only four of us left; it will not be strong enough, said Master Barwick.

We can only do what we can. I will count us in because a light will be too obvious now. Ready? Three, two, one.

As Gavin led Trouble to the tree by the stone, Tabitha began directing the witches into position. One of the guards escorted each of the woman to their assigned area.

Alain turned his full attention to the spell as he needed to finish before the other coven came too close. Because he had to speak in modern English he had written the words out phonetically to ensure he didn't make any mistakes.

Fire hot, fire bright,
I cast this spell to the candle's light
Threads of flame, fed on briar,
Weave a protection cloak made of earth's fire

As he stopped to burn the hawthorn, he heard the crunch of leaves nearby. If he burned the twig anyone close by would smell it, but if he did not the spell would not be complete. He had no option—he set the hawthorn in the correct place, finished the incantation and snuffed the candle. He took a moment to send his own silent prayer to the goddess. *Goddess, please look favourably on our work and strengthen the casting.*

Opening his eyes, he waited for a sign that he'd been spotted, but nothing happened. As his eyes adjusted, he caught sight of a member of the coven about five paces to the right of him setting up her altar. She seemed oblivious to everything else around her. Luckily for Alain, the man who guarded her directed his attention towards Gavin and Tabitha.

Alain swivelled his head for a better view of the clearing around the Rufus Stone. Gavin stood by the marker, the dog beside him held in place by the make-shift lead the eco-terrorist had fashioned from his belt.

On the other side of the stone stood one of the muscle men, and beside him, Tabitha directed her witches. Across from him he caught sight of Izzy setting up her altar near Trouble's workings. In the darkness, he could not make out the others from the coven, nor those from his own group.

As he waited, his legs began to cramp. Taking a deep breath, he tried to relax. How long would it be before they finished? He hoped it was not long, because he his legs were beginning to cramp.

'Are we ready?' Gavin asked, clearly no longer worried about keeping up the pretence that Tabitha was in charge.

'All right, begin your cast.'

As the woman in front of him began incanting her spell Alain's stomach sank. Without a fifth practitioner, their own casting would not be likely to counter the coven's spell. He stifled a groan as his muscle cramped again, brushing a branch with his arm, and the guard turned towards the noise. As he tensed to run, the air around him changed. It became thick and heavy, like a blanket had fallen over the area.

The witch in front of him stopped mid-cast. The guard turned and nudged her with his gun. 'Keep going.' The poor women trembled and almost dropped the vial she held. Taking a deep breath, she carried on.

After finishing her spell, she stood and looked around as if waiting for the others to complete their tasks. Soon, all five witches stood and looked towards Gavin.

'Shall I release it now?' He turned to Tabitha, holding a vial aloft.

Tabitha stepped from the shadows. 'There is no point; something is blocking us. Our spell has fizzled like a flame with no air.'

'Did you all cast?' Gavin glared at the witches, and they in turn would not meet his gaze.

'Check the altars,' he ordered his men.

'Over here. This one has two altars.' A guard held Izzy by the arm and hauled her into the centre of the clearing.

'Traitor,' Tabitha spat at the girl.

Izzy raised her head, as if daring Tabitha to do her worst.

Two altars? Had Izzy picked up Trouble's spell and finished the cast using his altar? Alain smiled. By casting both spells she had kept her actions in balance, and by doing theirs first she'd ensured their success rather than Tabitha's.

She had helped them and he could not let anything happen to her. Preparing himself to leap to her defence, he made to move as a hand clamped down on his arm.

'Look what we have here.' Teeth gleamed in the dark as the guard grinned menacingly, pulling Alain to his feet.

Within seconds, he found himself stumbling as the man pushed him into the centre of the clearing. Everyone waited while the guards searched the entire area. Soon Jo joined Alain, along with Master Barwick and Alice. Rather than cowering in the ring of armed guards, Alice stepped forward and confronted her nemesis.

'You are too late. Your evil spell will not work here now. We have seen to that,' she said.

Tabitha raised her arm and slapped Alice hard enough for the woman's head to snap back. 'How dare you,' she snarled. 'Your actions have doomed the forest—doomed it to years of overdevelopment.' Turning to Gavin, she nodded.

He stepped forward, holding the vial aloft. 'The spell might not work, but the bacteria will still spread without it. While saving others you have condemned yourselves to meet their fate.'

'You can infect us, and we may well die, but your bacteria will not infect others who come here,' Izzy boasted.

Gavin laughed. 'Your antics have merely delayed the inevitable. Tabitha and I will make more. There is another full moon in a month, but by then you will all be gone.'

Izzy opened her mouth, but no words came out. A guard shuffled uneasily beside Alain, and he turned to survey the faces of the men who held them captive. The surprise he found on them gave him an inkling of a plan.

'Are you so sure you are ready to die for your cause?' He spoke to the man behind him. 'Because if he releases that bacteria here, it will not only be us who become infected.'

The guard shoved him, but as he did he glanced at the man next to him, and then looked to his leader, the man standing beside Gavin.

Perhaps he sensed the change in his men's moods, or perhaps he'd worked out the danger himself. Whatever his motivation, the guard leader moved to confront the ecoterrorist. 'This is not what we agreed. We were to take the witches back to the car before you unleashed the bacteria.'

Confusion clouded Gavin's face, only to be replaced by a look of such cunning it sent a shiver down Gavin's spine.

'You don't think Tabitha and I would risk our own lives to set this bacteria loose, do you?'

The guard's face showed his uncertainty.

'We made an antidote which we will make available to you and your men after we leave here,' Gavin said.

'But you promised we would make the ultimate ...' one of the witches started.

'Shut up, Rosalind!' Gavin glared at her and she took a step back, white-faced, fear in her eyes.

'You can't do this.' Ruth stepped forward to stand beside Jo. 'You could bully me into setting a bacteria free that would attack random people, but I cannot stand by and watch you infect my friends. That is cold-blooded murder.'

Gavin laughed a hollow laugh. 'It always was, my dear.

You were just one step back from it.'

'I won't let you do this—not to us, or the forest.' Ruth stood taller as she uttered the words.

'You think you can stop me?' Gavin motioned to one of the guards, who grabbed hold of Ruth's arm.

'Let go of me.' Ruth jerked her arm out of his grasp and kicked him in the shin. The slap he delivered rang loud through the cold air. Ruth raised her hand to retaliate, but the guard would not be beaten twice. He took hold of Ruth's arm and, in a single movement, pulled it up behind her back. He marched her over to join the other captives. Ruth spat at him as he returned to his position.

'Anyone else want to join her?' No one moved, so Gavin said, 'All right, scram, the lot of you, unless you want to be infected too.'

Alain expected a flurry of activity as the other witches rushed to leave the clearing, but no one moved. Then, as if on some silent signal, all but one of them walked forward and stood beside Ruth. Rosalind alone remained.

Gavin sneered. 'All the more to act as a lesson to those who wish to harm nature. Rosalind, come here.'

Without missing a beat, the woman joined him under the tree, moving as if in a dream.

'Tabitha, if I open this vial can you call a breeze to disperse it over everyone?'

Tabitha nodded. 'I will call the wind. You wait for the count of three before releasing the contents.'

She began chanting, and a light breeze brush against Alain's cheeks. The longer Tabitha chanted, the stronger the breeze became. Gavin held his arm out in front, his thumb ready to pop the stopper of the vial. Tabitha stopped chanting.

'One ...'

Out of the corner of his eye Alain caught a movement.

'... Two ...'

Trouble jumped and clamped his jaw around Gavin's wrist. The man's arm jerked involuntarily, and the bottle slipped from his hand, stopping in mid-air. It was as if everyone had frozen with it until Trouble let go and dropped to the ground, landing on all four paws. Then, in a single movement, he leapt again, picked the bottle out of the air and took off into the woods.

No one moved, then everything seemed to happen at once.

Gavin swung around, yelling, 'Someone grab that mutt.'

Trying to move out of his way, Rosalind tripped and fell to the ground.

The guards pulled out their weapons and aimed them at the captives.

Everyone around Alain dropped to the ground to avoid being shot.

Alain found himself the only one standing in the circle of guards as he tried to find out what was happening with Trouble.

'Ah, the dog owner. In spite of all evidence to the contrary, I assume the animal has had some training. Make him bring the vial back,' Gavin commanded.

Alain shook his head.

'You have five seconds. If that mutt does not bring back my property, Andy, there, will shoot you.'

ALCHEMIST

While Alain was sure he did not want to die here in this faraway place, he was equally sure he couldn't save his own life at the cost of perhaps millions of others.

'Five ...'

Goodbye, Barabal. I hope you find someone else to love you as much as I do.

'Four ...'

Please take care of Barabal, Master Barwick. She can get herself into quite a bit of trouble and needs someone to keep an eye on her.

'Three ...'

It is the least I can do, young friend. I will make sure she wants for nothing.

'Two ...'

Alain closed his eyes and hoped being shot did not hurt too much, and that his death would be swift. He tensed for the final count ... but there was nothing. The tension around him eased and he opened his eyes one at a time and looked around.

Under the tree sat an obedient Trouble staring up at Gavin—his mouth empty. Alain searched for evidence of the bottle containing the bacteria, but could not see it.

'Where is my bottle, dog? Where did you put it?' Gavin's tone was friendly. Trouble stayed where he was—statue still. 'Where is it?' Gavin shouted, raising his arm to strike the animal.

'Here.'

The bushes rustled and the clearing illuminated as someone turned on strong lamps around the edges of it. A large number of soldiers in camouflage gear moved in from all sides, guns pointed at the group beside the Rufus Stone.

Once Alain's eyes adjusted, he turned his attention back to the scene under the tree, and found the balance had changed.

'Put down your weapons,' the man standing behind Gavin and Tabitha commanded. When no one moved, he said, 'Don't run. You are surrounded. And if you did by chance manage to get away, at this precise moment the authorities are processing images we sent and should have no trouble identifying you all within the hour. Best you surrender now rather than face further charges.'

As the guards laid down their weapons and raised their hands, Rosalind scrambled to her feet and made a run for it. At the edge of the clearing, one of the soldiers tackled her to the ground and handcuffed her before leading her back to the stone.

'It was all their idea,' she whined. 'They talked me into going along with their plan.'

'Oh, for goodness sake, shut up, you stupid girl,' Tabitha said.

'Do you have any idea what you are doing? Don't you want this forest safe for all humanity to enjoy? By stopping us you just signed its death warrant.' Gavin spoke passionately, like someone rallying support.

'An interesting defence,' Master Barwick said. 'He would kill humanity to save a forest for them.'

Slowly, the guards lowered themselves to kneel on the ground. Soldiers came forward, removed their guns and handcuffed their arms behind their backs before leading them away.

'I am Agent Morrison,' the man under the tree said as a group of soldiers led the guards away. 'You can all stand now.'

As they did, Alain caught a glimpse of Lee, Bebe and another man in a Macintosh coat joining the agents under the tree.

'All right, you two. Tell me which of these people are yours,' Agent Morrison said.

Not waiting for anyone to speak, Alice ran towards Lee and Bebe, and the remaining soldiers immediately raised their weapons.

Agent Morrison held up his hand, then looked to the twins, but before they could speak the man in the coat pushed past him, moving to meet Alice.

'Oh Alice, what mayhem have you caused now?' Although his words were admonishing, the tone was one of fondness. The man wrapped his arms around her, and Alice sunk in to his embrace.

A stern-faced soldier led Alain and Lee, along with Jo, Bebe and Trouble, into a side room of The Sir Walter Tyrell pub. He waited until they'd all found a seat before taking up a position by the door. It appeared they wouldn't be leaving anytime soon, so Alain slouched in the comfortable chair by the crackling fire and took a mug of steaming chocolate from the tray carried in by the pub's owner.

In the next room, he could hear Alice and Master Barwick talking to the men in charge, and occasionally the voice of Alice's husband could also be heard. Headlights illuminated the room as yet another military vehicle departed the car park.

'That looks like Tabitha's coven's military escort,' Alain said, peering through the window.

'Where are they taking them? Do you have any idea?' Jo asked.

'They are based in Southampton, so I guess that's where they will go,' Lee said.

'I hope Izzy is okay.' Jo wrung her hands, and added, 'And I hope they throw Gavin and Tabitha in the deepest, darkest cell.'

Alain shuddered, remembering the dungeon he'd rescued Jo's alter ego from a week or so ago. He would not send his worst enemy anywhere like that

They will spend the next few years behind bars, Trouble said from his place in front of the fire. He stretched and snuggled into the rug before continuing. *They will all be charged with malicious intent and terrorist activities for planning to release the bacteria. In this time, witchcraft is something from children's stories, so no one believes they manipulated Alabama Rot to become a deadly weapon. Although scientists will work on the contents of the vial, none will be able to replicate it.*

Thank goodness, Alain said. *What about the coven?*

The others will get a year's probation once Gavin's guard friends admit to threatening most of them.

The others continued their conversation as he and Trouble spoke, and Alain realised the Guardian's words were meant for his ears only. He returned to the conversation in time to hear Jo ask, 'So, want to tell us how we got here?'

'Of course,' Lee answered, a grin on his face. 'It all turned out to be a bit strange.'

'Stop mucking around or I will tell them,' Bebe said.

Lee shrugged, so she continued, 'When we drove past the car park we saw the guards. We pulled in to find out what was going on and caught sight of their guns. Lee and I panicked and drove off.'

'Which turned out to be inspired in the end,' Lee added, earning a glare from his sister. 'Once we'd doubled back to pick up the jack and things, we decided to stop at the pub and plan our next moves.'

'Anyway, in the end we thought it best to call the police. Lee rang and reported some suspicious activity in the car park by the Rufus Stone. He made sure to mention he thought he saw guns, as we didn't want anyone getting hurt, and I seem to remember the police here don't carry weapons,' Bebe told them.

'And the operator forwarded that call to me.'

The group turned as one to find the agent-in-charge from the clearing leaning against the doorframe, a steaming mug in his hand. He joined them by the fire, perching on the window ledge.

'Your friends here held me up earlier in the evening with their flat tyre stunt. My current intel led me to believe Gavin was up to something at The Sir Walter Tyrell. Helping Bebe and Lee fix their flat tyre meant I missed him. Like them, I stopped here to regroup. I was just enjoying a coffee when I received their call.'

'You were watching Gavin? Did you know what he was up to?' Jo asked.

'No. We picked up his trail when he entered the country. We knew he'd been in contact with some of his old friends and believed he was putting together a team.'

'But you didn't know exactly what for?' Jo was sceptical.

'No, we didn't. Bebe and Lee told me a fantastical story this evening, which I only half-believed until I watched what went on in the forest tonight. In fact, I am still getting my head around it. Fortunately, they mentioned armed men in the car park, which allowed me to call in my team and the rest, as they say, is history.'

'See? I told you—inspired. I am just not sure by what,' Lee said, grinning.

'Thank the goddess,' Alain murmured.

'I am not sure how much of what I witnessed tonight will be believed by those higher up, and even less will be able to be used to prosecute the accused. But with that vial of bacteria there is enough evidence to put the two of them away for a very long time.'

'Wait until you uncover what is at Tabitha's house,' Bebe said, but was silenced by Lee's punch to her arm as the agent turned a questioning gaze her way.

'What about my friend Izzy, and the other coven members?' Jo deflected the man's attention with her question.

'That will depend entirely on their level of involvement,' Agent Morrison said. 'None of them will get away scot-free, I fear.'

'Oh.' Jo's shoulder's slumped.

'What about us?' Alain asked.

'For you, home to bed for now. Donald will drive you all. Alice and Barnaby will give us the rest of the story tonight, but your statements can wait a few days. Please don't be going anywhere until we have spoken with you again.'

Alain's heart sank. Once Tabitha and Gavin had been taken into custody, and they were relaxing at the pub, his reason for being in 2017 was gone. His thoughts automatically turned to home. He would be sad to leave his new friends, but he couldn't wait to return to Stanislaus and Barabal, and his boring, uncomplicated life.

Trouble, can't we just leave?

Can you imagine what strife the others would be in if we just disappeared off the face of the earth? Trouble asked. *Besides, before we go I require clearance from the Council that our work here is done.*

'Are you guys ready to head home?'

Donald, Alice's husband, stood in the doorway, jiggling car keys in his hand.

'Yes,' Alain said wearily, along with the others. So much it hurts, he added to himself.

CHAPTER SIXTEEN
GOODBYES

'What did you think you were doing?'

Isolde was released with the other coven witches, much to her surprise. Especially given the fact it was she who'd directed Tabitha's attention to the spell to increase the bacteria's growth in the first place.

Tabitha had kept her role in proceedings secret. She had assured the authorities she and Gavin alone had developed the Alabama Rot bacteria—both the animal and human forms. She admitted to coercing the coven into helping them spread it, but denied any of them had a hand in developing it.

That, combined with the fact they had been threatened with violence should they not turn up and cast their spells, led the crown prosecution to charge them with minor offences, giving them all a year's probation.

ALCHEMIST

She had not been as surprised by her summons back home to face charges for her actions.

As beings without bodies, the Council could choose any form and any location to project when she answered the charges laid against her. It told her much that they chose a courtroom and appeared as three judges.

'I repeat, what did you think you were doing?

Holding her head high, Isolde said, 'Saving humanity, just as you tasked me.'

'Your mission was to assist Tabitha in defending the New Forest.' The judges spoke as one, which threw her off for a moment.

'Surely the idea behind saving the forest was to ultimately save the planet and humanity,' Isolde said.

'That is not your call to make. As a second-level operative your role is to follow orders, not bend policy to your will.' The middle judge peered at her from the raised dais, his finger wagging as if telling off a naughty child.

Tilting her chin defiantly, Isolde stared him down. 'Are we truly in the business of correcting the world at any cost? I saved millions of lives by stopping Tabitha.'

'You have no idea whether or not you saved anyone.' The head judge told her.

'Tabitha intended to release a new bacteria into the world to kill as many people as possible. Is there any real justification for that—ever?'

The three judges looked down at her in silence, each of them almost statue still. Micro movements of their faces were the only evidence they mind-spoke, discussing her case in front of her. None of their expressions gave anything away.

Minutes ticked by, and she tried not to shuffle from foot to foot as she waited. She did not spend the time idly though. Her own mind was busy as she considered her options should they tell her they countenanced the sacrifice of so many to their cause. Her stomach sank as she realised she would be forced to leave. Mass killings was not what she had signed up for.

'We are sympathetic to your plight.' The female judge on her left finally broke the silence. 'We could not foresee the one we chose to manipulate would fall under another's influence, one that would lead her to extremeness and endanger so many lives.'

'How did you miss such a critical fact?' Isolde pushed. If the Council allowed this detail to slip through the cracks, would they miss more important ones?

Another discussion took place before the other female judge, the one to her right, answered, 'It is not your place to question us.'

'No, we placed her in a precarious position; she has a right to know.' The comment came from the head of the Council sitting in the middle. 'Our major offensive took more resources than we anticipated, meaning we were unable to offer support to some of the satellite activities intended to stretch the Time Guardians.'

The judge on the right continued, 'The assassination of a prime minster, and the installation of a replacement who would make some real inroads on climate change was critical to our plans, all our attention was directed to that mission. By the time we got round to you we were too late to change anything—your plan was already set in motion.'

'Still, you didn't send help then either? I requested backup more than once.' Isolde attempted to keep the anger out of her voice, but the frowns on the judges' faces told her she had not succeeded.

'You only asked when it was too late for us to alter your course of action,' the head judge said. 'I could turn this around and ask why did you not call us in sooner?'

Isolde paused before answering. There was only one reason—Jo. She could not bear the way Jo looked at her when she knew of her involvement in Tabitha's plans. But the Council would not accept that as an excuse, so she said nothing.

The left-hand judge smiled at her sympathetically. 'If only you'd called us in earlier, we may have found a way to help you without having to work with Time Guardians.'

'And that is why our decision is that you should lose your current independent operating status,' the right-hand woman seemed pleased to be able to pass on this verdict.

The chief judge frowned at his co-judge, and she blushed. He turned his gaze back to Isolde. 'Our verdict is that you acted with the best intentions using your current level of abilities and training. We take responsibility for our failures in planning, but you must also take responsibility for allowing emotions to cloud your judgement. Because of this, you will be accompanied on your next assignment by a senior operative who will assess your work in the field.'

Isolde knew she should ask if she was being demoted, but she wasn't sure she cared. Her commitment to the cause was waning. These last weeks had shown her she and Jo could not be together in any life so long as they fought on different sides in the fight to improve the world.

She thought back to the time she'd first met Jo, before she knew her to be Jo or John. If she had stayed around, they might have had a chance at happiness then.

The judges all leaned forward in their seats as if expecting something. Of course, they wanted her to respond. She shook her head to clear her thoughts, then made a quick decision. For the moment she had no idea where her future lay, so she needed to buy some time while she considered her options.

'I thank you for your leniency.' She heard herself say as she sought the words she needed for her next move. 'Perhaps I need a break from assignments to reassess where I am in my life.'

Isolde took a deep breath before continuing. 'I heard it is possible to be returned to our original body at a point in time before we chose to join the World Fixers. We are given the option of reaffirming our commitment and returning here, or living our original lives until their natural end. Is that true?'

She raised her eyes to meet those of the main judge and found him shaking his head. 'Yes it is. I can see you are in distress and would be a prime candidate for such a journey under normal circumstances. However, there are so many critical missions in play at the moment we cannot afford to let you go. Perhaps after you complete your next assignment we might review that decision.'

'But if I am to accompany another agent, could you not perhaps send them alone?' Isolde pled her case.

Again the judges conferred before responding.

'In theory, yes. But our seers calculate minimal chances of success if you are not part of the team. Perhaps if I explain the task you will understand why your presence is critical.'

Isolde shrugged. 'All right.'

'The Time Guardians are sending Sigma to a particular event to ensure the flow of time proceeds. It is a critical time in human development because we cannot foresee any future beyond this event.'

'What do you want me to do about that?' Isolde asked, not sure she could face fighting against the Time Guardian she had just worked with; she respected him too much.

'Actually, we do not want you to do anything, as such,' the woman on the left said. 'We want the two of you to accompany the Guardian Sigma to ensure his actions benefit both the human race and the Earth.'

'How will I know whether or not his actions are within our guidelines if you can't direct me towards an end goal?' Isolde said. She had never heard of a mission without a specific action required to improve the future. Then again, a joint team was something completely new as well.

'We hope that, as your mission progresses, the future will become clearer, and we will send your instructions. In the interim, you are to use your common sense,' the head judge said.

'If this is so pivotal, why are you sending a screw-up like me?' Isolde said the words without thinking, but once they were out she could not take them back.

'Because you screwed up with Sigma,' the head judge shot back. 'You built a connection. No one else here has any sort of rapport with a Guardian, so we are forced to send you.'

'Oh, I understand.' Isolde did not, but if she had to get through this to earn a chance to be returned to her original life to see if she could fix her future then so be it.

'Never fear though; we are sending one of our most decorated agents with you to ensure nothing goes wrong.' The sneer on the right-hand judge's face highlighted that after her time in Burley she had made an enemy on the Council, one who would not easily forgive her transgressions.

The three judges stood, and Isolde bowed as they left. Standing alone in the now stark white room, she sighed. She had not known what to expect when she'd entered the court, and in the end it was not too bad. One more mission and she might earn a chance to find out what she wanted from life. It was not the worst outcome.

As she turned to leave, she saw a figure in the back of the room, the grin on his face telling her he had watched the whole proceedings. As her eyes met his, she sucked air in through her teeth, feeling as if she had been punched in the gut. 'Jason, so good to see you.' There was no way she would show him the effect he had on her.

'Isolde, it seems I am to take over your training once again. I told them not to send you out on your own—that you weren't ready—especially after that debacle in Athens.'

She was not having this. If they were to work together one more time, there at least needed to be honesty between them. 'The reports may not agree, but you and I both know exactly what happened last time we worked together. Beware, Jason, I am older and wiser now, and will not take the fall for your incompetence again.'

Sweeping past him, she left the room, not caring whether or not he followed.

ALCHEMIST

'Jo, you know I can't stay. My new mission starts almost immediately,' Izzy said, her words creating mist in the cool morning air.

'But what about your probation? If you abscond, you won't be able to come back without facing additional charges.' Jo's face crumpled and tears welled in her eyes as Izzy hugged her, as if she realised this was their final goodbye.

Alain looked down at his feet, trying to give the two of them some privacy.

'Will you be okay?'

'Of course, but I can't come back here. They won't let me—ever.' Even to Alain's ears, Izzy sounded uncertain.

'I love you,' Jo whispered.

'I love you too, now and through time itself,' Izzy said.

Are you ready? Trouble said, giving Alain something to do other than try not to listen to Izzy and Jo.

He stomped his feet to restore circulation in the cool winter air, and glanced around the clearing. The forest was a study of reds and browns hidden in a swirling mist. Although they had only arrived here a little over a week ago, the area felt more alive, and a hint of magic tinged the air.

'Here we all are then,' Master Barwick said as he joined them, Alice in tow.

Even after such a short time, Master Barwick looked odd back in his own clothes, and Alain thought he must too. They certainly itched more than he remembered.

'Alice, thank you so much for putting up with us,' Master Barwick said as he clumsily hugged their hostess.

'No, it is I who must thank you for everything you've done.' Alice wiped a tear from her eye.

'I hope you aren't in too much strife with Donald,' Master Barwick said. 'I didn't get much of a chance to speak with him to explain you were just helping us out.'

An early phone call the morning after the casting had called Donald back to work. Knowing the couple needed time alone, the others went out for the day, and by the time they returned he was gone.

'I told you, he was fine. He would have loved to stay and meet you all properly ... but ... well, he'll be back soon enough.' Alice smiled at them all.

Alain found tears welling in his own eyes as he hugged Alice and Jo goodbye, knowing that even though he'd only met them a few days ago, he would miss them. They were all reincarnations of people back home, but their own unique personalities had wormed their way into his heart—especially Bebe's.

They had said their farewells this morning, before she'd left for the hospital to meet with Ruth and her department heads. When Ruth had called the day before and asked Bebe to come to the hospital to talk about a volunteer position, and perhaps some part-time work, Bebe had been beside herself, almost skipping back into the room to tell them her news.

'When I apologised for drugging her, she just poo-pooed me. She said we all did things we were not proud of, and we need to put the past behind us and move on.'

'It was good of her to call, especially as the hospital

board placed her on probation after the hearing over her involvement with Tabitha,' Alice had said.

'I can't wait to tell Mum and Dad. They will be here in a little over a week, but I might just text them the news.'

With her future falling into place, Alain had thought his departure would be far down her list of priorities, but she'd proved him wrong when she'd cornered him in his room earlier that day. It was a bitter-sweet farewell. They clearly felt something more than friendship toward each other, but Alain's heart belonged to Barabal and Bebe would be concentrating on her studies for the next few years. Still, there would forever be a Bebe sized gap in his heart.

Are you ready? Trouble asked him again.

Almost.

He sighed as he remembered he still had to say his farewells to Lee.

It was almost as if his thoughts called the other boy over. They said their goodbyes as boys do, and Lee diffused the emotional scene by changing the focus.

'So, how do you do this, Trouble?'

I take everyone into the water and create a portal back to medieval England.

'Cool.'

Then I will be coming back. My new assignment requires me to leave from here.

Lee smiled wryly. 'It looks like everyone has something to do. Bebe is going to be working at the hospital with Ruth instead of doing a tour around Southern England with me. Jo is off to visit her grandparents. Alain is heading home and even Izzy says she has another mission.

My parents don't arrive for Christmas for another week or so—what am I going to do with myself?'

'I am sure you will find some mischief to get into,' Alain joked.

'I don't find it; it finds me.' Lee laughed. 'Problem is, after all this excitement I am looking at the world a little differently, and I'm wondering if I am cut out to be a soldier. Too much thinking like that does my head in, and I need to find something more constructive to do with my time.'

Alain laughed, but stopped abruptly as his body tingled all over. Trouble tilted his head to the side and appeared to go into a trance, which, in his dog form, looked odd. He then shook himself all over, and became dog-like again.

Can you meet me back here in an hour or so? We need to talk about something, Trouble said to Lee.

'Sure. Want to tell me what we need to talk about?'

Not now. I'll brief you when you return.

Lee shrugged and opened his mouth to speak, but closed it as the others joined them.

'It is time,' Master Barwick said, and Trouble nodded.

There was another round of farewells before Trouble led Alain and Master Barwick over to the stream.

'Are you sure this is the only way?' Alain said, suddenly reluctant to step into the freezing water.

'Unfortunately, yes.'

His master's response did nothing to calm the butterflies in his stomach.

'I bet Izzy has another way to travel,' he muttered under his breath as icy fingers of water clawed their way

up his leg. He stumbled and gasped as he submerged his body in the swirling icy stream. Everything went black, then a bright light blinded him. Opening his eyes, he found himself sitting under a gas lamp on the banks of the Thames. Beside him, Master Barwick slowly rose to his feet.

We are later than I planned. I believe it is the evening of the day we left. You will need to explain your afternoon's absence. It's up to you whether or not you tell them the truth. Barabal and Stanislaus should be around the stables if you want to go and find them. Trouble, the dog, grinned.

'Thank you, Sigma. That was a very informative journey.' Master Barwick's voice cut through the evening air. 'These old bones are weary and I want to be back in my own rooms. Until we meet again, old friend.'

Goodbye, Barwick. It will not be long until you join us for good.

As his master departed, Alain said, 'I must thank you too. I learnt a lot ... The future was interesting, and I shall miss the people and the food—but I am pleased to be home.'

What now for you? Trouble asked Alain. *Are you off back to the New Forest to agitate for the return of the land to the Saxons?*

'No, I think I will stay here,' Alain answered. 'Master Barwick still has much to teach me and ... well, we don't know how much longer he will be here.'

And you will be better placed to use your friendship with the King to lobby for a change of ownership?

I am not sure I will. Although my heart yearns for a return to the days before the Normans arrived, my head is saying perhaps I should wait a bit before rushing to action. In the long-term, it may be better for the forest to stay as it is. Perhaps I can persuade the King to love it again so he protects it for the future.

Trouble's muzzle formed a grin. *Then all that is left to say is, make the most of your time with Barwick. Soon he will be called to a higher task, and you will be left to fill his shoes. Goodbye, my friend.*

'Alain, where have you been? Stanislaus and I were supposed leave half an hour ago, but I made everyone wait until I found you.'

Alain turned to see Barabal striding along the docks towards him.

'Oh, Barabal, I am so pleased you did.' Alain swept the girl into his arms. 'I missed you so much.'

'Put me down, silly. We only spoke this morning. Please, Alain, someone will see and they will think I am a loose woman.'

'Maybe we should do something about that then. While you are away, I will speak with the King—that is, if you want me to.'

Barabal stared at him, and his stomach started to sink when she did not answer. Then, she placed her arm through his, giving him an affectionate squeeze, and said, 'You may escort me to my mount, and I am sure I could not stop you from talking to the King even if I wanted to.'

Looking back over his shoulder as Barabal drew him away, Alain watched Trouble leap from the wharf, and the dog was soon swallowed by the churning waters of the portal before he disappeared from sight.

ALCHEMIST

The house was toasty warm after their morning on the common. Alice made them a pot of tea and they drank it in the kitchen by the Aga. The room seemed so empty with just the two of them, and even emptier still when Alice excused herself to go to work.

Wandering round the house somewhat at a loose end, Lee headed up to the bedroom to get his tablet. He found it on top of Alain's copy of *The Lord of the Rings*. Reaching for the device, he almost dropped it as the book came off the dresser as well. He stood there with the book hanging from his tablet cover. On the floor, he found a note Alain must have left for him on the bedside table, beside the bottle of super glue. When he grabbed his tablet it must have fallen to the floor.

I could not resist. This glue is amazing, but I could not take it back with me. I had to use it at least once. Leave the tablet alone and try the book. Your friend through time—Alain.

Laughing, Lee went to his sister's room to find her nail polish remover so he could free his tablet. Once the job was done, he returned, lay on his bed and flipped open the cover, then closed it. Placing it back on the dresser, he rolled to his side and opened the book.

He was still engrossed in *The Lord of the Rings* when the alarm on his phone went off. Reluctant to leave the story, he placed the book in his backpack, wedged in between a water bottle and some food bars. He had no idea what Trouble had planned, but if it was a walk through the forest to check everything was back to normal, he wanted to be prepared.

After locking the door behind himself, he rushed down the street and turned the corner to be confronted with a moving van. Sliding to a stop, he narrowly missed careening into a sofa, only to lose his footing. A hand grabbed hold of him, saving him from an embarrassing fall. Once back upright, he checked everything was in working order. Someone held out his backpack, which had slipped from his shoulder as he fell.

'Thank you,' he said, looking up. The face in front of him was familiar, but different. Caught off guard, his mouth hung open. As he shut it, he whispered, 'Alain.'

The boy looked at him, frowning. 'Close. I am Allan. Do I know you?'

'Um, no, not really,' Lee stammered.

'Ah, you must be one of the guys staying with their aunt round the corner.'

'Yes, but how ...?'

'Mum was talking to a woman this morning. She said she had her niece and nephew staying, and that they were about my age. Pleased to meet you.' The boy smiled and held out his hand.

Confused, Lee shook it. 'Lee. Sorry, I am late for something.'

'Oh.' The boy's face fell and a wave of guilt washed over Lee.

'Look, perhaps we can meet properly later. I can show you around what little there is of Burley, if you like.'

'Sure, if it's no bother. But can we do it tomorrow? I am kinda busy with unloading today, and Mum'll skin me if I don't do my share.'

'Sure, catch you then,' Lee said as Allan picked up a box from the back of the truck and followed one of the removal men inside.

'Bye,' Lee said as he stepped around some furniture on the sidewalk and took off at a run, hoping he had not missed Trouble.

Arriving at the agreed spot a little late, Lee was relieved to find the dog sitting calmly waiting for him. He was not so happy to see Izzy standing by his side.

'Glad you could make it.' Izzy's smile had a sarcastic twist.

'What are you doing here?' Lee asked.

'I understand you are coming with us,' the girl said enigmatically.

'Coming with you? Where?' Lee looked at Trouble, but he sat still, almost smiling, and Lee wondered if the dog was indeed Trouble, or an actual Spoodle.

'To the future, of course!' Izzy said condescendingly, and Lee fought back the urge to say something to wipe the smile from her face.

Trouble? He begged the dog to intervene.

Something changed before when you questioned your future as a soldier. When you queried your role in the world, the Time Guardians decided to expand your experience so you might be better equipped to decide what you want to do.

'What?'

Like Alain, you have the potential to one day become a Guardian. When you reach a certain stage in your evolution, we like to test how you do on a mission. The

Council asked me to take you along on this expedition.

Izzy smirked. 'Yeah, we are finally all on the same page.'

Not quite, Izzy. Please give me a moment to explain, Trouble said. *Our next jump in time is going to be a joint mission with the Time …* Trouble stopped and cocked his head to the side. *Um, not the time for that word I think. We are joining up with Isolde and one of her friends. We are going to work together to ensure humanity survives and thrives.*

'You want me to leap through time with you. That would be so great. But I just made plans for tomorrow, and Bebe would miss me.'

Izzy placed a hand on his arm. 'You'll be back before anyone even notices you are gone.'

She is correct. We can time your return to be within minutes of having left. And we could do with a soldier to help with this particular task.

'I am not a soldier yet,' Lee said, stalling. He was not good at making snap decisions.

'But you were a cadet at school; Bebe told me,' Izzy said.

Taking a deep breath, Lee weighed up the excitement of going through a portal against his fear of the unknown. As he tried to work through the pros and cons, the devil in his head said, *If Alain can do it, so can you.*

'All right, I'm in.' Lee gulped down his fear and he voiced his agreement.

Good, let's go then.

Trouble and Lee headed towards the stream, but Izzy did not move.

'I never understood all this jumping into freezing liquid,' she said. 'Here, let me.'

ALCHEMIST

She moved her arm in a circle, her lips moving, and the air in front of her shimmered. 'Quick, I can't hold it forever.'

Trouble turned and went to stand beside Isolde. She held out her hand, and Lee took a few steps and grabbed hold of it. Taking a deep breath, he allowed her to pull him into the unknown.

EPILOGUE

'Surely you understand why it has to be him, Alpha. He is the only one of our kind to forge a relationship with a Time Wrecker, and this mission is too delicate to leave to chance,' Beta said. Why did all his conversations with Alpha seem like a visit to a torture chamber?

'I cannot help but feel he is being rewarded for a botched mission. He almost died, which would have stranded a potential Guardian and his helper in a strange world. He was unable to eradicate the bacteria, and he worked hand in hand with a Time Wrecker.'

Beta had no answer for this. Technically it was all true, although not everything had been Sigma's fault.

'If he would just turn up as a person for his missions he would not get into these messes.'

'Oh really, Alpha, you know that is not true. Just because you do not like his methods, there is no reason to vilify him for them.'

ALCHEMIST

Taking a deep breath, Beta thought of the best way to win Alpha over, or at the very least curb his antagonism towards Sigma. Until this critical mission was completed they needed to work as a team to provide the best guidance they could for their agents. Alpha thought of himself as a man of reason, so perhaps that was the best approach?

'Barnaby Barwick is back with his apprentice in his correct time, preparing things for his imminent death when he will join our ranks. All in all, no harm was done.'

Alpha snorted at this, but said nothing, so Beta continued.

'As you well know, although the Alabama Rot is still around, they prevented the mutated version from being released, and the people who created it are in prison. The disease will not skip to humans, and they averted a mass epidemic—that's due to the people on the ground who we left largely to their own devices because of critical issues elsewhere.'

'I will concede that.' Alpha's tone was grudging. 'However, he worked with a Time Wrecker—a Time Wrecker, Beta. He will still need to be sanctioned for that.'

It had taken a while, but they had come around to the real crux of the matter. Alpha was not the only member of the Council to feel this way, so Beta needed to tread gently. 'Sigma's helpers made this alliance while he was under anaesthetic. He was not a party to it, and no one was able to contact us for direction,'

'All right. It was John—Jo who brought the Time Wrecker in. She based her judgement on emotional connections, which is not how we do things.'

'True, Alpha, and I think we should all remember that although Jo was a long way through her reincarnation cycle, she was not yet at the level where we were considering her ascension to Guardian, so she was still prone to making very human decisions.'

'Humph. What about Barwick? He is almost a Guardian; why didn't he stand against including that Isolde in their plans?'

'The fault was not his either. Without Sigma to assist him he was left with an impossible choice. Unable to talk with us, and unable to operate in the time he was in without Isolde's help, but knowing he had to do something to stop an epidemic spreading. What other option was there?'

'I guess I can appreciate his dilemma,' Alpha conceded.

'The fault is ours as well. We took our eye off them—left them without support when they needed it most. We must discuss extending trainee's powers to allow them to operate a little more independently as they progress through the levels,' Beta pressed on.

'We can discuss that at the next Council meeting. Before that, we need to agree on Jo's punishment, for there must be some sanction for collaborating with the enemy.'

'Must there really?' Beta asked. 'It is because of their collaboration we find ourselves in the unique position of being able to launch our new mission.'

'I see why you would think that, but we cannot allow our Guardians to think they can work with Time Wreckers whenever they feel the urge.'

'You are right; that would cause chaos. Perhaps a minor sanction then—a nudge backwards on the evolutionary wheel,' Beta suggested.

'It is a shame. Her Guardian training was only one or two lifetimes away, but it is fair. After all, we do not want to lose such a promising candidate altogether. We cannot nudge her back too far though; we will need her to be ready for this new mission. Perhaps one hop back?'

'Done then?' Beta asked, and Alpha nodded his agreement.

'Right, now that is sorted, shall we go and tell Theta about her next assignment?' Beta said.

'Yes, let's. I am sure she will be thrilled to be working with her old partner again.'

'You still think this is a wise pairing?' Beta himself was not so certain.

Sigma and Theta had been Guardian trainees together. Along with himself and Alpha, the group had often worked as a team. The two trainees had fallen for each other. When they had realised they could not become Guardians and maintain their relationship, Theta had been torn, but in the end she'd listened to her mentor and ascended to Guardian without discussing it with Sigma first.

Sigma had been devastated, and it had taken a lot of convincing on Beta's behalf to have him ascend. The Council had been keeping the two apart ever since.

'Perhaps not wise, but when the Time Wreckers said they were sending two agents we needed to match that,' Alpha said. 'Theta is the only other Guardian Sigma has worked with, so it is logical to send her. Surely by now they are over their little misunderstanding.'

Beta frowned. Was it time for Alpha to step down and let a new Guardian take his place. Some Guardians stayed too long in the job, losing touch with their humanity. Alpha had been exhibiting the signs for a while now, and it was colouring the way he approached things.

'Sigma has already jumped with Lee; it will come as

quite a shock to him when Theta joins them. Perhaps I should warn him first,' Beta said.

'By all means, but let us go get Theta prepared. There's no time to waste. Recent reports indicate our catalyst has disappeared, so our agent's first task will be to find him at all costs.'

'Do we have a contact they are to meet with?'

'Not exactly. Because of the nature of the environment they will portal in to, there are few people evolved enough to assist us. I sent someone in to steal some supplies for them and alter some records to provide covers for everyone. I fear they are pretty much on their own this time, but I'm sure they will be fine.' Alpha reassured him.

Beta paused. There were so many new things in play, this was a risky mission—but there were always risks. They were sending their best agent—what could possibly go wrong?

ABOUT THIS BOOK
HOW MUCH IS FICTION AND HOW MUCH IS REAL?

This story came to me when I was visiting family in Southampton and we spent a couple of days in the New Forest in the middle of winter 2017. The misty atmosphere and magical history captured my imagination and the book was already forming in my head. The places in the book exist, and I have to thank the lovely village of Burley for playing host to this story. It is a picturesque village and really deserves a visit.

During my time in the New Forest I noticed warnings to dog owners to keep their animals on leads to prevent further cases of Alabama Rot. It was a serious problem in the area, and I took this idea, studied it and fed it into the mix.

The other thing that struck me during that trip to England was the unrest caused by the issue of whether or not England should stay a part of the European Union. As we spoke to people on different sides of the debate we realised the country was likely set for some big changes, and this also managed to weave itself into my story.

Everything else exists only in my head, and now in this book.

ACKNOWLEDGEMENTS

Although this Guardian's of Time book owes a little less to to my family than Swagman, I still owe some of Alain's antics to my father Allan. His story of blowing up his neighbour's letter box was legend in my family, as was his fascination with super glue.

A little thanks must also go to my writing companion, Trouble, who manages to make an appearance in this book. Your snores have kept me company on may writing stints.

As always I had a load of help to bring this book to you. To Daria and Sandy, thank you so much for giving your time to beta read and proof my story. Your support on my writing journey makes it less lonely.

My editor, Lauren McKeller, took my story, worked her magic, and turned it into a book. I could not have done this without you.

As always, Kim Last, worked her own special magic with the cover, which could be a piece of art in its own right.

As always, thanks to my lovely husband, Jim. Without your support and creative art work I would not have been able to visualise my story as clearly. I also would not have been able to meet any of my deadlines without your taking over the cooking duties.

And to all of you who have taken the time to read this book. I write because I love it, but nothing beats the glow of knowing someone else has appreciated your work. Please email or message me and let me know what you thought of the book.

ABOUT THE AUTHOR

Vivienne has been writing books since she was fifteen years old, but only friends and family were allowed to read them. Forced to give up work because of family commitments she was encouraged by friends and family to finally put some of her writing out there for others to read.

In the real world after leaving university with a BA in History and Politics she worked as a Personnel Officer, an Office Manager, a Project Manager, a DBA and IT Manager then as a Business and Data Analyst, adding an MSC in Information Systems along the way. In her world she continued to write.

Born in Invercargill (New Zealand), she has lived in; Dunedin (New Zealand), London (England), Petersfield (England) and currently lives with her husband and son and their dog Trouble and kitten Lola in Sydney (Australia).

For future releases and current news you can find
Vivienne at **www.viviennelfraser.com.au** or on
Facebook at **www.facebook.com/vivienneleefraser**